She was perfect for him. . . .

He smelled her.

Her distinctive clean, citrus-tinged scent wafted on the light spring breeze along with the smells of sweaty little boys, fresh-popped popcorn, and exhaust fumes from the cars arriving and leaving the ball fields. The scent twisted his gut, filling him with a want that had become as familiar as his own heartbeat.

The Line Creek Park contained a total of four baseball diamonds, and at the moment all of them were occupied by ball players of various ages.

The field directly in front of him held the youngest players, boys six and seven years old. But he hadn't come to watch the plays on the field. He'd come because of her.

She sat on the bleachers two rows in front of him, her blond hair shimmering in the early evening sunshine. His fingers ached with the need to reach out and touch the strands.

Not yet. Soon, but not yet, he told himself.

THE
PERFECT FAMILY

Carla Cassidy

A SIGNET ECLIPSE BOOK

SIGNET ECLIPSE
Published by New American Library, a division of
Penguin Group (USA) Inc., 375 Hudson Street,
New York, New York 10014, USA
Penguin Group (Canada), 10 Alcorn Avenue, Toronto,
Ontario M4V 3B2, Canada (a division of Pearson Penguin Canada Inc.)
Penguin Books Ltd., 80 Strand, London WC2R 0RL, England
Penguin Ireland, 25 St. Stephen's Green, Dublin 2,
Ireland (a division of Penguin Books, Ltd.)
Penguin Group (Australia), 250 Camberwell Road, Camberwell, Victoria 3124,
Australia (a division of Pearson Australia Group Pty. Ltd.)
Penguin Books India Pvt. Ltd., 11 Community Centre, Panchsheel Park,
New Delhi - 110 017, India
Penguin Group (NZ), cnr Airborne and Rosedale Roads, Albany,
Auckland 1310, New Zealand (a division of Pearson New Zealand Ltd.)
Penguin Books (South Africa) (Pty.) Ltd., 24 Sturdee Avenue,
Rosebank, Johannesburg 2196, South Africa

Penguin Books Ltd., Registered Offices:
80 Strand, London WC2R 0RL, England

First published by Signet Eclipse, an imprint of New American Library,
a division of Penguin Group (USA) Inc.

First Printing, March 2005
10 9 8 7 6 5 4 3 2 1

Chapter 1

It was a perfect evening. The Kansas City suburb called Cass Creek offered the best of the season: trees bursting with blossoms, lawns lush and green with new growth, and children throbbing with energy built up during a long winter.

As Marissa Jamison drove toward her son's Little League baseball game she noticed the signs of spring everywhere in the air. The rebirth of the earth resonated deep inside her.

It had been a long, hard winter, but for the first time since her husband's death she felt a new strength and focus. Business at the shop was wonderful, and her children were adjusting as well as could be expected considering their loss.

They were going to be all right. There had been a time when she hadn't been so sure, when she'd feared the grief would take her to a place from where she'd never be able to emerge. But somehow they'd gotten through it, and for the first time in a year she believed the bad times were really behind them.

"Mom, can we get pizza after the game?" Justin asked, as they turned into the park.

"It's a school night. You know the rules," she replied. "How about we plan to get pizza tomorrow night? It will be Friday Fun Night at the Pizza Place."

"And we'll get pepperoni pizza," Jessica exclaimed.

Marissa smiled. "Yes, pepperoni pizza," she agreed.

The park was crowded, and it took her a few minutes to find a parking space near the field where Justin's team would be playing.

As she walked toward the bleachers her two children ran ahead of her, their blond hair gleaming in the sunshine and their shouts of excitement riding the warm breeze.

Her love for them filled her heart, her soul. They were the beacons that had gotten her through the black storm of grief. It was the two of them who had forced her through the darkest days of despair, the deepest grip of heartache.

She and Jessica had been watching Justin's game for half an hour when some of the adult teams began to arrive to play on the other ball diamonds.

She smiled as she saw Kip Larson approaching. The young man wore the red-and-white jersey of the Cass Country Firefighters team. He sat next to Jessica and gave her a hug.

"When are you going to grow up so I can marry you?" he asked. Jessica giggled, accustomed to Kip's teasing.

"Who are you playing?" Marissa asked.

"Henderson's Dry Cleaning. They're supposed to be tough," Kip replied. He directed his gaze toward the field. "How's our boy doing?"

"At the moment he looks incredibly bored." Marissa smiled as she looked at her son.

Three more firefighters arrived and headed for Marissa and Jessica. As always, Marissa's heart filled with warmth. She knew these men always came early for their games to show Justin their support.

John had been a fireman, and since his death the men at his station had practically adopted her children, often showing up at their activities.

"Captain Morrison," Marissa greeted the middle-aged man who John had always liked and admired. "I hear you've got a tough game ahead of you."

He smiled. "They're all tough. But we're hungry for a championship win this year."

"We've been hungry for a championship win every year," Brett Tupelo, another fireman, said.

As they cheered for Justin and his team, Marissa's heart warmed and, not for the first time, she realized how lucky she was that John had worked with such fine men and that those men hadn't forgotten the family of one of their own.

He smelled her.

Her distinctive clean, citrus-tinged scent wafted on the light spring breeze along with the smells of sweaty little boys, fresh-popped popcorn, and exhaust fumes from the cars arriving and leaving the ball fields. The scent twisted in his gut, filling him with a want that had become as familiar as his own heartbeat.

The Line Creek Park contained a total of four baseball diamonds, and at the moment all of them were occupied by ballplayers of various ages.

The field directly in front of him held the youngest players, boys six and seven years old. But he hadn't come to watch the plays on the field. He'd come because of her.

Her shoulder-length blond hair shimmered in the early-evening sunshine. His fingers ached with the need to reach out and touch the strands.

Not yet. Soon, but not yet, he told himself. There was nothing as intoxicating as the ache of anticipation, the sweet savoring of expectation.

He watched as she bent her head to listen to whatever her daughter was telling her. Five-year-old Jessica had the same shade of blond hair as her mother. She was like a little fairy sprite with delicate features and big blue eyes.

He tore his gaze from mother and daughter and

looked toward the field where seven-year-old Justin seemed to be daydreaming at his position as short stop.

The perfect family. He knew everything he needed to know about them. He knew that little Jessica loved pepperoni pizza and ballet, that Justin loved baseball and dinosaurs. He knew the kids got up around seven each morning and went to bed at eight thirty each night.

Looking back at the blond woman, his heart swelled with the sweet fullness of a love that gnawed at him day and night.

Marissa Jamison.

Her very name sang through his veins. Being near her made his hands shake, caused his heart to pound so loudly that for a moment he heard none of the cheers of the parents, none of the shouts from the coaches, nothing but the pounding of his love for her.

He knew she liked to sip wine while taking a bubble bath after the kids went to bed. He knew she loved working at the little shop she owned that sold Tiffany-style lamps, and he knew she'd deeply mourned the death of her husband.

John Jamison had been dead for a year now, and it was time for her to move on with her life. He'd given her a reasonable time to mourn.

He'd show her now that he could take care of her, be the man who would make her life perfect again.

After all, he'd been in love with her for a long time. He wanted only what was best for her.

She'd made a mistake when she'd married John, but he'd corrected that mistake. Marissa and Jessica and Justin were the family he was supposed to have, the family he would have when the time was right.

Soon she would understand, and her gratitude would turn to love and she would bind her heart with his.

He was a patient man, but it was time to begin, time to prove to sweet Marissa just how much he loved her. Soon it would be time to claim the perfect family as his own.

Chapter 2

"Great job!" Marissa gave her son a high five, knowing that to hug him here on the ball field among his peers would be pure torture for him.

He grinned at her, a lopsided smile so like his father's it caused an ache in Marissa. "Did you see me catch that ball?"

"I saw you," Jessica said with all the pride of a little sister. "You catched it real good, Justin."

"Caught it, honey. He caught it real well," Marissa said as the three of them headed for her minivan.

The walk from the bleachers to the van had become a bittersweet one for Marissa as she watched fathers climb into cars to take their little ballplayers home.

Marissa wasn't the only single mother who was trying to be both father and mother to her son, but for the most part Justin's teammates came from whole families.

"Hey, Marissa! Good hands, Justin," Marc Carter called from across the parking lot. Marissa waved back, then loaded the kids into the van. Marc was one of the single parents who had become friendly with Marissa over the last couple of games.

"Everyone buckled in?" she asked as she started the engine. When both kids answered affirmatively she began to back out of the parking space.

The sharp blare of a horn made her slam on the brakes. She stuck her head out the window to see a small car just behind the van.

"Are you fucking blind?" a dark-haired young woman screamed out of the window of the compact car.

"Sorry," Marissa exclaimed.

"If you'd hit me you would have been real fucking sorry, you moron." The women sped away but not before she flipped Marissa a one-finger goodbye.

"She said a bad word," Jessica said with all the indignation of a five-year-old.

"Yes, she did," Marissa agreed as she carefully backed out of the parking space.

"Her mommy should put her in time out," Jessica said. "She's naughty."

"I think you're right." Marissa smiled. Jessica was already intimately acquainted with time out.

As they drove the fifteen minutes to their home,

Marissa listened absently as the kids cheerfully argued about whether it was better to own a dog or a cat. It didn't matter who won the argument; she'd told the kids no pets until they got a little older.

"Maybe I should practice a little catch before bedtime?" Justin said as she pulled into the driveway of the neat ranch house that was home.

"You'd better do your practicing in the bathtub because it's almost bedtime and I can smell your sweaty feet from here." She smiled as she heard her son giggle.

The rest of the evening flew by in the routine that brought comfort in its very familiarity. They sat down to dinner, took baths, and then each child was tucked into bed with good-night kisses and prayers.

With the kids asleep and the house quiet, Marissa poured herself a glass of wine and went into the master bath. Once the tub was full she undressed and sank down into the warm bubbly water.

There had been a time when the silence of the house had ached in her heart, when the absence of John's deep voice had created a void almost too big to bear.

In the last couple of months she'd grown more comfortable with the silence. She closed her eyes and leaned her head back against the inflatable bath pillow and took a sip of her wine.

It wasn't just John's voice she missed. She missed the intimacy of his glance from across the room, the brush of his thigh against hers in the middle of the night, the scent that had belonged to him alone.

She missed two toothbrushes in the ceramic holder on the sink, the sports section of the newspaper spread out on the kitchen table in the mornings, and having to fight for the remote control.

She was thirty-three years old and had learned through the tragedy of her husband's death that she was stronger than she'd thought.

She finished her wine and got out of the tub. She needed to get to bed relatively early. Tomorrow was a big day at the shop: the first day of a spring sale that she hoped would bring people in to spend their money on pretty lamps and home decor.

Clad in a thigh-length cotton nightshirt, she carried her wineglass into the kitchen. She washed it out in the sink, then went to the children's bedroom doorways for a final check on them.

Justin slept on his back, using the entire space of his single-size bed with sprawled arms and legs. He was such a good boy, with a heart of gold and a love for all creatures.

Jessica was curled up in a ball on her side, her favorite stuffed ballerina bunny clutched tight against her chest. As Marissa stood in the doorway and gazed at her daughter, a spike of irrational terror swept through her.

It was the kind of fear that occasionally woke her up in the middle of the night when the darkness was the most profound.

It was the terror of a mother afraid that something might happen to her children, the fear that no matter how hard she tried, no matter what measures were taken, she couldn't keep danger at bay.

Her heart banged against her ribs and she swallowed hard and mentally shook herself as the feeling passed as quickly as it had come.

The only difference between Marissa and any other person who might momentarily entertain these kinds of dark fears was that she'd already learned the reality of how much could be lost in the blink of an eye.

Chapter 3

The emergency operator got the call at nine fifteen on Friday morning. The call came from a pay phone.

"There's a body at Penguin Park," the male caller said. "You might want to get somebody over there before the kids get out of school and go over there to play."

"May I have your name, sir?" the operator asked. The caller hung up.

At nine twenty-two Detective Luke Hunter and his partner, Detective Sarah Wilkerson, headed toward the neighborhood park to check it out.

Sarah Wilkerson sat in the unmarked car next to Luke. She had been with the Cass Creek Police Department for only two weeks, having transferred from Chicago after her marriage bit the dust.

She had yet to get a good feel for her partner and was acutely conscious of the fact that everyone on the small force seemed to be holding their breath and waiting for the big-city female cop to screw up.

"Penguin Park—is there a story behind the name?" she asked to break the silence in the car. Luke Hunter was a man who seemed at ease with silence. She was a woman who was not.

"You'll see when we get there," he replied. "I'm not sure what the park was officially named, but it's been called Penguin Park for as long as I can remember."

She shot him a surreptitious glance. In the two weeks she'd worked with Luke she'd discovered that he hated paperwork, drove like a bat out of hell, and liked his tacos with extra cheese and sour cream. She also found him easy on the eyes . . . too easy on the eyes.

When they were within two blocks of the neighborhood park, the reason for the name became apparent. A huge black-and-white penguin rose up against the beautiful blue morning sky. Sporting a red bow tie and a grin, it stood like a giant sentry in the center of the playground.

"It's a slide," Luke explained as he pulled into the lot and parked next to a patrol car already there. "The stairs are inside the base, and the slide curves around and shoots the kids out at the feet."

"Let's see what they've got," she said. They got out of the car and approached a young patrolman who stood guard near the giant penguin.

"What's up?" Luke asked.

"A dead woman." The officer looked a little green around the gills. "A murdered dead woman. I've called it in. The crime-scene boys are on their way."

"Did you touch anything?" Sarah asked as she scanned the general area.

"No. Me and my partner, we just stepped inside the base." He pointed toward the smiling penguin. "We saw her and immediately backed out."

"Where's your partner now?" Luke asked.

"He's at the back of the penguin, guarding the entrance."

"Guess we'd better check it out," Sarah said. Together she and Luke headed for the entrance to the big slide.

She smelled death before they reached the structure. It was the coppery tang of blood, the overly sweet odor of the first stages of decomposition.

"You'd think you'd get used to it," Luke murmured. "The smell, I mean."

"You never get used to it," she replied. There had been many nights in the past that she'd thought she'd carried that odor home with her, that it not only clung to her clothes, but had somehow managed to seep into the very pores of her body. There had been a time when she'd thought maybe that's what had chased her husband out of her life, the smell of death.

The victim lay on her back next to the slide's stairs. There was no question she was dead, nor was there a question about the death being of natural causes. Natural causes didn't include a throat nearly slashed in half.

But it wasn't the gaping throat that twisted Sarah's stomach into knots. It was the bow. A bright red bow decorated the center of the victim's forehead, an obscenely cheerful bit of ribbon.

Careful not to disturb anything, she pulled on a pair of latex gloves and knelt down as close as possible to the body, frowning thoughtfully. The victim appeared to be a young woman between the ages of eighteen and twenty-five. Her long dark hair splayed around her head, and Sarah tried to discern if it had fallen that way naturally or had been combed out after her death.

She stood, aware of Luke standing just behind her. She could hear his shallow breathing. "There's no doubt she was killed here," he said. "There's blood splatter everywhere."

"Should I check her for ID?"

"We'd better wait for the lab guys to get here. I don't want to disturb the scene by trying to move her to check her pockets. I'll go outside and check the area to see if there's a purse or something that might have belonged to her, or something from our perp."

She nodded, and he left the penguin.

Once again she knelt down. The victim's fingernails were painted a deep purple. None of them appeared cracked or broken off. Sarah suspected there would be no skin or DNA matter found beneath them. There also didn't appear to be any defensive wounds on her forearms or hands.

She was clad in a pair of worn jeans and a hot pink T-shirt that advertised an alcoholic beverage. There were no obvious signs of sexual assault.

The bow bothered Sarah. She wanted to rip it off the victim's forehead. She found it as offensive as the wound that had taken her life. She frowned and leaned a little closer as she realized there was something beneath the bow.

Something white. A piece of paper? A note of some kind? Her heartbeat accelerated as she pulled a pair of tweezers from her pocket. With the care of a skilled surgeon, she grabbed the edge of the object and pulled.

A small tug of resistance, then it came free. It was a gift card, one of the little ones that often accompanied flowers.

"No purse or anything else that we can find," Luke said as he came back into the base of the slide. "What have you got?"

"Our first clue." With her tweezers she held out the card for Luke to read. It said, *To Marissa, Love Blake.* "I'd say our first order of business is to find this Marissa and ask her who might be leaving her this kind of gift."

Chapter 4

"Jessica, stop playing with your cereal and finish eating. We've got to leave here in fifteen minutes." Marissa rummaged on the cluttered counter, seeking the car keys that she'd sworn she'd tossed there the night before.

"Mom, I can't find my other sneaker," Justin hollered from his bedroom.

"Look under your bed," Marissa yelled back.

Saturday mornings always held a kind of frantic energy as she got the kids ready to take to her in-laws so she could work the day at the shop. Justin and Jessica adored their grandparents, who often watched the children while Marissa worked.

"Finish up, Jessica," Marissa said, then breathed a sigh of relief as she finally found the keys.

Jessica picked up her cereal bowl and held it to her mouth, slurping up the last of the Granola

Crunch and milk. "Done," she announced with a milk-mustache smile.

"Okay, go brush your teeth and we're off." As Jessica left the kitchen, Marissa quickly rinsed the bowls and put them in the dishwasher. From the freezer she pulled out a package of hot dogs and placed them in the fridge, knowing that after a long day at the store she wouldn't feel like cooking anything more elaborate.

"Let's go," she cried from the front door. Minutes later they were in the van headed for Edith and Jim Jamison's place on the outskirts of town.

When she'd fallen in love with John, she'd also fallen in love with his parents. Edith and Jim lived on seven acres of beautifully wooded land, and they were salt-of-the-earth kinds of people. Uncomplicated and without artifice, they had embraced their only child's spouse as if she were one of their own, and Marissa had embraced them back.

Marissa's parents had divorced years ago. She had no relationship with the father who had disappeared from her life, and her mother had remarried a wealthy widower two years ago and moved to Florida, where she'd adopted a lifestyle that left little time for her daughter.

The attractive ranch house where her in-laws lived held an aura of welcome. Pots of spring flowers hung on either side of the front door, a smiling leprechaun whirligig was planted in the ground near the walk, arms moving as if by magic in the light morning breeze.

She had no sooner pulled into the driveway than Edith and Jim were out the front door, smiles riding their faces as the kids tumbled out of the van.

Marissa got out and was immediately enveloped in a hug from Edith. It didn't matter how often she saw John's mother, Edith always greeted her with a hug.

"You got time for coffee?" Edith asked.

"No, not this morning, although I'll take a rain check," Marissa replied.

"You got it." Edith ruffled Justin's hair. "Your grandpa's got quite a day planned for you and your sister. He's hoping you two will help him plant some vegetables in the garden."

Jim grinned at his grandkids. "I figure we'll plant some turnips; then, in a couple of months, your grandma can make us some turnip stew."

"Yuck!" Justin exclaimed, wrinkling his nose in disgust.

"Yuck," Jessica parroted her older brother.

Jim laughed. "Okay, then maybe we won't plant turnips."

Knowing the kids were in good hands, Marissa said her good-byes, then headed the van in the direction of the shopping mall that was home to her store.

When Marissa was younger, the Oak Tree Mall had been one of the most popular malls in the county, but in the past ten years it had gone the way of so many big malls. Stores had closed in response to the competition of strip-mall shopping.

The management of Oak Tree Mall had begun to fight back by offering low rent to new businesses and hosting special events that drew people into the mall.

Marissa entered her store, Tiffany Rose, through the side door and, as always, a sense of pride mingled with a whisper of regret that her store had been born through John's death. It had been insurance money that had enabled her to achieve this particular dream.

With the security gate still across the store entrance, she walked around, turning on the lamps on display, enjoying the muted jewel tone light each one displayed.

She sold not only lamps, but also chairs, chaises, small accent tables, original paintings, and plants. The items for sale were aesthetically displayed, and the shop breathed with the aura of quiet style and class.

John would approve, she thought with comfort. He'd been an active participant in her dream of owning a shop like this. While he was alive they had worked together to save pennies and dimes, hoping that one day the dream would become a reality. In death, he'd given her the dream.

At precisely ten o'clock she pulled open the security gate, then sat at the chair behind the cash register and waited for customers. She didn't sit idly. She thumbed through catalogs and made notes of items she thought might sell well. She reevaluated what wasn't selling and whether she should display it differently or cut the prices.

The morning passed quickly. She sold three lamps and was pleased that one of the customers had bought in the store before. Repeat customers were always welcomed.

At noon her assistant, Alison, came in. An elegant older woman with snow-white hair and a style all her own, Alison McCade had proven herself invaluable to Marissa, not only as a terrific saleswoman but also as a friend.

"A little slow this morning," Marissa said.

"Things should pick up this afternoon. The piano store is giving some kind of free music lessons in the center court. Hopefully some of the people who attend will drift down in this direction."

"Let's hope so," Marissa replied. "If you can man the front, I'll spend a little time in the back unloading some boxes that came in yesterday."

"I'll be fine," Alison assured her.

The back room of the store held shelves of overstock, a computer, a restroom, and a small microwave for the days when employees brought their own lunches.

Two large boxes sat on the floor, awaiting a box cutter and Marissa's gentle hands in unpacking the delicate glass figurines inside.

As she worked, she heard Alison waiting on customers and she thanked the good fortune that had sent the older woman into her life. There was a certain comfort in her friendship with Alison, who, unlike most of Marissa's friends, had never known John.

There were no memories of John with Alison, and as much as Marissa had loved her husband, she was ashamed to admit there were times when it was a relief not to have the memories.

The friends she and John had shared together either talked too much about him or never mentioned his name at all. John's death had transformed their friends into awkward acquaintances, and Marissa had found herself becoming more isolated.

It took her nearly an hour to unpack and catalog into the computer the newest inventory; then she left the shop to go to the food court for lunch.

She bought a salad and a diet soda, then carried the tray to an empty table nearby. The food court was busier than usual. Maybe Alison had been right: The promise of free music lessons had brought more people than usual into the mall. More people in the mall could only be good for business.

She was halfway through her salad when she saw him.

He walked with the easy, loose gait of a man comfortable with his place in the world, a man confident in who he had become in his thirty-three years on the planet.

It had been sixteen years since she'd seen him, but recognition was instantaneous. His hair was shorter than she remembered, but still as dark and curly as when he'd been a teenager.

He glanced at her as he started to walk past her table, then did a double take and halted, his eyes wide in obvious surprise.

"Marissa." His deep voice evoked a rush of crazy memories that spun through her head. He held out his hands and she stood and grabbed them and warmth swept through her at the physical touch.

"Marissa Guthrie." He used the maiden name she hadn't heard in years.

"Alex Kincaid." His name felt strange on her lips. It had been so long, so very long. "What on earth are you doing here in town?"

"I'm living here now." He smiled, that sexy half smile she remembered from a lifetime ago. "My God, you look wonderful." He squeezed her hands, then released them and gestured her back into her chair.

He took the seat opposite her, and for a moment she felt as if she were sixteen again and they were sitting across from each other in the high-school lunchroom.

She'd forgotten how blue his eyes were, not the blue of a summer day, but more the shade of a twilight sky. The good-looking teenage boy had grown into a very handsome man.

"Tell me everything," he said. "Tell me what

you're doing, who you married, if you have children."

She laughed, an exuberant burst of laughter that had been absent for a long time. "First tell me when you moved back to town."

"I've been here about two months."

"You by yourself? No wife? No children?"

"No. I'm not married. I lost my mother several years ago, and my father passed away four months ago. With both of them gone, I decided to make some changes in my life. The first thing I realized was that I wanted to move. Cass Creek always held good memories for me, so here I am. Now, your turn."

"I have two children. Justin is seven and Jessica is five."

"And your husband?"

"John passed away a year ago."

He winced, the gesture doing nothing to distract from his sculptured features. "I'm so sorry. It must be tough, being a single parent."

She smiled. "My kids make it easy. They're great kids." She pushed the last of her salad aside. "What are you doing here in the mall?"

"I'm having new tires put on my car at Sears and decided while the work was being done to walk down here and get something to eat. What about you? What are you doing here?"

"I own a shop."

His dark brows lifted. "Really? That's great. What kind of shop?"

She'd forgotten Alex's ability to focus on a person so intently he made him or her feel as if they were the most important person in the universe. It had been part of his charm as a teenager and it was a charm she felt at the moment.

She told him about her store, about the kinds of things she sold and how much she enjoyed being a proprietor. In turn he told her that he was an architect and was working on the plans for a new community center where an old movie theater now existed.

"You still run?" she asked.

"Every morning." He grinned. "You still leading cheers?"

She laughed. "Only in the privacy of my room and after too many daiquiris." Alex had been a high-school track star and Marissa had been a cheerleader. Looking back, those days had been wonderfully idyllic, filled with promise and hope for the future.

Minutes later he walked with her back toward her store, and they continued catching up, not speaking of anything too personal, but sharing bits and pieces of the last sixteen years.

She was surprised that he wore the same cologne or something similar to what he'd worn years ago. The familiar scent evoked memories of slow dancing with her face burrowed in the crook of his neck, of hot kisses shared in the back of a car, of hands touching her where nobody's hands had ever touched her before.

Alex had been her first boyfriend, and she'd loved him with the intensity that only a teenage girl can feel. She knew it was crazy, but even after all these years his nearness caused her heart to beat in the erratic rhythm of teenage memory.

"Have dinner with me," he said as they reached her shop. "I want to hear everything about your life since high school."

She contemplated the offer. It was the first time since John's death that such an offer had been made by a single, attractive man. She was surprised to discover a touch of anxiety at the thought of going on a date, so to speak.

"When?" she asked, and with the question realized she'd made the decision to go. It wasn't really a date, she told herself. It was just two old friends getting together to catch up on old times.

"Tonight . . . tomorrow night . . . whenever."

"I can't tonight. I'd need to arrange for a sitter."

"You could bring the kids along," he replied. "We could do pizza or something that they'd like."

"That's very kind, but I think maybe it would be best if I get a sitter." There was no way she intended to introduce into her children's lives any man, even an old boyfriend. "How about tomorrow evening?"

"Great." He pulled a business card from his pocket. "This has my home number on it. Why don't you call me sometime later this evening or tomorrow and we'll set up the time?"

She took the card, recognizing that in agreeing to call him, in setting up a dinner date, she was taking a momentous step into life after death.

"Mrs. Jamison? Marissa Jamison?" a deep voice said from behind her.

She turned to see a man and a woman approach from the direction of her store. "Yes? I'm Marissa Jamison." She looked toward the back of the store where Alison stood by the register. She shrugged her shoulders to indicate to Marissa she didn't know what they wanted.

The slender dark-haired woman pulled out a wallet and displayed a badge. "I'm Detective Wilkerson and this is my partner Detective Hunter. We have some questions to ask you and we'd like to ask them down at the station."

Marissa was aware of Alex taking a step closer to her as she stared at the woman in confusion. "Questions? Questions about what?"

"If you could just come with us, we'll get it all straightened out at the station," the tall blond man said. There was a kindness in his eyes that wasn't present in the woman's.

"She's not going anywhere until we see some ID from you," Alex said to the man.

He nodded and pulled aside his jacket to expose not only the badge clipped to his belt, but also a shoulder holster fully loaded. "Look, if you'd feel more comfortable, you don't have to ride with us. We can follow you and you can drive yourself."

Alex touched her arm. "You want me to come with you?"

"No, I'm fine. I'm sure this is all some kind of a mistake or something." She forced a smile. "You go on. I'll call you later."

He hesitated a moment, then nodded before he turned and left. Marissa once again focused her attention to the two detectives. "Can't you tell me what this is about? Am I in some kind of trouble?"

"Have you done something that would make you think you're in trouble?" Detective Wilkerson asked, her dark brown eyes intent.

"No . . . I mean, nothing I can think of." Marissa flushed, surprised to discover she felt guilty just standing in the presence of the two.

"We'll explain everything at the station," Detective Hunter said.

Marissa nodded, recognizing they intended to tell her nothing. "I'll drive myself. I know where the station is located and my car is in the parking lot just outside the side door of my shop. I just need to speak with my assistant for a moment."

The detectives waited as she checked with Alison to make sure she could handle things until Marissa returned. Minutes later Marissa drove toward the police station the children referred to as the bumblebee building because of its bright yellow-and-black paint, but frivolous nicknames were the last thing on her mind.

What could they want with her? Crazy thoughts shot through her head as she drove toward the station, acutely aware of the dark sedan following closely behind her.

Was it possible she'd gotten some parking tickets and didn't know about them? Had they caught her on some video camera running a stoplight or speeding?

Even as the questions appeared, she dismissed them. She was a good, cautious driver. She didn't ignore parking tickets and she didn't run stoplights or speed. Besides, if it was a traffic issue they wouldn't have come hunting for her. Surely they would have just sent her something in the mail.

John. Her hands tightened on the steering wheel. It had to be something to do with John. Maybe they'd finally gotten a break, learned something about the person who had run him down in the grocery store parking lot. Maybe finally she would gain closure by learning exactly what had happened on the night of John's death.

If it hadn't been for a lucky break, Sarah and Luke would have still been searching for a woman named Marissa. Without a last name the traditional search methods were impossible. They couldn't call information for a phone number, couldn't check DMV for a driver's license record.

The victim's identity had been established within hours of the body being found. Her car had been located across the street from the park in a no-parking zone in front of a business. Her purse with her identification had been in the front seat.

Jennifer Walsh had been twenty-two years old at the time of her death. She lived in a dreary low-rent studio apartment, worked at a convenience store, and had a fair amount of cocaine in her system at the time of her death.

They had interviewed her parents and coworkers, but none of those people had been much help. They were still trying to locate any friends Jennifer might have had.

It wasn't until that morning when Sarah and Luke were sitting at the desk that they shared when fellow officer Guy Woodson had stopped by to shoot the breeze.

Luke had mentioned their frustration in trying to find the elusive Marissa. Guy had frowned thoughtfully. "Marissa. Marissa. Why does that name sound so familiar?" He'd snapped his fingers. "The fireman."

"What fireman?" Sarah had asked.

"He was killed last year in a hit-and-run. His name was Johnson . . . Jackson . . . no Jamison. That's it, John Jamison. I think his wife's name was Marissa."

Luke didn't bother to grab a pen to write it down. In the couple of weeks he'd been working with

Sarah he'd quickly discovered she was not only a compulsive talker, but also a compulsive note taker, which worked for him, since he hated taking notes.

They'd found an M. Jamison in the phone book and had called the number. An answering machine had picked up, indicating that nobody was available to take the call and encouraging the caller to come in and browse at Tiffany Rose.

They had learned the location of the store within minutes and had gone there. Now Marissa Jamison sat in an interview room, waiting for Luke and Sarah to tell her why she was there.

Luke turned to Sarah, who was pouring herself a cup of coffee. His new partner intrigued him, with her boyishly slim hips and small breasts, her intelligent eyes, and slightly manic energy.

He knew she was almost forty years old, but with her spiked dark hair and smattering of freckles she looked much younger.

She hadn't shared much of her personal life with him in the weeks that they'd worked together. Initially he'd thought she might be a lesbian, but she'd mentioned a divorce and he'd seen the way she looked at men and knew his initial assessment had been wrong.

He liked her, even though she was anal to a fault and could be brusque and tough. More than that, he trusted her, and in a world of crime and partnerships, that was the most important thing of all.

"You ready?" he asked. He clutched the file

folder they would need for the interview. She nodded, and he followed her toward the room where Marissa had been placed when they'd arrived at the station.

Marissa Jamison sat with her hands folded on top of the table. As they entered the room she looked up, her blue eyes filled with worry.

She was a pretty woman, all blond hair and blue eyes and dainty features. She was the kind of woman that men lusted after and women didn't trust.

"Before we get started, can I get you anything?" Luke asked. "A soft drink or a cup of coffee?" Sarah looked at him as if he'd just offered a prisoner the key to the handcuffs. It was obvious she intended to play the bad cop. That meant he got to play the good cop.

"No, thank you. I'm fine. I just want to know why I'm here," Marissa said.

"We have some questions to ask you." Sarah took the file folder from Luke and sat at the end of the table. Luke took the chair next to Marissa and let his partner take the lead.

Sarah withdrew a sheet of paper from the folder and shoved it across the table toward Marissa. "Do you know this woman?"

Luke knew the paper held a copy of Jennifer Walsh's driver's license photo. He watched as Marissa picked up the paper, looked at it, then set it down.

"No," she replied. "I don't know her. Why?" She frowned and picked up the paper once again. "Wait . . . maybe . . ."

Sarah leaned forward, and Luke straightened in his chair. "Maybe what?" Sarah asked.

"I don't know her, but I think maybe I saw her."

"When?" Luke asked.

"What's happened to her?" Marissa asked.

"Just answer the questions," Sarah replied.

Fear leaped into her eyes as she looked first at Sarah, then at Luke. "At the ball field on Thursday evening. At Line Creek Park." Her gaze went to the paper once again. "I think she and I might have had a slight altercation in the parking lot."

"A slight altercation? What does that mean?" Sarah asked, her dark eyes cold and hard.

"It wasn't really a big deal. I was backing out of my parking space at the ballpark and she was in a small car behind me, in my blind spot. She honked and I stopped, but she was quite irate and yelled some obscenities at me."

"Then what happened?" Luke asked with a gentleness in his voice that his partner's lacked. Sarah was already acting as if the woman were guilty of something, but they had no idea what was going on yet. Luke was willing to give the fragile blonde the benefit of the doubt.

"Nothing," she replied. "She roared off and I went home." She looked at the photo again. "I'm not even sure it's the same woman."

"Did anyone else see this?" Sarah stood, as if unable to remain seated another minute longer.

"I don't know . . . Maybe. Please, won't you tell me what this is about?"

"I'll tell you what it's about." Sarah opened the file folder, grabbed a photo, walked around the table, and slapped it in front of Marissa.

Marissa gasped, and Luke winced, knowing she was seeing one of the crime-scene photos. However, whatever photo it was, it wouldn't include one important piece of evidence . . . the red bow. That and the presence of the note card were being withheld from the public. They needed something to use to discredit the nuts that would fall out of the woodwork to confess to the crime.

"It's about murder, Mrs. Jamison. Jessica Walsh was murdered within hours of your 'slight altercation' with her." Sarah returned to her seat.

Marissa stood, her face bloodless as she flipped the photo over on its face. "How dare you show me something like that without preparing me first?" she said with the first stir of anger she'd displayed.

"Where were you Thursday night after you left the ballpark?" Sarah asked, unaffected by the woman's outburst.

"Home with my children." Once again her gaze flickered from Sarah to Luke. "This is insane. You can't believe I had anything to do with this."

Sarah opened the file folder again, and Luke saw Marissa flinch, as if expecting another shock.

"We have to believe you had something to do with this, or know something about this," she said as she handed Marissa the final piece of paper from the file. "This is a copy of a note card that was on the body."

Luke had thought Marissa's face was bloodless before, but as she read the sheet of paper, she paled even more. She sank back down into the chair, her hand trembling as she laid the paper on the table.

"This is crazy. I don't understand. I don't know anyone named Blake."

"Apparently somebody named Blake knows you," Sarah returned.

Marissa raised a hand and rubbed the center of her forehead, as if a headache pounded there. "This is some sort of horrible mistake, a terrible coincidence of some kind. I don't know anyone capable of doing something like this."

"We'll need a list of all the people you can remember being at the ballpark that night," Luke said.

She looked at him as if he'd just ask her for a list of every plant form on the face of the earth. "The park was full that night, there were games or practices going on at all of the diamonds. I can't . . . I don't . . ."

"Do the best you can," Luke replied.

"And we're keeping the information about that note card under wraps, so don't mention it to anyone else."

She nodded, her eyes still awash with horror. "Can I go now?" Her need to escape was obvious.

Luke looked at Sarah, then nodded.

The three of them stood, and Marissa walked toward the door. "Mrs. Jamison," Sarah said, stopping Marissa in her tracks. "You might not think anyone you know is capable of murder, but Jennifer Walsh is dead after yelling obscenities at you in a public parking lot. I'd say you'd better reevaluate the people close to you."

"And I think you'd better find another Marissa, because this has absolutely nothing to do with me," she said, then turned and left the room.

"She's probably a dead end," Luke said. "She didn't have a clue about the murder."

Sarah raised a dark eyebrow. "And why would you think that?"

"I don't know. She appeared truthful, was obviously shocked. It's just my initial gut reaction."

"And she looks like a pretty fairy princess, and princesses don't have anything to do with murder?" There was an edge to Sarah's voice. "I suppose that's the type of woman you like, all blond hair and big boobs and blue eyes."

Luke raised an eyebrow. "Did she have big boobs? Damn, I didn't notice. I'm more of a leg man myself."

"Let me tell you something, Luke Hunter. If there's one thing I've learned in my experience, it's that not just ugly women kill. Pretty little blondes with big boobs kill, and Marissa Jamison isn't off my suspect list and she'd better not be off yours." She left the interview room, slamming the door behind her more forcefully than necessary.

Luke scratched his head thoughtfully, wondering what in the hell had bit her behind.

Chapter 5

Marissa didn't go directly back to the shop after leaving the police station. Instead she drove aimlessly, trying to absorb what had just happened. She felt as if she'd been plunged into a horrible nightmare.

Maybe the victim wasn't the same girl she'd nearly backed into at the ball field parking lot. Maybe she had just looked similar to the young woman. Marissa hadn't really gotten a good look at the driver in the car behind her.

Surely there was another Marissa somewhere in the town, a Marissa who would know who this Blake was, a Marissa who would have some clue as to what had happened and why. This couldn't have anything to do with her, it just couldn't.

Still, no amount of rationalization could still the frantic beat of her heart or remove the taste of horror that lingered in her mouth as she thought of that photograph the female cop had shoved in front of her.

The photo had been like none other she had ever seen in her life and hoped never to see again. The victim hadn't worn the mask of death well. Her skin had looked waxy and beyond pale and her eyes had stared as if accusing in death. The slash across her throat had been gaping. She shuddered and gripped the steering wheel more tightly with trembling hands.

She drove up and down residential streets, then discovered herself back at the ballpark. She parked, got out of her car, and sat on the set of bleachers where she'd sat to watch Justin's last game.

It was too early for any ballplayers to be on the fields. She was alone, needed to be alone.

The late-afternoon breeze was pleasant, bringing with it the scent of freshly mowed grass and newly bloomed spring flowers. The overhead sky was a pastel shade of blue, and the pretty scene was in direct contrast with the vision of death that lingered in her head.

She thought again of the picture of Jennifer Walsh. It made her nauseous to think that a human being could do something like that to another.

Who would have done such a thing? And why? It surely had nothing to do with the woman yelling obscenities to her. Surely it had nothing to do with her.

She'd told the officers the truth when she'd said

that she knew nobody capable of such a brutal act. There was no way she'd believe that anyone in her life had the potential for murder. It had to be a terrible coincidence of some kind.

Closing her eyes, she raised her face to the sun for a moment. The officers had said that they'd need a list of people who had been at the ball field that night, but there was no way she could provide them with a complete list.

She didn't even know all the players and parents on Justin's team, let alone all the people from the other teams that had been on the fields that night.

She gasped and snapped her eyes open once again. A sound. She'd heard something. A whisper of footsteps against the grass? A brush of clothing against the benches?

Jerking her head from left to right, she saw nobody around, but was suddenly struck by the fact that she was alone in an isolated ballpark.

Heart pounding, she grabbed her keys from the bench next to her and hurried back to her car, not breathing easily until she was locked inside with the engine running.

Deciding not to return to the shop, she placed a quick call to Alison from her cell phone, then headed in the direction of Jim and Edith's to pick up her kids. She needed desperately to see her children.

Numbness still claimed her as she pulled into the

driveway of the ranch. Unlike that morning, nobody greeted her arrival.

A thrum of panic edged through her as she got out of the car. Where was everyone? She never made it to the door before one of the kids ran out to greet her, or Jim or Edith appeared.

She yanked open the front door. "Justin? Jessica?"

No reply.

Panic crawled up her throat. Where was everyone? She ran through the living room and into the kitchen, relief sweeping over her as she saw the four of them out the window in the backyard.

For a moment she leaned weakly against the round oak table and watched her children working in the garden. Get a grip, Marissa, she scolded herself. You're here early. Nobody was expecting you here.

Apparently the events of the afternoon had wound her far too tight. There was absolutely no reason to suspect any threat toward herself or her family. She drew several deep breaths to steady herself, then stepped out the back door to greet her family.

They stayed for dinner with Jim and Edith. The pleasant banter and laughter that accompanied the meal eased some of her tension.

"I have a favor to ask," she said as they prepared to leave.

Edith placed an arm around her shoulder as they walked toward her car. "What's that?"

"Would you mind watching the kids for a couple of hours tomorrow evening? I've been invited to have dinner with an old friend."

Edith tightened her arm around Marissa's shoulder and smiled. "You know we'd have those kids here every minute of every day if we could. Why don't you just let them stay tonight and tomorrow night? Jim will drive them to school Monday morning."

"Oh, that's too much," Marissa protested.

"Honey." Edith dropped her arm from Marissa and faced her. "You know it's not too much for us, and besides, you look tired. You could use a little break. You've been running yourself ragged for the last several months. Leave the kids here for the rest of the weekend and you go home and enjoy some peace and quiet."

Marissa was torn. Justin and Jessica hadn't spent the night away from her since John's death. She'd held them tight for the past year. Her instinct was to continue to hold on, but she knew that wasn't healthy.

She knew Justin and Jessica would love to spend more time with the grandparents they adored, and for the first time since her husband's death the idea of quiet time without the needs of the kids sounded appealing.

"What about clothes?" she asked. "They only have what they have on."

"We've got spares here, and I do have a washer and dryer," Edith assured her. "Don't worry. They'll be fine." Edith pulled her into a hug, and again Marissa thanked God that he'd seen fit to bring her such wonderful in-laws.

"All right," she agreed.

Minutes later she was once again alone in her car, this time headed home. The kids had been thrilled at the idea of a two-night sleepover and had practically pushed their mother back into the car and on her way.

As she drove home her thoughts filled with Alex Kincaid. With everything that had happened she'd scarcely had time to assess her emotions at seeing him again.

He'd looked marvelous. For a moment, staring into those blue eyes of his, she'd felt as if she were a teenager again and he was the man who held all of her dreams, all her love.

She and Alex had met in the third grade when his family had moved to Cass Creek. They had become not only best friends, but also boyfriend and girlfriend. In high school they had gone steady and had talked about a future together, dreaming about the day they would be married and share a life.

Disaster had struck when they had been juniors in high school. Alex's family had moved from Cass Creek, Missouri, to Boise, Idaho. The two teenagers had tried desperately to figure out a way for Alex to remain in Cass Creek, but ultimately he had moved away with his parents.

She could still remember the day they'd said good-bye to each other. It had been a chilly autumn day and they had clung to each other, promising love forever more.

Both of them had been too young, too idealistic to recognize the difficulty of a long-distance relationship. Although for several months they had written long, passionate letters to each other, had shared as many phone calls as their parents would allow, eventually the letters had become less frequent, the phone calls had stopped altogether, and life and love resumed for each of them separately.

She had no idea if he'd been serious about getting together for dinner with her the next night or if it had been the kind of superficial banter people made with no intention of follow-through.

It would take only minutes of a phone call to him for her to assess whether he really wanted to go to dinner with her or not.

Purple shadows of twilight painted the sky as she pulled her car into the garage. She entered the house and turned on the lights to ward off the coming night.

Without the children the house seemed unusually silent and empty. Saturday nights she had a routine. Some women found manicures and spa treatments relaxing. Marissa baked.

It had been a routine established when John was alive. She'd bake on Saturday nights; then Sunday morning she would take her goodies to the fire station where John was on duty.

John's death had not stopped the routine. Although for the first couple of Sundays after John's death going back into the station house had been extremely difficult for her, she'd also found some comfort in feeding the men who had been like brothers to her husband.

Besides, the fellow firefighters had become like favorite uncles to her children. They'd already lost their father. Marissa hadn't wanted to deprive them of the fine men who had been John's "family."

As she got out the ingredients for a batch of blueberry muffins she checked the clock on the oven. Almost eight. If she was going to call Alex she needed to do it soon.

Surprised at the nervous energy that coursed through her, she picked up her phone and dialed the number on the business card Alex had given her earlier in the afternoon.

He answered on the second ring, and his familiar deep voice sent a rush of heat sweeping through her. "Alex. It's Marissa."

"I was hoping it was you," he replied. "Is everything all right?"

She knew he was asking about the police presence when he'd walked her back to her store. She didn't want to discuss it. She didn't even want to think about it at the moment.

"Everything is fine," she replied.

"Were you able to line up a babysitter for tomorrow evening?"

"Yes, that is, if you still want to have dinner together."

"I can't think of anything I'd like more," he replied. "However, I need your help in choosing the restaurant. There have been so many changes in town in the years I've been gone, and since I've gotten back I haven't eaten out much."

Marissa took a moment to consider the restaurants she knew. There were several in the vicinity that had been favorite haunts of hers and John's. She didn't want to go to any of them with Alex. It wouldn't feel right.

"Café Italian is a great place," she offered. The restaurant wasn't far from her home, was medium priced, and had delicious food. "It's on the corner of Oak and Walnut Streets."

"Sounds good to me," he replied. "Why don't I plan on picking you up around a quarter of seven."

"Why don't I meet you there," she replied. She wasn't sure why, but she preferred he didn't pick her up. That felt too much like a date, and this wasn't a date, she reminded herself firmly. It was just two old friends having dinner together.

"Sure," he agreed easily. "Then I'll see you tomorrow night at seven at Café Italian."

The instant she agreed and hung up, she wanted to call him back and cancel. She wasn't ready for any kind of social activities, especially with a man who had once owned her heart so completely.

"Don't be ridiculous, Marissa," she murmured aloud as she got to work on the muffins. She wasn't a teenager anymore, and whatever she had once felt for Alex Kincaid had been left behind long ago. She had no idea what kind of man he had become, had only memories of the boy he had been.

As she worked, she tried desperately to shove thoughts of the dead woman away from her mind. She turned on an easy-listening radio station and poured herself a glass of white wine.

Marissa had discovered the joy of baking in the first year of her marriage to John. John had loved freshly baked pies and cakes, muffins and cookies, and in an effort to please her handsome husband, Marissa had learned how to bake. In the process she'd discovered it was something she found both relaxing and enjoyable.

Tonight it was difficult to keep her mind on the baking and off that damned photograph. Had it been the young woman that she'd almost hit in the parking lot? She couldn't be positive.

By the time she pulled the last of the blueberry muffins from the oven, she was pleasantly buzzed from a little too much wine and relaxed by the music and savory scent that filled the house.

She stored the muffins for the night, turned off

the lights, checked to make sure the doors were locked, then went into the master bathroom for a long, leisurely bath.

She carried with her one last glass of wine, suspecting that she'd be sorry in the morning that she'd overindulged. As the water ran in the deep over-sized tub, she undressed and stared at her reflection in the mirror.

Sixteen years of life and the birth of two children had transformed her body from the seventeen-year-old she had been when she'd last seen Alex. Her breasts were larger and a little less perky. There were several faint white stretch marks across her lower abdomen, but all in all, Marissa wasn't un-happy with her reflection.

She was a realist and knew that time and gravity and life experiences worked on youth and supple-ness. Would she take away her children to erase the stretch marks? Not a chance. Would she give back the years she'd spent with John to reclaim the youth she'd had when she married him? No way.

Turning away from the mirror, she shook her head, knowing that the moments of self-examination had been prompted by her dinner engagement the next evening with Alex.

She lit half a dozen candles that were scattered around the sunken tub, then turned off the over-head lights and slid into the warm, perfumed water.

A large picture window was at tub level and looked out on the heavily wooded backyard. It had been this, as much as anything, that had sold Marissa on the house. If she positioned herself just right in the tub she could see out the window to the stars up in the sky.

The bedroom had the same view of thick woods full of wildlife. The nearest house couldn't even be seen from this vantage point. Many nights she and John had made love with the curtains wide open and the sound of the forest whispering in through open windows.

She grabbed her glass of wine and leaned her head back against the bath pillow, the warm water and soothing heat easing the last of the tension from inside her.

With the faint light of the candles, she could see the night sky filled with stars so close it appeared that she could reach right up and grab a handful.

She thought of her children, and a smile curved her lips. Jim would probably already be in bed. There wasn't much that kept her father-in-law from his early bedtime hour. Edith and the kids would be in the living room, watching movies and eating popcorn out of a butter-slippery bowl and drinking soda from glasses without coasters. In the morning the kids would probably have a bowl of the sugary cereal Marissa didn't allow in the house.

An occasional indulgence didn't hurt them, she told herself. Besides, that's what grandparents did, indulge their grandchildren.

She finished her glass of wine, set the glass on the tub rim, then grabbed her favorite loofah.

It was as she dragged the soapy loofah sponge across her shoulders that the skin on the nape of her neck prickled uncomfortably. Despite the warmth of the water that surrounded her, a chill walked up her spine.

For the first time in the ten years that she had lived in the house, she grabbed the end of the wand that controlled the blinds over her window and quickly twirled it, shutting out the outside world.

The blinds closed and he breathed a sigh of disappointment as he slid among the trees and away from her house. Even though he would have liked to watch her a lot longer, the glimpses he'd gotten were enough to sustain him through the night.

He would dream about her. He'd dream of that silky skin, of her long golden hair and sweet smile. He wondered if she would dream about him. Did she know of the gift he had left for her? The foul-mouthed bitch who had yelled at her? If she didn't know yet, she would know soon enough.

It took him only minutes to get to his car parked two streets over from her house. He slid behind the wheel and leaned his head back against the headrest, savoring for a moment the memory of that kill.

It had been remarkably easy. Of course, the young woman had been doped up and looking for excitement. From the ballpark he'd followed her to

an area of the city that was known to law enforce-
ment as Dealers' Corner. She'd parked, obviously
looking for a connection.

She'd found one. Him.

She was certain that with his connections whatever he could provide her would be far better than
the shit she could buy on the streets. She'd agreed to
follow him to Penguin Park and have a little party
with him. So easy.

He started the engine of his car and pulled away
from the curb, his thoughts returning to Marissa.
"She'll be mine, Mama," he murmured aloud. "The
perfect wife for the perfect man."

A deep sense of satisfaction swept through him.
His mother had spent her days drinking, watching
soap operas, and beating the hell out of him.

"You'll never amount to anything," she'd rail, her
eyes bleary and her breath stale. "You're nothing.
You'll always be nothing." After she'd beat him,
she'd weep, railing at God for not sending her a perfect son. "Why can't you be like Blake?" Blake was
the name of her favorite character on her soap
opera.

His hands tightened around the steering wheel as
he remembered those horrid days of his youth and
the mother who had raised him. She'd been a miserable bitch, foul-mouthed, filthy, and mean. But
he'd shown her.

He'd gotten the perfect job, where he was respected and admired. He lived an exemplary life.

He didn't drink, he didn't smoke or gamble. His small apartment was neat and clean.

He had become perfect.

He had become Blake.

It amused him that only after her death had he become the perfect son. Her death had been his freedom. Just like he'd freed Marissa from that ugly bitch who had screamed obscenities at her.

She knew him now. He knew the police would question her, that they probably would show her the note he'd left on the body. Yes, she would know him soon if she didn't already. She'd know his name was Blake. What she didn't know yet was that he was her destiny.

Chapter 6

Strange to wake up without the sounds of the kids fighting over the remote control or demanding breakfast. Instead the sound of birdsong awakened her. A mockingbird and a redbird sang, heralding in the morning with sweet melodic tunes.

For a long, luxurious few minutes she remained in bed, listening to the birds without any real conscious thought intruding. Sundays were special. It was the only day of the week she didn't go into the shop.

Usually the day was devoted to the children. They'd go to a park or to a movie or simply spend the day in the house playing games. Today the day was hers to spend as she wished. First on the agenda was to deliver the muffins to the station house.

It was only when thoughts of Jennifer Walsh's murder intruded that she pulled herself from bed, the beauty of the morning tainted by thoughts of violence and death.

It took her only a few minutes to dress for the day, then she loaded up the muffins and headed toward the fire station where John had worked for twelve years before his death.

Despite the trauma of the previous day she had slept deep and without dreams. She made herself believe that whatever had happened to Jennifer Walsh had nothing whatsoever to do with her. The police would realize that soon enough and catch the killer.

It had nothing to do with her and she refused to allow it to play in her mind. Instead she focused on the evening to come. It surprised her how much she looked forward to dinner with Alex.

A nice restaurant. Adult conversation. The enjoyment of old memories. It sounded like a wonderful way to pass a couple of hours.

A two-story brick building housed the Cass Creek Fire Department Station No. 5. Two garage bays and an office comprised the bottom floor. When Marissa pulled up in the visitor parking, one of the fire engines was parked out front and the other was inside the bay.

Several firemen worked on the engine, polishing paint and spit shining chrome. All three stopped what they were doing as she approached carrying the huge basket of baked goods.

David Harrold was the first to reach her, and she

smiled warmly at the tall, handsome blond who had been her husband's closest friend.

"Ah, it's the angel of muffins," he said as he took the basket from her. "Where are the munchkins?"

"At John's parents. They had a sleepover last night."

"Hey, Marissa," Kip Larson, one of the other fire-fighters shouted. "What is it this morning? Banana nut? Cinnamon?"

"Blueberry," she replied. "Haven't you heard? Blueberries are good for the brain. You might want to eat an extra muffin, Kip," she teased. He laughed and gave her a thumbs-up.

Although there were only three firemen in the bay area, Marissa knew there were at least six more upstairs in the area that served as living quarters while the men were on duty.

As she followed David into the bay, Captain Michael Morrison came out of his office to greet her. Tall, with premature salt-and-pepper hair, Mike radiated a quiet authority. All the men liked and respected Mike. John had always described him as tough but fair.

"Marissa." He nodded and smiled. "I don't know what the men will do when they no longer have your goodies to look forward to on Sunday mornings."

"If it wasn't for you, we'd all be eating Kip's left-over chili for breakfast on Sundays," David exclaimed.

"So did you beat the dry cleaner boys the other night?"

Mike smiled and nodded. "It was a shut out, five to one."

"Good for you," she exclaimed.

"You doing all right, Marissa?" he asked.

She nodded. "Fine. We're doing just fine."

"The kids seem to grow an inch every time I see them."

Marissa smiled. "Yes, they are growing by leaps and bounds."

Mike excused himself and returned to his office and closed the door behind him.

"Why don't I go up and tell the other guys you're here. You know they'll want to say hello."

"No, that's all right. I'm not staying today." Normally, Marissa would hang around for a half an hour or so and visit with all the men in the station. "I've got a ton of things I need to do at home today."

"All right. Then I'll walk you back to your car." He set the basket of muffins on a workbench and together they headed back toward her car.

"Got a girlfriend yet?" Marissa asked.

He grinned and shook his head ruefully. "All the women I meet are either married, gay, or just plain crazy." His grin fell away. "How are you doing? How's life treating you? We never get a chance to really visit when I see you at the ball fields."

For a brief moment she thought about telling him about the murder and the questioning by the police, but the impulse lasted only a second, then was gone. "Things are okay. The kids are doing well, and between them and the shop I'm always busy."

"John would be so proud of you."

"I hope so." She smiled at him and for a moment memories of the man they had both loved filled the space between them. "And now I'd better get out of here before Captain Mike yells at you for standing around," she said, breaking the moment.

"Tell the kids I'll stop by sometime this week. I've got a little surprise for each of them."

"David, you spoil them," she chided.

He grinned and nodded. "Yeah, but that's what kids are for." His eyes darkened slightly. "Besides, if things were different, John would have spoiled my kids for me. I'll call you."

Back in her car and headed home minutes later, she thought of David. He and John had started working for the fire department at the same time. David had been the first person John had introduced her to when she and John had started dating.

At the time she first met him, he'd been married, but a year after John and Marissa's wedding, David's wife divorced him. Divorce certainly wasn't uncommon at the fire station.

Like police officers, firefighters often found themselves married to women who couldn't handle the danger, the shift work, and the pressure of their husbands' jobs.

Certainly there had been times over the course of

their marriage when Marissa had secretly wished her husband had a nine-to-five job, a job that when she heard sirens didn't start her heart thumping with a touch of anxiety. But John had loved being a fireman, and she had loved being married to a man who was passionate about his work.

But John was gone and tonight she would have dinner with Alex. She tightened her grip on the steering wheel, amazed that after all these years the thought of Alex Kincaid still had the power to make her pulse race more than a little.

Alex Kincaid sat on a stool nursing a beer in the bar area of the Café Italian restaurant. He checked his watch for the third time since he'd arrived. Quarter until seven.

He'd arrived far too early, like an overeager schoolboy on a first date. It was crazy, how much he had wanted this to happen, how much he'd wanted to see her again, spend time with her.

She had been the first thing he'd thought of when he'd awakened that morning. While he'd worked at his drafting table thoughts of her had intruded over and over again.

Looking into those blue eyes of hers, he'd remembered a hundred moments from his youth, another hundred from his adolescence, and each of those memories had been filled with the heat of turbulent, wild hormone-driven yearnings.

Amazing how teenage angst and lust could

survive undiluted through adulthood. Marissa had been the one who had gotten away, the one who had been taken away at a time when both of them had been young and powerless to fight the whims of fate.

They weren't powerless anymore, and the whims of fate seemed to be blowing their way. Still, he was nervous, and that surprised him. He couldn't remember the last time a woman had made him nervous. He certainly hadn't expected having a meal with her to make him so anxious.

The restaurant door opened, and he turned on his stool to see her step inside. For a moment he remained unmoving, watching her.

The black dress she wore clung to her in all the right places. The black strappy shoes seemed to emphasize the slender curve of her calves and the length of her shapely legs. Gold earrings sparkled along with a gold necklace that complemented the gracefulness of her neck.

She looked casually elegant, and despite his admonitions to himself to take it slow, he couldn't help the pulse that quickened in a lingering emotion from the past.

He saw the moment she spied him. Her eyes widened and a smile curved her lips, and in the warmth of that smile all his nervous energy ebbed away.

He stood and went to greet her. "Marissa." He grabbed one of her hands and at the same time gestured to the hostess that they were ready to be seated.

"You look wonderful."

"Thank you," she murmured. He dropped her hand as the hostess approached and indicated they should follow her.

Within moments they were settled at a small candlelit table that afforded just enough privacy for intimate conversation. The hostess left and there was a moment of awkward silence. They both spoke at once in an effort to break it, then laughed. "You first," he said.

"I was just going to say that it's nice to see you again," she said.

"I was going to say the same thing."

Before they could say anything more the waitress arrived to take their drink orders. They each ordered a glass of wine, and when the waitress had departed they eased into a conversation talking about old schoolmates and friends.

As she caught him up on the doings of people he'd lost contact with sixteen years before, he found himself studying her, seeing glimpses of the girl he'd once loved in the woman she'd become.

Her eyes were just as blue as he remembered, her smile just as warm and bright. There were fine lines radiating out from the outer corners of her eyes that hadn't been there years before, but they only added to her attractiveness, adding a touch of character to her beauty.

It wasn't just on the outside that he caught glimpses of her youth. She still had a wicked sense of humor coupled with a keen intelligence he'd always found challenging.

It wasn't until the waitress had served their meals that he asked her about her husband. "John Jamison? Did we all go to school together?"

"No. John was four years older than us. He was finishing up college when we were graduating from high school."

Alex twirled a forkful of spaghetti. "How did you meet?"

She smiled. "I was cooking bacon and started a grease fire. I went blank, couldn't think of how to get it out, so I called 911, and within minutes John and a handful of other firemen stormed into my tiny kitchen and put out the flames. I was mortified."

She dabbed at her mouth with a corner of her napkin, then reached for a piece of garlic bread. "Anyway, we dated for almost a year, then got married."

"Was it a good marriage?"

She paused a moment to take a sip of her wine, a whisper of sadness darkening her eyes. "Yes, it was a good marriage. Not perfect, but good. I'm not one of those women who canonizes her husband in death. John was a good man with faults, and I certainly have faults of my own. Like any marriage, we had our ups and downs, but mostly it was ups."

"You must miss him," Alex said softly. "Was it an illness that took him?"

"No." She hesitated a long moment before continuing. "It was murder."

"My God, Marissa. What happened?"

Marissa picked up her wineglass again and took another sip before replying. In the first weeks after the murder she'd lain awake for hours wondering exactly what had happened, if John had seen his death coming in the headlights of the vehicle, what his last thoughts had been, if any.

"The night of his death he and I had spent the evening watching old movies together. It was after midnight when we finished the last one and I discovered we were out of milk."

"And the kids would need milk for breakfast," Alex replied.

She nodded. "So John left to go to the grocery store near our house. It's open twenty-four hours. The rest I know only from what the police were able to surmise. Apparently John made it to the store and bought the milk, but when he was on his way back to the car he was struck by another car and killed. There were no witnesses, and the driver didn't stick around. There were also no skid marks, no indication that the driver tried in any way to miss hitting John."

Alex's features wore both horror and sympathy. "How terrible. Have the police caught the person?"

"No. As I said, there were no witnesses, no leads

to follow. They found some pieces of a headlight and in the next couple of weeks checked out all the repair shops in the area for cars with front-end damage, but nothing concrete turned up." She waved a hand in the air. "But you don't want to talk about this."

"No, no, if you need to talk about it, then I want to talk about it," he replied.

Marissa smiled as a wave of warmth swept through her. "That's one of the things I remember from when we were dating, that you always had a gift for listening."

He grinned, the sexy half grin that had been the first thing she'd noticed when they'd been nothing more than schoolkids. "That's because I always found everything you had to say fascinating."

"I appreciate the sympathetic ear," she replied, and meant it. She rarely talked about John's death to anyone. "Are you enjoying being back here?" she asked, deciding a change of topic was in order.

"I am. I remembered Cass Creek as a warm, friendly place, and I'm glad to discover my memories weren't wrong."

"I can't imagine living anyplace else," she replied.

"I can tell you I'm definitely happy to be back here now that I ran into you."

For a long moment their gazes remained locked and the old magic she'd once felt whenever he was near shimmered in the air between them. She looked away, disconcerted by the surge of sweet, familiar emotion inside her.

Since the moment she'd arrived at the restaurant and joined him, she'd been aware of a subtle sizzle in the air between them. It frightened her just a little bit. She knew she was in a vulnerable state, lonely and ripe to fall into a relationship for all the wrong reasons.

She leaned back in her chair to escape the pleasant scent of him and the power of his eyes. "So tell me about the women in your past. I'm sure there have been a bevy of beauties."

"No bevy, just two. At least two who were important enough to remember. I dated a woman named Elaine through college, but the relationship didn't sustain life after we graduated. Then there was Susan. Susan and I dated for five years, talked about marriage, but it never happened."

"Why not?"

He frowned thoughtfully, the gesture doing nothing to detract from his attractiveness. "I'm not sure. The timing never seemed right, and neither of us had any real driving need."

"Why did you break up?"

"We didn't exactly break up. We just drifted further and further apart until eventually it seemed right not to be together rather than right to be together. That was three years ago and I haven't really dated since then. I've been focused on my work for the last couple of years."

"A workaholic?" she teased.

"Maybe a bit," he agreed. "It's easy to be a workaholic when there's nothing much else to distract you. Speaking of distractions, I took a little time yesterday and drove around to some of the old haunts. Did you know our tree is gone and a story-and-a-half house now stands in its place?"

She knew exactly what tree he was speaking about, and thoughts of that old tree evoked myriad memories. They had always ended their dates parked beneath the same huge old oak tree where they would make out until both of them were breathless and wanting more.

"The Sweet River Development. It was built about four years ago, and the tree was one of the first taken out when they began building."

"Kind of a shame." His eyes twinkled with a light that cast a whisper of heat through her. "There were many nights I thought I might die beneath that tree."

She smiled. "There were many nights you tried to convince me you might die."

"Ah, but you were stronger than me."

"I was determined to be a virgin on my wedding night."

One of his dark eyebrows rose. "And were you?"

A slight flush warmed her cheeks. "When we were together, Alex, I was a seventeen-year-old schoolgirl. I was twenty-four when I met John, at a different place in my life than when I was with you.

So, to answer your question, no, I wasn't a virgin on my wedding night."

"My timing has always been bad," he said, his eyes warm with a teasing glint.

"Oh, I don't know about that. You invited me to dinner at exactly the time I was yearning for a little adult company and a meal that didn't include finger food."

His expression grew more serious. "Did those detectives have news for you about John's murder?"

It would be easy to make something up, to keep the horror of the dead girl's photos away from Alex, but she found that she wanted to tell somebody, needed to talk about it with someone completely uninvolved. Even though it had been sixteen years since she'd had anything to do with Alex, the trust that had once existed between them still remained.

"No, they didn't come to discuss John's murder with me. They wanted to question me about another murder." She shoved her plate aside, appetite gone as she thought of the murder of Jennifer Walsh.

Even though the police had told her not to mention the note left at the scene, she couldn't tell Alex about the murder and her involvement without mentioning the note. Besides, she desperately needed to talk to somebody about all of it.

It took her only minutes to fill him in, starting with the incident in the ball field parking lot to the interview with the two detectives and the note that had been left at the crime scene. As she talked his features radiated a number of expressions: sympathy, horror, then thoughtfulness.

"And you don't know for sure if the dead woman was the same as the woman in the parking lot?" he asked when she was finished.

Marissa shook her head. "I just don't know for sure. I've played and replayed that moment in the parking lot in my mind, but I can't get a real clear picture of the young woman who cussed me out."

"And you don't know anyone named Blake?"

"If I did, believe me, I would have told the detectives," she replied. "I just keep hoping that what they'll find out is that there is another Marissa somewhere in the area, a Marissa who knows a Blake and that all this has nothing to do with me." She fought the chill that threatened to walk up her spine.

Alex reached across the table and wrapped his hand around one of hers. The contact was both comforting and electrifying and forced her to recognize how hungry she'd been for even the most simple of male touches.

"I hope you're right," he said. "But in the meantime, I hope you're being extra careful about your own safety. It sounds like there's a nut loose in the area."

"Since John's murder I've never forgotten the fact that I'm a single woman living with two small children in my house. I take our safety very seriously."

She knew she should pull her hand from his, but reluctance kept her in place.

"Still, you need to be careful, Marissa." His eyes darkened with concern. "I'll follow you home from here." She started to protest, but he squeezed her hand. "I won't ask for an invitation inside, at least not this time. I won't bother you at all, but I need to see that you're safely home."

At least not this time. The words promised another dinner, another time, and she welcomed the promise.

She had no idea where a relationship with Alex might lead, whether simply to a friendship or to something deeper, but she had learned to take life one day at a time and see where it went.

Chapter 7

"Y ou wearing perfume?" Luke looked at Sarah, who sat next to him in the passenger seat.

Sarah's cheeks warmed. "Yeah. I always wear perfume. Why? A cop can't wear perfume?" A touch of defiance deepened her voice.

He cast her another quick glance. "I just haven't noticed before today. It smells good."

"Thanks." She waited for him to say something derogatory, but when nothing was forthcoming, she relaxed. Back in Chicago she'd worn perfume only once while on the job. She'd taken so much ribbing from her fellow officers she hadn't made the mistake again.

She wasn't sure why she'd put it on every day for the last week, but she knew it had something to do with Luke Hunter. She wanted him to view her as a valuable partner, a competent fellow cop, but somewhere deep inside her she also wanted him to take note of the fact that she was female.

It worried her just a little bit, how acutely conscious she was of him. Since her divorce over a year ago Sarah hadn't been remotely drawn to any other man, had sworn that she would live the rest of her life alone. But something about Luke Hunter made her miss having a man in her life.

They were now on their way to Jennifer Walsh's funeral and hoped to meet up with some of the young woman's friends. Jennifer's parents had been no help in their investigation.

Jennifer had moved out of her parents' home two years ago, and the relationship between parents and child had been strained. They had no idea who she hung out with, how she spent her spare time, or where she had worked.

Sarah had found the situation tragic and had gone home and called her own parents, needing to touch base and check in with them and let them know she was doing fine. Five years ago they had moved from Chicago to a retirement village in Arizona. When she'd mentioned making a move of her own after the divorce, they had encouraged her to move to Arizona, but the Cass Creek job had looked more promising.

"Nice day," she said, breaking the silence in the car.

"I heard we're supposed to get rain by this afternoon."

She looked out at the bright blue sky. No hint of rain clouds at the moment. "Hopefully it will hold off until after the funeral. There's nothing worse than a rainy funeral."

"There's nothing worse than a funeral, period," he replied. "Marissa Jamison called this morning. This afternoon she's bringing in a list of people who were at the ball field on Thursday."

"I did a little checking on Marissa Jamison late last night."

He slid her another look. "When you're off duty, you should stay off duty, otherwise you'll burn out quicker than a short wooden match."

"I didn't have anything else to do," she replied. She had yet to meet anyone to socialize with, and television held no appeal. "Anyway, I learned several interesting tidbits."

"Like?"

"Like the fact that her husband's death remains on the records as an unsolved murder. She used the insurance money from his death to open her store."

"Not a crime," he replied.

"True, but don't you find it odd that most people live their entire lives and don't experience any random acts of violence, yet she has already been touched by two murders."

"I'd say she's been unusually unlucky. Besides, we haven't absolutely confirmed that she's the Marissa the note was intended for."

"She's the only Marissa we've been able to find in the Cass Creek area," Sarah replied.

"But it's possible the Marissa we're looking for is in Kansas City or any of the dozen outlying towns," he countered easily. "Hopefully we'll get a little more information at the funeral about Jennifer and see how or if the two women might tie together. It will all sort itself out sooner or later."

Sarah tamped down frustration. Everyone knew the first forty-eight hours following a homicide were the most crucial. Every hour that passed after that made it less and less likely that the crime would be solved.

She wanted action. She needed to slap handcuffs on whoever was responsible for this crime. She needed to solve this. This was her first murder case as a Cass Creek detective. It was vital that she prove herself not just to Luke but to the other men on the force.

She slid another glance toward her partner as he turned into the cemetery gates. This was the first time since she'd started working with him that she'd seen him in a suit and tie. His normal attire was dress slacks and a sports jacket or jeans and a shirt.

His sandy hair was tousled, as usual, and she'd never seen his eyes radiate anything other than the lazy glint that lit them now, but the navy suit and subdued tie gave him an aura of polish that increased his attractiveness.

She frowned and focused her attention out the front car window. The last thing she needed was a case of the hots for her partner, especially since other than commenting on her perfume he had given her no indication that he was aware that she was female.

It took only moments to assess the fact that the funeral for Jennifer Walsh would probably yield little. Investigators always tried to attend the funeral of murder victims in the hopes that the perpetrator of the crime would attend to see the aftermath of grief and tragedy.

Whoever killed Jennifer would be a fool to show up at a funeral where it appeared only a handful of people had come. As Luke parked the car a wave of depression swept through Sarah as she saw how few people had turned out for the last good-bye to Jennifer Lynn Walsh.

As she got out of the car and smoothed a hand down the front of her navy blazer, she wondered who would attend her funeral. Certainly her parents, if they were still alive, would attend. But who else? It was only after her divorce from Max that she realized their friends had been his friends, and when he'd left her, their friends had left her as well.

She hadn't been in Cass Creek long enough to get acquainted with anyone other than her fellow officers, and none of them had invited her to socialize.

As she and Luke walked toward the group of people gathered to say their final good-byes to

Jennifer, Sarah had the craziest impulse to make Luke promise that if something happened to her he would attend her funeral. She wanted him to vow that he would send flowers and perhaps shed a single tear for her.

She mentally shook herself and focused on the task at hand. Jeez, she wasn't just getting maudlin, she was dancing on the edge of insanity expecting Luke Hunter to give a damn about her.

They were greeted solemnly by Jennifer's parents and introduced to the others who stood nearby. There was an aunt and uncle who looked as if they'd rather be anywhere but here, a girlfriend of Jennifer's with a pierced eyebrow and a belligerent attitude, and a guy friend named Sam who appeared to be under the influence of drugs.

Luke exchanged a glance with Sarah, letting her know they would probably get nothing here.

The service was blessedly short, and afterward Sarah and Luke spent a few minutes talking to the parents, the aunt and uncle, then chatting up the young man and young girl who had been friends with Jennifer.

Sarah looked up at the tall, unnaturally thin Sam. "You and Jennifer, you were good friends?"

He picked at a scab on his cheek with dirty nails and shrugged. "We hung out pretty often." His gaze refused to stay still, indicating to her that his drug of choice was probably meth.

"She ever mention anyone named Marissa?"

He frowned and found another scab to pick on his forearm. "Nah, I never heard her mention no Marissa."

"Jennifer like to hang out at the Line Creek ball fields?"

He grinned, displaying uneven yellow front teeth. "Yeah, she hung out at lots of ball fields. She was a real baseball freak. Loved to watch the big boys throw their balls around." He laughed at the double entendre. Sarah didn't.

"I need your full name and address. We might need to talk to you as we further investigate Jennifer's death."

It took her only minutes to get the information from Sam, although her instincts told her the hyped-up loser probably had nothing to offer them. At the same time Luke finished up with the young woman and together they headed back to their car.

"Get anything?" he asked.

"Jennifer liked baseball," Sarah replied. "It's very possible she was at the Line Creek ball field when Marissa was there."

"Yeah, that's what I got, too." They got into the car.

As they pulled out of the cemetery gates Luke's cell phone rang. "Yeah. Yeah. Got it." He snapped the phone shut and yanked at his tie. "That was the station. Just got a call about a body found in a trash Dumpster. Looks like Jennifer Walsh is going to have to go on the back burner."

Sarah knew this was the way it went, a four-day-old murder replaced by a fresh one. Cases were shuffled and energies divided.

Still, it would take more than a fresh case to put Jennifer Walsh's murder on Sarah's back burner. That red bow stuck on Jennifer's forehead would haunt her until the killer was found.

Chapter 8

Dread filled Marissa as she returned to the ball field. Even though she knew Jennifer's murder hadn't taken place here, even though she had almost convinced herself that the young girl's murder had absolutely nothing to do with her, tension rippled through her as she turned into the parking area.

Tuesdays were practices and Thursdays were games. Although she would have loved to skip the practice tonight, she couldn't do that to Justin, who lived and breathed his baseball.

"I wanna go home," Jessica whined from the backseat.

"After Justin's practice," Marissa replied as she pulled into a parking space.

"But I want to go home now."

Marissa sighed. Jessica had been out of sorts all day, plaintive and whining about anything and everything. She always got that way when she was overtired, and she hadn't slept well the night before. Jessica suffered from allergies, and spring was always difficult for her.

Marissa shut off the car engine and turned around to look at her daughter. "We'll go home right after practice, and you can get right into bed and I'll read you a story."

"What story?" the little girl asked, her lips pursed into a pout.

"*Swan Lake Barbie*," Marissa replied without hesitation. For the last month that particular book had been the choice reading material. There was nothing better than Barbies and ballerinas.

"Okay," Jessica relented, and Marissa breathed a sigh of relief. Jessica was the sweetest girl, but if she was overtired or ill, she became a monster child.

"Come on, let's go," Justin exclaimed. "Coach doesn't like it if we're late."

Within minutes she and Jessica were seated on the bleachers and Justin was on the field with his team. There were always fewer people here on Tuesdays for the practices than on Thursdays for the games.

As Jessica occupied herself with a book, Marissa found her attention divided between the field and the people seated on the bleachers. They were the same people she'd seen here every Tuesday and Thursday for the last three weeks, ever since the team had come together.

She wasn't sure what she was looking for? A deranged killer lingering in the crowd? A homicidal maniac with bloodlust in his eyes?

If what the police believed was true, then somebody here had seen her altercation with Jennifer Walsh and the result had been Jennifer's death.

Her gaze caught Marc Carter's eyes and he smiled warmly and instantly stood and headed in her direction.

She swallowed a small groan. For the past couple of weeks Marc had been giving her signals that he'd like to go out sometime. All she knew about him was that his wife had left him eight months ago, they shared joint custody of their son, Timothy, and that Marc worked as an accountant for a law firm.

The other thing she knew about Marc was that he radiated a kind of desperate need to get a woman, any woman, back in his life. The last thing Marissa needed in her life was a desperate man.

Marc slid onto the bleacher next to her with an overly bright smile and smelling like he'd bathed in a pine-scented cologne. "Hey, Marissa, how's it going?"

"Fine, just fine, Marc."

"How are things at that shop of yours?"

"Busy. Business has been good."

"Great, that's great. Must be fun to have your own business like that."

"It's fun, but it's also a lot of work."

He turned his gaze toward the field. "Justin sure

is getting good out there. He looks better and better at every practice."

She looked out at her son and smiled. "He loves baseball."

"Timothy can't decide between baseball and martial arts," he said.

"Thank goodness they don't have to decide their careers when they're seven."

"Yeah, right." He laughed as if somehow she'd managed to say something delightfully witty. "So I was wondering if maybe you'd like to have a drink with me some evening."

Marissa had felt this coming and her mind whirled to come up with a graceful reply. "Oh, Marc, that's really nice of you, but most evenings I'm working at my shop, and if I'm not at the shop I try to be home with the kids."

"Then maybe a weekend barbecue with the kids included," he said, apparently not discouraged by her initial reply.

The last thing she wanted to do was hurt his feelings, nor did she want to encourage him. A week ago she would have rejected his offer simply because she didn't feel ready to pursue any kind of a romantic relationship. But that had been before the dinner with Alex. Since that night her head had been filled with thoughts of the handsome man she'd once thought she'd marry.

"Thanks, Marc, but I'm just not in a place right now to do the social thing."

His smile fell, and he shifted positions on the bleacher seat. "Okay, that's cool." His smile returned. "Maybe later in the summer?"

"Maybe," she replied, and returned his smile.

She sighed in relief when he finally murmured a good-bye and moved to another area of the bleachers. He seemed like a nice enough guy, but there was no spark, no magic for her where he was concerned.

She'd had spark and magic with John, and when he died she never imagined she'd feel that way again with another man. She'd been wrong.

Alex had fired a spark. There had been a sense of magic when they'd had dinner, a magic that had continued with phone calls from him the last two nights.

As nice as it was to feel that giddy warmth, that crazy kick of hormones and feminine pleasure, she told herself to go slow. She didn't want to make the mistake of building any kind of a relationship with him that might be built on nothing more than the sweet memories of youth.

"Mommy, I want to go home now," Jessica said, pulling Marissa back to the here and now.

"Soon, baby." Marissa placed an arm around Jessica's shoulder and pulled the little girl closer against her side. No matter how things went with Alex, her children came first.

Marissa had to admit that she was lonely, but she wasn't about to introduce man after man into the lives of her children. If Alex wanted to date her, he'd have to do it on her terms.

It was almost nine when she pulled into the driveway, eager to get the cranky Jessica into bed. After the practice session she had stopped and gotten them all ice cream cones, thinking the unexpected treat would cheer up Jessica. It had worked for a few minutes, but the moment the cone had been consumed, Jessica had resumed her plaintive whines.

A good night's sleep would put her right again. Justin, on the other hand, had grown quiet, a sure indication that he was tired as well.

She saw the flowers the moment she stepped out of her car. The glass vase holding the red roses shone in the gleam of the porch light and the sight of them constricted her heart with a sharp, unexpected grief.

"Hey, Mom, look!" Justin ran toward the porch. "There's flowers just like what Daddy used to get for you. Where did they come from?"

"I don't know." Marissa and Jessica joined him on the porch. Marissa picked up the vase with one hand and unlocked the front door with the other.

"Maybe Daddy sent them from heaven," Jessica said.

Again Marissa's heart squeezed painfully as she heard the longing in Jessica's voice. She carried the vase into the kitchen and placed it on the counter as the pungent fragrance filled the air.

"Justin, bath time. Jessica, pajama time." As the kids left to get ready for bed, she checked the roses for a card. No card, no note, there was nothing to indicate who had sent the flowers or where they had come from.

She touched one of the lush red blooms, remembering all the times in the past when John had surprised her with her favorites, long-stemmed red roses. It would be nice to think he'd sent her this bouquet straight from heaven, but of course that was impossible.

They had probably come from Alex. He knew they'd be at the ball field tonight, and he must have left them as a surprise. He wouldn't have known that red roses had always been John's gift to her, but he might have remembered from long ago that she'd always preferred red roses to any other kind of flower.

"Are you gonna read me a story?" Jessica appeared in the kitchen doorway, rubbing her eyes with a fist.

"Of course, honey." Marissa followed Jessica to her bedroom and tucked her into bed.

"I want Daddy to send me a new Barbie doll from heaven," Jessica said.

Marissa smoothed Jessica's fine bangs away from her forehead and breathed in the scent of childhood that lingered on her daughter. "You know, honey, those roses didn't come from Daddy in heaven, and

Daddy can't send you a new Barbie doll. All Daddy can send us from heaven is his love."

"I miss Daddy."

Marissa leaned down and kissed her daughter's cheek. "I do too, sweetheart. Now let's find out about *Swan Lake Barbie*."

It took only ten minutes of reading before Jessica fell asleep. Marissa turned off the bedside lamp and left the room.

Justin was freshly scrubbed and in his bed. He had several little plastic dinosaurs in bed with him, and when he saw her he gathered them up and placed them on the nightstand.

She sat down on the edge of his bed and fought the impulse to reach out and thread her fingers through his hair. He'd never been a particularly demonstrative child, and since John's death he was less so, as if hugs and kisses were for babies and he was now the little man of the house.

"I was just remembering when me and Dad made that dinosaur out of paper mâché. Do you remember that?"

"I do. It was a fine-looking dinosaur." The sight of those roses hadn't just affected her, but had brought forth memories of John for both of her children.

"It kind of looked more like a bear than a tyrannosaurus," Justin said, "but I didn't say anything 'cause I didn't want to hurt Dad's feelings."

"I thought it looked just like a tyrannosaurus,"

she replied. She had encouraged her kids to talk about their father often, to remember him always. "Your dad would have loved to have been sitting in the bleachers this evening watching you practice."

Justin smiled wistfully. "Yeah, I know." He yawned and snuggled deeper beneath the covers. "Night, Mom."

She stood and leaned forward to press her lips against his forehead. "Good night, honey."

She didn't linger at the door, but instead went back into the kitchen, where she fixed herself a cup of hot tea and sat staring at the flowers.

For a brief moment she allowed herself her memories of red roses and John. She'd mentioned she loved red roses on their first date, when they'd visited a botanical garden in nearby Kansas City. The next date he arrived at her apartment with a dozen long-stemmed American Beauties. She thought that just might have been the moment she'd fallen in love with him.

Through their marriage he'd often surprised her with a bouquet. Sometimes they were to mark a momentous occasion, like a birthday or an anniversary, and sometimes they were simply given to her for nothing more than a whim on his part.

She sipped her tea, lost in memories until the ringing of the telephone jolted her out of her reverie. She jumped up and grabbed the cordless from the counter.

"Too late?"

She smiled into the receiver at the sound of Alex's deep voice and sank back down at the table. "No, I was just having a cup of tea before turning in."

"How was practice?"

"Good." She frowned and thought about Marc Carter. Surely he hadn't left the flowers for her? There was only one way to find out if the roses had come from Alex. "Alex, did you leave something for me on my front porch this evening?"

"Like what?" he asked.

"Like red roses."

"No, although I wish I had. So I have some competition?"

"No . . . not at all." She stared at the flowers. "If you didn't send them, then I can't imagine who did." Marc Carter, perhaps? Or maybe the firemen at the station had left them as some sort of thank-you for her weekly delivery of baked goods.

"Even though I didn't send you flowers, I'd love to have dinner with you again, maybe this Saturday?"

As much as she'd love to agree to another dinner, she hesitated. "I don't know, Alex. I feel as if I've taken advantage of my in-laws in the past week and really shouldn't ask them to babysit again so soon."

"We could take the kids with us. You know I'd love to meet them."

"We need to go slow, Alex. My kids are vulnerable right now." She didn't want to tell him how vulnerable she was, that she was both thrilled and frightened by his obvious interest in her.

"Marissa, I'm not going to pretend that I just want to be your friend." His deep voice evoked a sweet rush of warmth inside her. "I know it sounds crazy, but I feel like fate brought us together again, and I'm willing to take this as slow as you need me to."

His words increased the warmth inside her. "Thank you, Alex. I appreciate your understanding."

He laughed, that low, deep laughter she remembered from years ago. "Don't thank me. My motives are strictly selfish. I want to spend time with you, and if the only way to do that is on your terms, then that's fine with me. And now I'll just tell you good night and let you go. I know you get up early in the mornings."

"Good night, Alex." She hung up the phone with a smile curving her lips, but the smile faded as she once again stared at the roses.

She found it difficult to believe that they had come from the firemen at the station. She'd been delivering baked goods there every Sunday morning for years. Why would they suddenly decide now to send her a thank-you bouquet? And even if they had sent them, there would have been a card or a note.

Besides, she'd just seen most of the firemen at the ball field an hour before. She couldn't believe that they had sent the flowers and nobody had said a thing or mentioned it earlier.

She also found it as hard to believe that Marc would have brought them to her, especially in the aftermath of her declining his offer to get together for drinks or a barbecue.

To Marissa, Love Blake.

In the days since Jennifer Walsh's death there had been several follow-up news reports indicating that the police were following several leads. However, nowhere had she heard or read anything telling about the note that had been left with Jennifer's body. Thank goodness.

She knew the police were keeping that secret from the public in order to use it later in the investigation. She wondered what else they might be keeping not only from the public but also from her?

Even though nobody except Alex knew about that note, the memory of the card was burned into her brain. As she stared at the flowers, a chilling thought filled her head.

"No," she murmured softly, finding the thought too horrible to entertain. She got up from the table and carried her cup to the sink. As she rinsed it she tried to keep the awful thought out of her mind.

Jennifer Walsh's death had nothing to do with her. That note hadn't been written for her benefit. There was another Marissa somewhere who knew about that murder.

And there was a logical explanation for the roses.

Still, when she looked at them once again she realized she didn't want them. The very sight of them now made her sick to her stomach.

She grabbed a garbage bag from the pantry and threw the flowers, vase and all, inside. She knotted the top of the bag several times, then carried it out the door that led into the garage.

Even as she got ready for bed, the vision of those red roses haunted her. She absolutely refused to dwell on the fact that the card that had accompanied Jennifer's body had made it sound like her death had been some sort of a gift.

But what if the roses were the second gift?

Chapter 9

The morning had started poorly. Jessica had awakened grumpy, Justin had been unable to find his homework, and Marissa tried to function on too-little sleep.

By the time she got to the shop and opened the doors she was ready to return home and crawl back into bed, only she was afraid of the dreams.

Sleep had eluded her for half the night. When she had finally fallen asleep, horrifying dreams had disturbed her rest. Jennifer Walsh had risen from her grave to chase Marissa through a dream landscape.

In the dream Jennifer cursed Marissa like she had that night at the ball field, and each time she cursed she threw a bloodred rose and its jagged thorns ripped into Marissa's throat, tearing the skin until her throat was nothing more than a gaping, bloody wound.

She had awakened both exhausted and edgy,

irrationally fearing that somehow the horror of her dreams would find a way to bleed into her life.

The morning passed slowly. Business was never good on Wednesdays and this one was no different. The mall was quiet. Only an occasional *slap, slap, slap* of sneakers sounded, marking the rhythm of one of the many people who walked the mall for exercise.

She sat behind the counter, thumbing through a catalog without interest, trying to forget the nightmares of the night before.

She hadn't heard anything from the police since she'd dropped off the list of people she remembered seeing at the ball field last Thursday night. Each time the phone rang she expected it to be the police with more questions, but that hadn't happened.

Maybe they had found another Marissa, she thought with a surge of hope. She knew the edginess she'd felt for the past several days wouldn't go away until Jennifer's murder had been solved and she knew it had absolutely nothing to do with her.

In the meantime she simply had to get through each day moment by moment and try to keep her mind away from the memory of the picture of the murdered woman.

It was just before noon when Alex walked in, and warm pleasure splashed through her at the sight of him. "Alex," she exclaimed and stood from her chair behind the counter. "What a pleasant surprise."

He flashed that grin that increased the warmth flooding through her. "If the mountain won't come to Muhammad . . ." He placed a large brown shopping bag on the counter.

"What's this?"

"Lunch. I figured since you weren't comfortable making another dinner date, lunch was the next-best thing." He frowned. "You haven't eaten lunch yet, have you?"

"No."

"Great!" He reached into the bag and began to unload containers. "Sit," he commanded.

With a smile, she sat back in the chair and watched as he continued to unload the bag. She wasn't sure whether it was his thoughtfulness that made her slightly breathless or the fact that she'd never seen him look more handsome.

Clad in a pair of worn jeans and a light blue dress shirt that did amazing things to his eyes, he looked casual and sexy.

"My goodness, it looks like you've thought of everything," she exclaimed as he pulled out paper plates, napkins, and soft drinks.

"I tried." He offered her a sheepish grin. "A nice girl at the deli counter helped a bit."

She eyed one of the containers. "I'll bet that's not as good as your mother's potato salad."

"Probably not," he replied. "Mom's potato salad was world class."

She had a sudden burst of memory of Sunday

afternoon barbecues at Alex's house when she'd been a teenager. Unlike many teenage boys, Alex hadn't minded spending time with his parents on an occasional Sunday, and he'd usually invited Marissa to join them.

"I used to love time at your parents' house," she said. "They were always so nice to me, and I have wonderful memories of those days."

He smiled, that slow, sexy lift of the corners of his lips that evoked a new heat inside her. "I have great memories of lots of things." His eyes twinkled with a slightly wicked gleam. He laughed. "You're blushing, Marissa."

"You're making me blush." She busied herself taking the lids off the containers. "I'm sorry about your parents, Alex."

"Thanks. They were good people," he replied.

"Yes, they were."

He sat behind the counter in the chair next to hers. "You've mentioned John's parents. Are you close with them?"

"Very." She watched as he filled her plate with servings of fried chicken, potato salad, chunks of cheese, and bread and butter. "John's parents embraced me from the moment I started to date him, and since his death they have been pillars of support and love. Truthfully I don't know what I would do without them."

"That's nice." He handed her the plate, then

began to fill his own. "Too often all you hear about in-laws are horror stories."

"Not in my case."

As he leaned closer to grab a napkin she could smell him, a clean slightly spicy masculine scent that stirred her on some base level. She tried to ignore it.

They began to eat, talking about her kids and her in-laws and about his work. No customers came in to disrupt the pleasant interlude.

"It's nice that you can take off in the middle of the afternoon to bring me lunch," she said.

"One of the benefits of self-employment. I can pick and choose the hours that I work in the comfort of my own home."

"Is all your work done from your house?"

"Mostly, although when I'm working on drawing up blueprints I often visit the site where the building will be and meet with the client to discuss his vision and what is viable for the site."

"Sounds complicated."

He grinned. "No more complicated that running a shop, keeping track of inventory, and working with employees."

"Mine is a labor of love. I dreamed about this kind of shop for years before finally being able to get it."

"It's nice, isn't it? Doing something that you love."

"For a lot of years I did things I didn't love in an effort to achieve this particular dream," she replied.

"Like what?" One of his eyebrows rose with curiosity.

She paused with a piece of chicken halfway to her mouth and shrugged. "I delivered newspapers, cleaned houses, babysat, whatever I could do to put money into the fund for Tiffany Rose. John did the same. He worked extra shifts when he could and put that money into the account for the store."

"So he supported your dream."

"One hundred percent." She picked up the leg of chicken once again. "I sometimes feel guilty that my dream came true because of the insurance money, but then I tell myself that John wouldn't have had it any other way." She finally bit into the chicken.

Alex looked around the attractive shop. "I'm sure he would be pleased with what you've accomplished here."

She smiled. "Yes, I know he would be."

A customer walked in and interrupted the conversation. Marissa got up to assist the woman, who was shopping for a specific kind of lamp she didn't carry.

As the customer wandered the store, she stood nearby, her gaze drawn again and again to Alex. The man was dangerous, with his slightly wicked eyes and his sexy grin.

He was dangerous in that her life had settled into a calm routine and he had the potential to shake things up, to shake her up. He was dangerous in that she had finally accepted a life alone, but with him she recognized just how lonely she had been in the last year. The customer drifted out of the store and she returned to her chair next to Alex.

"I notice you carry a lot of Victorian pieces," he said. "You should come and see my house. I bought one of those old Victorians on Cambridge Street and I'm in the process of restoring it."

"How wonderful. I'd love to see it sometime."

"I know evenings are problematic for you. When would be good for you to see it?"

Her heart beat a little more rapidly at the thought of being alone in his home. My God, she thought, I'm responding to him like a teenager. "How about tomorrow afternoon? Alison is scheduled to work, so I don't have to be here, and the kids will be in school."

"Great. Why don't I pick you up at your place around one? What time do the kids get home from school?"

"Around four."

"Then I'll make sure you'll be home right before four."

Certainly she'd be home long before four, she thought. After all, how long could it take to view his home? Unless of course he had something else on his mind to pass the time. She fought a little shiver, wondering if she was emotionally ready to take their relationship to a more intimate level.

*   *   *

For the last several days Luke and Sarah had been investigating the latest murder case, a Kansas City businessman found shot and stuffed in a Dumpster. The pressure on the two detectives to solve the case was enormous, as the businessman, Jerrod Nichols, had been a personal friend of the mayor.

Sarah had felt the need to solve the Walsh murder because it had been her first murder case since joining the Cass Creek Police Department and because that damned red bow on the body had stirred her on some visceral level.

Her need to solve the Nichols case was driven by political pressure from the media and the demands of their chief.

Luke handled the demand of both cases with his usual aplomb, showing no indication that he felt the pressure of needing to get results.

The two were now seated at the desk they shared in the police station, reading over ballistic reports and studying crime scene photos and the coroner's report. But nothing new jumped out at either of them.

It was almost eleven, and the station held the nighttime hush that never occurred during daylight hours or on weekend nights. It was the Wednesday night quiet when it appeared that the criminals were resting up after the past weekend and in preparation for the next weekend's crime sprees.

In the several weeks that Sarah had been working with Luke she'd learned that he liked working late on Wednesday nights even though officially they weren't on the clock.

Sarah sighed in frustration and threw the coroner's report to the desk. "There's nothing here we haven't read or seen a hundred times in the last two days." She bolted out of her chair, unable to sit still another minute.

Luke closed the manila folder containing the ballistic reports he'd been studying. "You're right." He raised his arms over his head and stretched, emitting a sound like a grizzly bear coming out of a long hibernation. "Want to get a drink at Harry's before calling it a night?"

She worked hard not to show her surprise at the invitation. "Sure," she agreed.

Minutes later the two sat across from each other at a small table in the tavern that was half a block away from the police station.

Harry's was a cliché, owned by a former cop and mostly frequented by cops. The interior was dark and smoky and smelled of cheap whiskey and beer. There was nothing remotely romantic about Harry's, and that's the way the patrons liked it.

They each ordered a beer and for a few minutes sat in silence, sipping the cold brews. Sarah felt as if she'd somehow passed a test, gained approval, by the invitation to share a beer with her partner.

"I know the chief wants the Nichols case solved

as soon as possible, but that doesn't mean I'm not working the Walsh case just as hard," she said to break the silence between them.

She leaned forward in her chair and wrapped her fingers around the chilled glass mug in front of her. "I still think Marissa Jamison knows more than she's telling. Did you know that on the night her husband was killed her alibi was that she was home with the kids, asleep in bed. There was no way to corroborate her alibi, and her husband's insurance money was immediately put to use for her sole benefit."

"So you think she went home from the ball game, locked her kids in their rooms to play, found Jennifer Walsh, slit her throat, wrote a note to herself, then drove home, and tucked her kids into bed. You're working way too hard, Wilkerson." Sarah flushed. "No shop talk. This is supposed to be decompression time."

"I don't decompress well," she replied.

An eyebrow shot up lazily. "I've noticed." He took a sip of his beer. "Is that what screwed up your marriage?"

"No. What screwed up my marriage is that I married an asshole."

One of his thick eyebrows raised again. "I suppose that would do it."

"What about you? Have you ever been married?"

"Once, briefly, when I first joined the department. It didn't work out."

"Been tempted to try it again?" she asked.

"Never. Cops and marriage just don't work well together."

Sarah took a sip of her beer and shrugged. "Some cops seem to get it right."

"The exceptions, not the rule," he replied. "So did the asshole leave you, or did you leave the asshole?"

"It was a mutual decision. The last year of our marriage we were like two strangers sharing the same space. He resented my job and I resented his resentment. We had nothing in common, nothing to talk about. By the time he filed for a divorce I was ready to let go."

"No kids?"

"No. When I wanted a baby he didn't think the time was right. The time was never right for him and then it was just too late."

"Any regrets?"

"No, I suppose not. What about you? Anything you regret in your life?"

"I don't believe in regrets," he said. "Regrets are nothing but a waste of time and energy. I don't ever look back and I try never to look forward."

"Then how do you know where you've been or where you're going?"

He shrugged. "Doesn't matter where I've been and I'll know where I'm going when I get there."

"You're way too laid-back, Luke," she observed.

"And you're way too intense, Wilkerson," he replied, then raised his beer. "And I'll drink to that."

Sarah raised her beer mug and did the same.

The can of pink paint was just where he'd left it. He spied it the moment he walked into the small bedroom, and the sight of it filled his heart with sweet anticipation.

He set to work. He opened the can, stirred the cotton-candy color, then poured it into the paint tin to roll onto the walls.

He'd already painted the other small bedroom. The walls in there now sported a fresh coat of blue paint, not too light, not too dark. Perfect for a little boy's room.

The scent of paint filled the room as he rolled the walls with the feminine color, and with each stroke of the roller the buzz of excitement roared in his head.

The perfect room for the perfect daughter.

So much to do, but with each hour of his spare time this house was becoming the perfect home for his family. After this room, there was only one left to do . . . the master suite. He hadn't decided on a color for it yet.

He knew Marissa's bedroom in the home where she now lived was peachy beige, but he wanted something different for the bedroom they would share. The color and the furnishings needed to be something that would reflect their passion, their love, the commitment she would eventually come to feel for him.

He wasn't naive enough to believe that when he came for her she'd be ready for him. He knew that it would take time to gentle her, time for her to know his ways and grow to love him.

Once he got her and the children here, in their home, they'd have all the time in the world for her and the children to adjust.

It's all going to be perfect, Mama, he thought. Too bad you aren't here to see what I've managed to accomplish.

For a moment he allowed himself to relish the memory of the last time he'd seen his mother. His final vision was of her going head over heels down the basement stairs.

She'd been so slobbering drunk, it had taken only a small push. She hadn't uttered a single sound on the way down. The only noise was the *thunk, thunk, thunk* of her body slamming into each and every stair. When she hit the concrete floor at the bottom he knew she was dead.

He'd gone to the movies and when he returned he ran from the house, sobbing and screaming for somebody to help. The authorities came, her body was taken away, and few questions were asked. Everyone in the neighborhood knew she was a drunk, and a fall down the stairs or some other deadly household accident had been forecast by more than a few.

It had been the best day of his life. But soon he'd have even better days, for he'd be together with the woman he loved.

Two hours later he stood just outside the small bedroom and gazed at the walls with satisfaction. He'd already bought a bed with a pink canopy for the room. Pink walls and pink lace bedspread . . . sugar and spice and everything nice. When he was finished, it would be the perfect room for sweet little Jessica.

Chapter 10

Marissa stood at her front window, waiting for Alex to pick her up and take her to see his home. Standing by the window peering out to the street, she felt a strange sort of déjà vu.

How many times in her youth had she stood at her mother's window waiting for Alex to arrive to take her out for the evening? And no matter the fact that they'd known each other forever, had been romantically linked together since high school, butterflies still swirled in her stomach before each and every date.

The butterflies were there now, and she placed a hand on her lower abdomen, surprised to feel them. Would the prospect of being alone with any man make her feel the same way? Somehow she didn't think so.

Alex had always been special. Even though she had been happily married to John, would have remained happily married to John for the rest of her life, there had been a little piece of her heart that had remained hidden away, nurtured by those tumultuous teenage years and forever stained with Alex's mark.

Guilt assaulted her for a moment, the feeling that somehow she was about to commit a grievous sin, embark into the treacherous waters of adultery. But of course that was ridiculous. She wasn't contemplating adultery, she was moving forward with her life.

John had been a loving, giving man. He wouldn't have wanted her to spend the rest of her life alone. She had a feeling that if Alex and John had met, they would have liked each other.

The butterflies swooped another round in her stomach as Alex's car pulled into her driveway. She didn't wait for him to get out of the car, but instead hurried through the front door.

"Hey," he greeted her, his eyes lit with an appreciation that made her foolishly happy that she had decided to wear the pink sundress that she knew showed off her figure and complemented her coloring.

"Hey, yourself," she replied and slid into the passenger seat.

He got back into the car, bringing with him his scent, which was becoming both comfortably familiar to her and wonderfully exhilarating.

"All set?" he asked as he buckled his seat belt.

She nodded, and he started the engine and backed out of her driveway.

As they drove down her street toward the highway he slid her a quick sideways glance. "You look absolutely beautiful, as usual."

Pleasure swept through her. It wasn't just the compliment that pleased her, but the obvious warmth in his eyes as he looked at her. "Thank you. I can't believe it's supposed to be so warm today, far too warm for May."

"You know what they say about Missouri weather: If you don't like it, wait a minute and it will change."

"Isn't that the truth," she agreed. She clasped her hands in her lap, surprised to find her fingers cold with nerves. Calm down, she told herself. Alex had given no indication that he had anything on his mind except showing her his home.

No indication except the underlying tension that seemed to sizzle between them, no indication except the heat that emanated from his eyes when he looked at her. She clenched her hands more tightly together.

The area where he'd told her he'd bought his home was a fifteen-minute drive from her neighborhood, but the two neighborhoods were completely different worlds.

Marissa's neighborhood was middle class, occupied for the most part by blue-collar workers struggling to raise children and get ahead.

The Cambridge Circle neighborhood where Alex had bought his home was upper class, the residents professionals who had already gained more than a modicum of success.

"You must be doing well in your work," she said as he turned down a tree-laden street.

"I was very lucky. I was invited into a very successful firm when I first got out of school. I stayed with the firm for ten years and made a lot of valuable contacts, so when I struck out on my own I already had things in place to be successful."

She felt herself relaxing with the easy conversation. "I'm not surprised that you became an architect. I remember when we were younger that you were always doodling and drawing buildings."

"Yeah, and you were always thumbing through home furnishing magazines. I figured you'd become an interior decorator."

"I thought about it for a while, but I decided to get a degree in business instead. Then John and I got married, and I never really had a chance to put my degree to work."

She sat up straighter in the seat as he turned into the driveway of a lovely three-story brick Victorian. "Oh, Alex, it's beautiful," she exclaimed.

He pulled the car to a halt and shut off the engine, for a moment staring at the place he called home. "You should have seen it two months ago. I had the bricks sandblasted clean, the trim sanded and repainted, and some landscaping done. I got the house for a song and dance because it needed so much work."

"But it's a labor of love," she replied.

He turned and smiled at her. "Definitely." He unfastened his seat belt and she did the same. "I have to warn you, I'll show you the downstairs, which I've pretty much managed to get done, but the upstairs is off-limits until I get finished up there. I hate to show anyone a work in progress."

She smiled. "Then I'll look forward to seeing the upstairs when it's no longer a work in progress."

She could tell her words pleased him as they indicated a future relationship. Together they got out of his car and walked toward the front porch.

The landscaping was lush. Mature trees with thick, leafy heads occupied most of the yard, their leaves casting shadows over the area. The sidewalk was lined with pink and white begonias, their blooms lush and full.

A stone fountain trickled water from its position in the center of a nearby flower bed, the base surrounded by a profusion of multicolored petunias. None of the flowers were expensive or exotic, but she couldn't imagine any species more perfect.

They stepped onto the large front porch and Alex fumbled with his keys to unlock the door. They entered into a foyer and the first thing she noticed was the woodwork.

Highly polished cherrywood ceiling trim and gleaming wood floors gave the interior of the home a rich elegance and warmth. A round table in the center of the foyer held a freshly cut bouquet of flowers, their sweet scent filling the air.

"Alex, it's lovely," she exclaimed.

"Yeah, a good first impression, but the rest of the rooms down here have become my makeshift living area." He took her elbow, his simple touch increasing the beat of her heart. "This is the dining room, but as you can see, I've transformed it for the time being into my office and bedroom."

Again the room was richly embellished with wood accents. A drafting table stood where a dining room table would normally be and a single-size bed was against the wall.

"Are you always so neat?" she asked, noting that the bed was made and the drafting table held only a large topographical map.

He dropped his hand from her elbow and laughed. "Of course not. I cleaned up because I wanted to make a good impression on you."

She smiled. "Alex, you made a good impression on me when we were in fourth grade and you beat up Kevin Simpson for pulling my hair."

"And got grounded for a week by my parents."

"Yes, but Kevin sported his black eye longer and never pulled my hair again." For a moment their gazes remained locked and she knew he was remembering those long-ago days just as she was.

"Those were good days, weren't they?" His soft voice was like a caress.

"They were." Her voice was just as soft.

"I hated my parents for moving. For months afterward I thought they'd destroyed any chance I might have had for happiness."

"I hated them, too," she confessed. "Those first few months after you left were horrible." Afraid the conversation was getting too deep, too personal, she added, "Thankfully, youth is resilient and we both managed to survive."

He apparently sensed her reluctance to dwell too deeply in the past. "Come on, I'll show you the parlor."

In keeping with the age of the house, the parlor was smaller than most modern living rooms. The focal point was a huge stone fireplace with a thick wood mantel. It was easy to imagine how cozy the room would be on a cold wintry night with a crackling fire providing both heat and atmosphere.

"As you can see, interior decorating is not my strong suit." He placed his hands on the back of a recliner chair. "Maybe you can help me find the right pieces for this room."

"I'd love to," she replied without hesitation, her mind already whirling with possibilities.

"And now, the kitchen." He reached out and grabbed her hand as he led her into the airy kitchen complete with eating nook. "I had the entire house rewired and new plumbing put in when I first moved in. I didn't want to zap a meal in the microwave and blow all the fuses at the same time."

She ran a hand across the granite countertop, then looked longingly at the state-of-the-art appliances. "Now this is a kitchen to cook in."

He motioned her toward a chair at the table. "You like to cook?"

"Love it. It's one of my passions, although I rarely take the time to really cook anymore."

"Glass of wine?" he asked as he opened the refrigerator door and pulled out a bottle of chilled white wine.

"All right." She watched as he pulled two crystal glasses from a cabinet, then poured the wine into each.

"So what's your specialty?" He joined her at the table with the wine. "Every good cook has a specialty."

"I make a mean spaghetti sauce, but my real love is for baked goods. In fact, every Saturday night I bake, and first thing Sunday morning I bring goodies to the fire station where John worked."

"You're still close to the people there?"

"Very." She took a sip of the wine. "When John was alive the firefighters were extended family, and when he died I thought it was important to maintain contact with them if for nothing more than the children's sake. John was an only child, and you know I am, too, so the men down at the station became special uncles to the kids."

"That's nice. Did you ever solve the mystery of your roses?"

A chill swept through her as she thought about

the flowers. She frowned. "No. I have no idea where they came from. I threw them away."

It was his turn to frown. "They frightened you." It was a statement, not a question.

She nodded. "I'm not sure why, but they did. I guess I'm still spooked by that poor dead woman and being questioned by the police."

"Have you heard any more from the police?"

"No, but it's been on my mind." She took another sip of her wine, then waved a hand. "But, please, let's not talk about it. I'm having much too nice a time to talk about such horrible things."

He smiled, reached across the table, and lightly touched the back of her hand. "You're right. It's not every day I ply a childhood girlfriend with wine in my home."

For the next hour they drank wine and talked about old times, and Marissa didn't know if the glow she felt was from the alcohol or from the pleasant memories.

She spoke a little bit about John, and he told her a little bit more about the women he had dated. They talked about love and relationships in general terms, and before long she realized it was time for her to get back home.

"I know, I know," he said, as he caught her looking at her watch for the second time in as many minutes. "As much as I hate for the afternoon to end, I know you need to get home."

"I do," she said, and stood, also reluctant for the

time with him to end. She carried her wineglass to the sink, conscious of him following directly behind her.

He set his glass next to hers, then took her hand and stood so close to her she could see the faint silver shards in the blue of his eyes. Her heart seemed to stop beating for a moment.

"You know, I'm thirty-four years old, but whenever I'm with you I feel like a teenager again." He stood so close to her she could smell the wine on his breath.

"We have to be careful, Alex. There's a lot of power in our past, and I don't want to confuse where we've been together with where we are now. We need to take things slow."

"I agree." He took a step closer and placed his hands on her shoulders. "We can take it slow right after I do this." He wrapped his arms around her and took her mouth with his.

His mouth was warm and tasted of wine. It also tasted of youthful desire and sweet longing. She had thought she wasn't ready for him to kiss her, but her mouth opened to him as her arms reached up to wind around his neck.

His hands caressed down her back as he deepened the kiss, his tongue dancing with hers in a heated tango. Her response to him almost frightened her. Her legs weakened and her nipples hardened and a deep ache crashed through her.

Just when she thought she could stand it no

longer, he broke the kiss and released her. "I needed to know if it was as good as I remembered," he said, his voice deep and husky.

"Was it?" she asked half breathlessly.

"It was much better than I remembered." He swept a hand through his hair and averted his gaze from hers. "And now we'd better get out of here before I kiss you again."

Minutes later they were back in his car, silent as if the kiss had somehow changed things between them, complicated things.

"You know I intend to pursue you," he finally said.

"You've made that clear."

He shot her a glance, his gaze warm. "How fast do you intend to run from me? You know I'm older than I was years ago. I'm probably not quite as fast as I was then."

She reached up and touched her mouth where the imprint of his lips still burned. "Oh, I don't know, you seem pretty fast to me."

He laughed. "So when am I going to see you again?"

"I don't know. Why don't you call me and I'll see what I can work out."

"Maybe sometime I can talk you into making some of that special spaghetti sauce for me in my kitchen."

"I could do that," she agreed.

They pulled up into her driveway. She was torn,

reluctant to part and yet feeling the need to escape and think about that kiss, about this man who had swooped back into her life.

"Thank you for showing me your home," she said as she unbuckled her seat belt.

"I'll be eager to show you the second floor when it's finished. And I haven't forgotten that you said you'd help me with the decorating."

"I'd be delighted. Don't get out," she said as he moved to unbuckle from his seat belt. "Thank you, Alex, for a wonderful afternoon."

He nodded. "I'll call you."

She slid out of the car, waved good-bye, then hurried toward the house.

Once inside she sank down on the sofa and stared out the floor-to-ceiling windows that looked out on the lush woods behind her house.

For the first time in a long time she wished she had a girlfriend, somebody she could talk to about personal issues, about Alex.

Her best friend, Judy Codsbury, had moved away from Cass Creek three years ago. They had tried to maintain their relationship through letters and phone calls, but during the past year and a half the phone calls had become infrequent and the letters had stopped as the reality of raising families and responsibilities intruded.

The person Marissa considered one of her dearest friends was John's mother, and she couldn't very well talk about Alex to Edith. In truth, she had no idea how Edith and Jim would react to the discovery that she was seeing someone.

Would they think it too soon? Would they resent another man coming into her life?

She had reservations herself. It was so difficult to separate the man Alex had become and the boy he had been, so hard to know if the attraction she felt toward him was steeped in the very fact that he was familiar and felt somehow safe.

She touched her mouth again, remembering the raw desire that had been in his kiss. He'd felt safe and familiar until that kiss.

That kiss had awakened a desire in her she thought had been buried with John. For just a moment she'd wanted Alex to take her, she'd wanted him to strip her clothes off and make love to her.

Too fast, she warned herself.

Glancing at her watch, she realized it was time for the school bus. She got up and went to the front door and watched for the vehicle that would bring the kids home from school.

Another two weeks and school would be over. She'd arranged a day-care situation for the weekdays of the summer, refusing to take advantage of Jim and Edith any more than she already did.

Right on time the bus lumbered down the street and stopped in front of her house. Children spilled out, girls with flying hair ribbons and boys pushing and shoving one another. Justin was among the group of boys, his laughter audible as he juggled books and papers threatening to erupt from his arms.

Jessica was the last off the bus, a dainty ballerina dancing toward the house. You're missing so much, John, Marissa thought. They're growing up so fast.

They brought their school day with them when they entered the house, sharing with Marissa every detail that each deemed important. She listened, commiserated, and laughed when appropriate until they were spent and bored with her company.

Jessica went to her room and Justin went out to the backyard to play catch with a friend until dinner was ready. Marissa busied herself with the normal activities of the day and tried to keep her mind off Alex and the kiss that had awakened her in a way that was both thrilling and unsettling.

They had just finished dinner and were clearing the table when the doorbell rang. "I'll get it," both kids yelled simultaneously.

Marissa hurried behind them as they flew out of the kitchen and toward the front door. A smile curved her lips as Justin opened the door to reveal David Harrold.

"Uncle David," he exclaimed as the tall fireman stepped into the living room.

"Hey, buddy!" He dropped the bags he carried just inside the door, then leaned down to hug each of the kids. "How about a ballerina kiss?" he asked Jessica, who promptly responded by throwing her arms around David's neck and kissing him on his cheek.

He stood once again and flashed a grin at Marissa. "I hope you don't mind my dropping in without a phone call, but I had these things for the kids."

"Don't be silly. You know you're always welcome here," she replied.

"What things for the kids?" Jessica asked, eyeing the two large bags with interest.

He handed her one of the two bags and she pulled out a doll complete with pink tutu and ballet slippers. "She's beautiful," Jessica exclaimed. "Thank you, Uncle David!"

"You're welcome, doll. Here you go, big guy," he said to Justin.

Justin opened his bag to find a dinosaur activity set, complete with dozens of plastic dinosaurs, a play mat, and molded mountains, trees, and boulders to complete the scene.

"Wow, it's awesome. Thanks!"

"You can take it in your bedroom and play," Marissa told her son. "David, want a cup of coffee? I was just clearing the table after dinner."

"Sure, coffee sounds great." He followed her into the kitchen and sat at the table as she started a fresh pot, then finished cleaning off the table.

"How's life?" she asked as she put the last dish into the dishwasher.

"You know, same old same old. Go to work, fight fires, go home and fight boredom."

"I keep telling you that you need a girlfriend." She poured two cups of the freshly brewed coffee, then joined him at the table.

"I'm working on it. These things take time." He took a sip of his coffee and eyed her over the rim of the cup. "John was a lucky man, Marissa."

She smiled wistfully. "I was the lucky one. He was a good man."

"I still miss him." David set his cup down and sighed. "I'll be at the station and somebody will say something funny and I'll start off to find John so I can share it with him; then I remember he's not here anymore."

She reached across the table and covered his hand with hers. "I know and we'll both probably miss him for the rest of our lives."

He turned his hand over and gave hers a squeeze, then leaned back in his chair. "So tell me what's new at that shop of yours."

For the next hour she and David visited. They talked about nothing in particular, and the conversation was light and easy. Several times she thought about mentioning Alex to him, but in the end decided not to.

By the time he had finished three cups of coffee he stood to leave. She walked with him to the front door, where he turned once again to look at her. "You know, you don't have to keep bringing muffins to the fire station. I mean, the guys would understand if you decided not to."

"I know, but right now I enjoy doing it."

He gazed at her for a long moment. "Don't hang on forever, Marissa. We all need to move on." He stepped out of the door and waved.

She watched him walk to his car, his last words swirling in her head. Was that what she was doing with her weekly trips to the fire station? Hanging on to what had been? Nurturing the last link she had with the husband she had lost?

The psychological elements didn't matter. At the moment all that mattered was that her weekly trips to the station where John had been so happy felt right.

The evening flew by, filled with homework and the usual nighttime routine. By nine o'clock the two kids were asleep and Marissa had taken her bath and had curled up on the sofa with a book.

She intended to read for only an hour or so, but instantly got caught up in the story. The phone rang, jarring her as she glanced at the clock and realized it was nearly eleven. Who would be calling at this time of night? Alex certainly knew better than to call this late.

She grabbed up the receiver. "Hello?" No reply, although it wasn't a dead line. She could hear somebody breathing. "Hello? Who is this?"

No voice answered her. All she heard were the steady, even breaths of whoever was on the other end of the line. "Hello?" she said one last time, then hung up.

Wrong number, she told herself, but that didn't stop the disquiet that seeped through her veins as she got up from the sofa, intent on making sure all the doors and windows in the house were locked.

Blake hung up, sated for the moment, pleased that hers would be the last voice he heard before going to sleep.

Chapter 11

It had been over a week since Marissa had been to Alex's house. The days had flown by in a flurry of activity. Friday night had been dress rehearsal for Jessica's dance recital and Saturday night had been the big event.

Sunday had been Edith's birthday, and they had spent the day having a picnic and had come home exhausted from all the fresh air and exercise.

The shop had been unusually busy, and twice during the week Alex had visited her there. She should have been feeling good about life, but two things had her on edge and nervous like she'd never been before.

A new bouquet of roses had appeared on her porch the night of the dance recital, and the strange, silent phone calls had occurred every night.

Just like the last bouquet, there had been no card and no marking of any kind to indicate where they had come from. The phone calls came at around the same time, around eleven each night. Not a single word was spoken except by her, but each night she hung up feeling verbally and physically threatened and frightened beyond words.

She'd finally decided to change her phone number to a private one. The change would happen the next day, and she now sat in the parking lot at the police station.

She was here for two reasons; to check in with Detectives Wilkerson and Hunter about the Walsh murder and to let them know her new number.

She knew she was being paranoid, but she hadn't wanted to call them to give them the new number. She almost felt as if by speaking it aloud over a phone line the mysterious caller would somehow magically get the new number. At least she'd received no calls on her cell phone . . . yet.

What she hoped was that she would talk to the two detectives in charge of Jennifer Walsh's murder and they would tell her they had a suspect in custody and had found the Marissa indicated in the gift card left behind.

She'd pulled into the station on her way to work. It was going to be a busy day. She'd work until three thirty, then hurry home to get the kids ready to spend the night at Jim and Edith's. It was Friday, so the kids didn't have school the next day, and tonight Marissa had a date with Alex.

It surprised her, how much she anticipated

spending time with Alex again. The more time she spent with him, the more time she wanted to spend with him. Still, she was determined to take the relationship slowly, not so much for her sake, but for the sake of her children.

They didn't deserve any more loss in their lives and she didn't want to introduce Alex into their lives, allow them to get close to him, then discover he wasn't the man she wanted or needed after all.

She glanced at her watch and realized she couldn't put it off any longer. If she wanted to get to the shop on time she needed to go inside the police station and take care of her business there.

She hoped to speak to Detective Hunter. His eyes had been kind on the day they had questioned her. Detective Wilkerson had come at her like a hard-ass bitch and Marissa had no desire to go another round with the woman.

Unfortunately, the clerk informed her that Detective Hunter was out at the moment, but Detective Wilkerson was in. Marissa sat on one of the straight-backed chairs to wait for Wilkerson.

It took only moments for the tall, dark-haired detective to appear and motion Marissa through a door and into the same interrogation room where she'd sat before.

"What's up?" The detective motioned her into one of the chairs at the table, but Marissa didn't sit. She refused to put herself in a position of subordination.

"I was hoping you could tell me how things are progressing on the Walsh murder."

Wilkerson's dark expression gave Marissa her answer. "They aren't. Unfortunately, we've got a full caseload at the moment, and although we're doing the best we can, we've come up empty-handed on the Walsh case."

Marissa's heart plummeted. She'd hoped for a different answer.

"I can tell you this," Detective Wilkerson continued. "We've been unable to locate another Marissa either here or in the general Kansas City area."

Marissa nodded, heaviness weighing down her heart. "I also stopped by to tell you that I'm changing my phone number to a private one."

"Why?" Wilkerson's dark eyes studied her as if she were a particularly interesting species of insect.

"I've been getting some phone calls."

"Phone calls? What kind of phone calls?" She leaned a slender hip against the table.

"Every night for a little over a week my phone rings, and when I answer nobody speaks, but I know somebody is on the line." Now that she'd said it aloud she felt rather ridiculous. "I'm sure I'm over-reacting. It's probably just kids making prank calls, but they come late and are disturbing."

"Don't you have caller ID?"

"Yes, but the calls come up anonymous," Marissa replied.

"Anything else odd happening in the last couple of days?"

Marissa hesitated a moment. "I've gotten a dozen roses twice from somebody, and I don't know who gave them to me."

Wilkerson straightened up. "What do you mean? Were they sent to you from a florist?"

"No. Two different nights a vase with a dozen roses was left on my front porch."

"No card? No markings? Where are the roses now?"

"I threw them away."

"Everything? Vase and all?" Wilkerson cursed beneath her breath as Marissa nodded affirmatively.

"Surely you can't think the roses had anything to do with Jennifer Walsh's murder?" Marissa asked, her heart thudding painfully.

"I'll tell you what I think, Mrs. Jamison. I think you're the key to that murder. I think Jennifer Walsh was murdered and left as a gift to you. I think somebody in your life has a sick mind and some kind of twisted emotion where you are concerned."

She began to pace back and forth, her slender body vibrating with energy. "I would recommend that instead of changing your number you call and have the phone company put a tap on it and if you get any more flowers left on your doorstep you call me and I'll bring them to the lab to be dusted for fingerprints. Finally, I recommend you be very wary of anyone trying to insinuate themselves into your life and that you take a hard look at the people who are currently in your life."

Each word from the detective's mouth was like a knife stabbing into Marissa over and over again. Deep in her subconscious she'd been afraid that she was the cause of Jennifer's death, that the phone calls and the roses were all related, but she hadn't wanted to take out that fear and examine it in the cold hard light of day.

Now that fear was out, illuminated by the harsh voice, the dark eyes of the detective, and Marissa felt as if the earth beneath her feet had shifted and become treacherous ground.

"Am I in danger?" Although Marissa's question was about herself, her real fear was for her children.

Wilkerson stopped pacing and once again her gaze bore into Marissa's with an unflinching intensity. "Hell if I know. We don't have enough information to draw any kind of a psychological profile of the killer. I suppose it's possible there is another Marissa somewhere, that the phone calls you've been receiving are pranks, and that the flowers simply mean you're a lucky woman."

"But that's not what you believe."

Detective Wilkerson shrugged. Once again she leaned her hip against the table as some of the energy seeped out of her. "Some of these punk kids with their filthy mouths can drive a person to do something they normally wouldn't do." Her tone was light, conspiratorial. "I know more than once

I've wanted to bust the head of a foul-mouthed young girl."

Marissa recognized what Wilkerson was doing and it offended her. Playing "girlfriend" with that soft, "we're all in this together" tone. "If you're waiting for me to break down and confess, you'll wait until the end of time because I had nothing to do with Jennifer's murder."

"Just keep in mind, Mrs. Jamison, that if there isn't another Marissa, if those phone calls you've been getting aren't pranks, if those flowers weren't some kind of delivery mistake, then you have to accept the fact that somebody in your life or on the periphery of your life is a murderer."

"Then what are you and Detective Hunter doing to catch the person?"

Marissa thought she saw a tiny crack in the tough exterior as Wilkerson released a small sigh. "We're doing the best we can," she replied.

Minutes later, as Marissa drove toward her shop, her mind whirled with bits and pieces of the conversation she'd just had, and all her thoughts were darkened by a deep apprehension.

She would do as the detective had directed her and instead of changing her number she'd have the phone company put a trace on the phone. Hopefully they could discover who was making the calls each night. And the next time she got flowers on her porch, she would place them, vase and all, into a paper bag and take them to the police station.

Those were easy and relatively nonthreatening steps she could take. What worried her more than anything was the woman's certainty that somebody in Marissa's life or on the fringes of her life was a murderer.

Alex. His name jumped into her head unbidden. Her hands clenched more tightly around the steering wheel. He had reentered her life on the very day that the police had questioned her concerning Jennifer's murder. The arrival of the flowers and the phone calls hadn't begun until she'd started to see him. Was it all simply coincidence?

What did she really know about him? It had been almost sixteen years since she had dated him. How did she know what those sixteen years had done to him, what they had made of him?

Alex would have known her favorite flowers were red roses. She pulled into a parking place at the mall, shut off the engine, and lowered her forehead to the top of the steering wheel, for a moment overwhelmed by fears and doubts.

She wanted to think with her heart, to embrace the belief that Alex would never, could never, have anything to do with anyone's death. But she knew the danger of thinking only with her heart.

How long had Alex really been back in town? He'd told her he'd moved back two months ago, but for all she knew he'd been here a year . . . two years . . . watching her and acquainting himself with her life.

As she exited the car and walked toward her shop, she realized the last thing she wanted to do that evening was have dinner at Alex's place, not with the doubts swirling around in her head.

The moment she got inside the shop she dialed Alex's number, glad to get his answering machine. She left a brief message, canceling their plans for the evening, then opened the shop to begin a day that had already been ruined.

It was a long day. Between customers she continued to think about Detective Wilkerson's words. *Somebody in her life or around the periphery of her life.* The thought haunted her.

She also dreaded each ring of the phone, afraid that Alex would call her to see what the problem was and she didn't want to talk to him. She needed to think.

She began a list of everyone she could think of, friends and acquaintances, and no matter how many names she added to the list, Alex's seemed the most damning.

She'd known all the men at the fire station, the people in the mall, and her neighbors for years. Only Alex was new to her life. Was he a murderer? Did he have some sort of deep, dark obsession with her?

By the time she left the shop for the day, she was tired of her thoughts, tired of the fear. Even though she had changed her plans for the evening, there was no way she could change the plans for Jessica and Justin, who were looking forward to a night at Grandma and Grandpa's.

It was just after five when she arrived at Jim and Edith's place and as usual the two greeted them before they could get out of the car.

Marissa didn't feel like small talk. Although she was pleasant and tried to act as natural as possible, she just wanted to get back home.

She declined Edith's invitation to go inside and instead pled tiredness and inventory work to do at home. She kissed her children good-bye and left. She wasn't sure why, but she wanted to be inside the safety of her home before dark.

Minutes later she pulled into her garage and went into the house. The first thing she did was make sure all the doors were locked; then she changed out of her work clothes and into a pair of baggy sweatpants and a T-shirt.

In the kitchen she walked over to the built-in desk and checked her answering machine. Two calls. The first was a recorded advertisement for a high-speed Internet connection. The second was Alex.

"Marissa, it's me." His deep voice filled the room. "I just got your message about this evening. Is everything all right? You sounded stressed or something. Anyway, please give me a call."

She deleted the message and rubbed the center of her forehead wearily. Too much thinking, she thought as she went to the refrigerator. First she needed dinner. Then she intended to curl up on the sofa and watch a couple hours of mindless sitcoms.

No matter how much she thought, no matter how much she stewed and analyzed, she wasn't going to solve Jennifer's murder. She could only hope that what Detective Sarah Wilkerson had told her was true, that she and Detective Hunter were doing the best they could.

She ate a frozen pizza in front of the TV. As much as she wanted to relax, she couldn't. For the first time she realized how easy it would be for somebody to slice a screen and open a window, how flimsy the locks were on all of her doors.

It was crazy. She'd never been afraid after John's death. She'd always felt safe and secure here. But tonight nothing felt safe and nothing felt secure.

Stop it, she chided herself. Nothing had changed from yesterday to today. There was no reason to believe that either her or her children might somehow be in danger.

She had to cling to the belief that Jennifer Walsh's death had nothing to do with her, that there wasn't some horrid person in her life who was capable of murder. Those things happened in novels or in made-for-television movies, but they didn't happen in real life.

Did they?

Twice the phone rang. Both times it was Alex, who left messages again asking her to call him. She didn't want to talk to him at the moment. Her thoughts were too jumbled where he was concerned.

At ten o'clock she changed from her sweats into her nightshirt, then returned to the sofa. She had just settled back in when the knock fell on the front door. It fell so softly, for a moment she thought it had come from the television. Then it came again, this time a little bit louder.

She froze. Irrational fear shuddered through her. Who would be at her door at this time of night? She got up off the sofa and crept to the front window. Peering out the slats of the miniblinds, she saw Alex on her front porch.

Dammit. She should have returned his calls. It's Alex, for God's sake, a little voice whispered inside her. It's the boy who once fought a bully for you, the young man who gave you your first grown-up kiss.

During those years that they had spent together wouldn't she have seen a hint of a monster beneath his handsome facade? Wouldn't she have sensed some sort of darkness in his soul, an evil lurking just beneath the surface? Were murderers born or made? What might have happened to him in the years they'd been separated that would have transformed him from the loving, caring person he'd been into a monster?

His third knock broke her inertia. There was no way she could pretend not to be home. The lights were on, and he could probably hear the blare of the television through the door. Drawing a deep, steadying breath, she cracked open the door.

"Marissa, thank God. I was worried." His eyes, those blue eyes she'd once dreamed of, gazed at her with concern. "Are you all right? The kids okay?"

"We're fine. Everything is fine, Alex. I'm sorry about tonight. I . . . I wasn't feeling well." She didn't open the door to invite him in.

His gaze held hers for a long moment, and she saw a shadow of disbelief. "Is there anything I can do?"

"No. I was just getting ready to go to bed."

He shifted from foot to foot, as if reluctant to leave, yet he didn't press to come inside. "You sure everything else is okay?"

"It's fine, Alex. I'll call you tomorrow."

He held her gaze for another long moment, then uttered an audible sigh. "All right, then good night, Marissa."

"Good night." She watched as he left the porch and walked to his car. When he began to back down the driveway she closed and locked the front door.

Better to cut ties now before her heart got too involved, she thought. Surely it was best to put some distance between them as long as any uncertainties lingered in her head.

Eventually Jennifer's murderer would be caught, and if Alex had nothing to do with the madness occurring, maybe it wouldn't be too late to pick up where they left off.

Relief battled with regret as she went back into the living room and turned off the television. As much as she hated it, she couldn't help but be suspicious of Alex, and the last thing she wanted or needed in her life was somebody she didn't entirely trust.

She turned out all the lights in the living room and kitchen, then went into the bedroom. She crawled into bed, missing the children, missing the presence of another human being in the house.

A deep, abiding loneliness filled her, and for the first time since John's funeral she felt the sting of hot tears. She pressed her eyelids tightly together, willing the tears away.

Maybe she'd spent the whole day overreacting because of the conversation with Detective Wilkerson. Nothing really bad had happened since Jennifer's murder. There was no real reason to believe that a killer lurked in Marissa's life. There had to be a logical explanation for the phone calls, for the roses. And there had to be another Marissa somewhere.

She'd almost fallen asleep when the telephone rang.

Chapter 12

The weekend had been difficult. Marissa had spent the days running, going shopping, to the park, out to dinner with Justin and Jessica. She hadn't wanted to be home, where Alex might show up unexpectedly.

He'd called several times, getting her machine each time, and she hadn't returned any of his calls. It was a machination as old as time: Disinterest on the female part usually sent the male scurrying away for more inviting pleasures.

Monday morning she pulled into her parking space at the mall and got out of her car. She'd just unlocked the outer door to the shop when a hand touched her shoulder. She gasped and whirled around to see Alex.

"We need to talk," he said without preamble.

"Alex, I'm getting ready to open for business."

"Wait five minutes. I'm not going anywhere until you talk to me."

She remembered that determined thrust of his chin, the thin slash of his lips that indicated he would have his way. She sighed with resignation and went into the shop, aware of him following her close behind.

He waited by the counter as she went into the back room and turned on all the lights. At least with the lights on and the security gate across the front entrance, the people in the mall could hear her scream, they would be able to see if anything happened.

"What's going on, Marissa?" he asked the moment she walked back into the main area. "You cancelled our date; you've been avoiding my phone calls. Something has happened, and I can't fix it if I don't know what it is."

"There's nothing to fix," she said, unable to meet his gaze. "I've just realized that this isn't a good time for me to be pursuing any kind of a relationship."

"And just when did you make this decision? Was I moving too fast?" His soft voice flowed over her, through her, stroking all the lonely places.

"No, it's nothing you've done." She met his gaze, saw the warmth there, the worry, and she had a flash of the young man he had been, a young man who had been kind and gentle.

He'd been the type of young man who had often

indulged in little acts of kindness, not in an effort to impress anyone, but simply because that was the kind of person he had been.

Was that the background of a coldhearted killer? Did murderers spring from loving parents and carefree childhoods? She hated this. She hated her thoughts and she hated the person who had made her think such thoughts.

"Marissa?" He placed his hands on her shoulders and without conscious thought she jerked and took several steps back from him.

She wildly met his gaze and saw his eyes widen slightly. "Marissa, are you afraid of me? For God's sake, tell me what's going on."

"I'm afraid." The words came out of her without volition, but she realized in that moment she was going to tell him everything. Maybe by confronting him she would know the truth. "I've been afraid ever since Jennifer Walsh's murder." She sank onto the chair behind the register.

"Has something else happened? Have you talked to the police again?"

"I got more roses and I've been getting phone calls."

"Phone calls? What kind of calls."

She explained to him about the calls, then about the flowers. As she told him she watched his face carefully, looking for any glimmer of foreknowledge, any hint that he might be responsible. But all she saw was the boy of her childhood, the young man who had made her laugh and had captured her heart.

"And you think I sent you those roses? I'm making those phone calls? You think that I had something to do with that girl's murder?" He gazed at her with incredulous wonder and a touch of hurt. "Marissa, what are you thinking?"

"I don't know." She jumped up off the chair and paced the narrow aisle between the counter and the sales floor. "All I know is that none of these things started happening until you came back into my life."

"Let me tell you something, Marissa Jamison. I loved you as a young man, and since I've been seeing you I've come to care about you again, a lot, but that doesn't mean I'd kill for you. And if I were going to send you flowers you can be damned sure I'd put a card with them. I'd want the credit. As far as the phone calls are concerned, if you really think it's me making those calls, then let me come to your house tonight and sit with you, and one of those calls will come in and I'll be sitting innocently on your sofa."

He drew a deep breath, as if his impassioned diatribe had depleted all his energy. "Marissa, I had nothing to do with that woman's death. I didn't send you flowers and I'm not making weird phone calls to you. The last thing I want to be is somebody who frightens you."

Marissa sat once again in the chair, suddenly

weary. She raised a trembling hand to the center of her forehead and rubbed the spot where a headache attempted to take hold. "I'm so confused, Alex. I'm confused and I didn't realize until just now that I've been so afraid." She dropped her hand to the counter.

He leaned forward and covered her hand with his. "Marissa, I swear to you that it's just a coincidence that all this started happening when I came back into your life. I had nothing to do with any of this. You should know me better than that."

With the warmth of his hand on hers, memories once again swept through her, memories of Alex consoling her when her cat had disappeared, memories of him making her laugh when her mother had been indifferent or harsh. Could this be the same person who was subtly tormenting her? She drew her hand away from his.

He raked a hand through his hair. "You said the calls come every night. I'm serious, Marissa. Let me come over tonight. Invite anyone you want to be there and you'll see it isn't me making the calls. You'll see that you can trust me."

She wanted to know, needed to know. Even though her heart was certain that Alex would never do anything to harm her, she needed to know for sure.

"All right. Tonight. Come to my house around nine. The calls usually come between ten and eleven."

"Is there anything else I can do?"

Yes, hold me, she wanted to say. Hold me and tell me that woman's death had nothing to do with me. Convince me that nobody killed that woman as some sort of twisted gift to me. Hold me tight like you used to when we were teenagers.

She shook her head. "No. I'll just see you tonight." She was grateful when he left. As she opened the security gate to the shop and busied herself preparing for the day, she thought of the night to come.

She would ask Jim and Edith to keep the kids. She didn't want them there with Alex there. As much as she wanted to believe that Alex had nothing to do with anything that was going on, she knew she'd be a fool to be alone with him in her house.

Even though nothing that had happened appeared to be an overt threat to her, Detective Wilkerson had been clear that she should be careful. So who could she invite over? Jim and Edith were out of the question, nor did she want to invite David over.

She'd ask Alison. Once she explained the situation to her employee, she knew Alison wouldn't mind coming over for an hour or two. It didn't matter that Alison was an older woman. What mattered was that there be somebody in the house besides Marissa and Alex.

It was after six that evening when she arrived home after dropping the kids at Jim and Edith's.

She checked her messages, finding nothing unusual, then went into her bathroom and took a
quick shower.

She changed into a pair of light blue sweats with
a matching T-shirt, then went back into the kitchen
to find something for dinner.

At least there had been no roses on her front
porch, no strange calls on her answering machine.
Tomorrow morning she intended to call the phone
company and see what they could tell her about the
late-night calls.

She had no idea what she'd do, what she would
think, if a call didn't happen tonight while Alex
was there. She'd face that problem if it occurred.

At precisely eight thirty Alison arrived, carrying
a knitting bag containing her latest project, a coral
sweater for her granddaughter.

"I can't tell you how much I appreciate you coming," Marissa said as she greeted the woman.

"Nonsense. I don't mind a bit." Alison headed
for the sofa and made herself at home.

"Can I get you something to drink?"

"No, thanks. I'd much rather you sit and tell me
again why I'm here. You were pretty vague earlier."

Quickly Marissa explained about the phone calls
and her suspicions of everyone in her life, includ-
ing Alex. "If a call comes in tonight while Alex is
here, then I'll know for certain that he isn't making
the calls. I'm probably being paranoid by asking

you to be here, but until this is settled I'm not comfortable being alone in the house with him."

Alison wielded one of her knitting needles like a weapon. "You have nothing to worry about while I'm here."

Marissa laughed in spite of her nerves. For the next half an hour the two women chatted about children and grandchildren.

At nine the doorbell rang and Marissa knew it was Alex. If he was surprised to see Alison there he didn't show it. He was gracious and warm as the three of them converged on the kitchen for coffee and pastries.

Although the conversation was pleasant, with each tick of the clock Marissa's nerves grew more taut. Her heart banged against her ribs and she found it difficult to focus on anything but the telephone mere inches from where she sat.

At precisely ten forty-five it rang. Her gaze shot to Alex, who appeared as relieved as she felt. "Answer it," he said softly.

She jumped out of her chair and went to the phone. The caller ID read anonymous, as it had for each of the late-night calls.

She picked up the receiver. "Hello?"

As usual she heard only the sound of breathing, letting her know there was somebody on the line, but as always they had no intention of actually speaking to her.

"Who is this? What do you want? Why do you

keep calling me?" She leveled each question calmly, refusing to allow the caller to know the chill that these calls created inside her.

In the back of her thoughts, a little voice sang. It wasn't Alex. She'd known all along in her heart that it wasn't him. Now she had her proof.

"Please won't you talk to me? Tell me why you are calling."

There was a soft click, and Marissa knew the caller had disconnected. She hung up the phone and turned to Alison and Alex. "Whoever it was hung up."

Alison's forehead wrinkled in concern. "You said these calls come every night?"

Marissa nodded. "They started about a week ago and they've come every night between about ten thirty and eleven."

"And nothing is ever said?"

"No. I can hear somebody breathing, but that's all. I've had the phone company put a tap on my phone. Tomorrow morning I'm going to call and see if they can tell me the phone number the calls are coming from. Alison, thank you so much for being here."

Alison stood. "No problem, Marissa. But now it's time for this old woman to go home and get to bed."

Alex remained at the table as Marissa walked Alison to the front door. "You sure you're all right?" Alison whispered when the two reached the door.

"I'm fine."

"He seems very nice, and he's definitely easy to look at. You'll be all right with him alone?"

"I'll be fine." The two women said their good-byes, then Marissa returned to the kitchen, where Alex hadn't moved from his seat.

"I owe you an apology," she said as she sat in the chair next to his.

"No, you don't," he countered. "With everything that's happened you'd have been a fool to completely trust me." He leaned toward her and took her hands in his. "Marissa, I would never, ever, do anything to harm you or your children."

The warmth of his hands seeped up her arms. "I knew that, but I just needed to be sure."

"I'll tell you again: I had nothing to do with that woman's death. I didn't send you roses, and I'm not making calls that obviously unsettle you."

Despite the steadiness of his grip on her hands, tears burned at her eyes. "Then who is?" she whispered.

He rose and pulled her up with him and instantly embraced her. She wrapped her arms around his neck and leaned into him, savoring the strength of his arms, the broadness of his chest, the sweet safety implied there.

She burrowed her head in the crook of his neck, the familiar scent of him stronger there and creating an ache inside her that had nothing to do with the need for comfort.

His long legs pressed against hers, his thighs firm and solid. He stroked a hand up her spine while at the same time he kissed the side of her neck. It was a gentle kiss, without any real heat, but it stirred a fire in her that hadn't been stirred in a very long time.

"I should go," he murmured against her hair.

"Not yet," she replied. She raised her head to look at him. The heat that had been absent from his gentle kiss on her neck was there in his eyes, and her breath caught in her throat at the sight of that raw, deep hunger.

"Marissa." There was a warning in his voice, the warning of a man who could make no promises about his actions if she encouraged him in the least.

She knew she had a split-second decision to make. She could step back from him and send him on his way, or she could pull him closer and finish what they had begun so many years ago.

"I want you to stay."

Before the words had completely left her, his mouth crashed to hers in a fiery kiss of possession. She welcomed him, opening her mouth and molding herself to him as he tangled his hands in her hair.

The kiss held not only the hunger of young teenagers in the first flush of passion, but also the knowledge of adults already touched by desire, already knowing of its heady heights.

His hands untangled from her hair and moved

down the length of her back, stopping only when he cupped her buttocks and pulled her more tightly against his arousal. "I feel as if I've spent my whole life wanting you," he said when he tore his mouth from hers.

"I feel the same way," she said, breathless from the kiss and his intimate nearness. She stepped back, her legs unsteady, and took his hand. There was no doubt in her mind that they were going to make love, but it wasn't going to happen in her kitchen.

They moved halfway through the living room when she suddenly stopped, unsure that she could make love to Alex in the same bedroom, in the same bed, where she and John had made love.

He seemed to read her thoughts. He released her hand, shut off the living room light, and moved to the sofa. "Come here," he said, his voice husky. "Come here and let me make out with my best girl in the moonlight."

This was the young man she'd once loved, the young man who had been kind and thoughtful and in tune with her wants and needs. She joined him on the sofa, and immediately their lips sought each other's again.

The kiss was long and filled with the kind of desperate need reminiscent of the kisses they had shared in the past. When his mouth left hers, he kissed down the line of her jaw and into the hollow of her throat.

There had been a time when his kisses had frightened her, when his touch had scared her because it evoked such want, such need in her.

She'd been afraid of being caught in the middle of one of their make-out sessions, afraid of saying yes to him before she was emotionally prepared to accept the consequences. She'd been afraid of getting pregnant or, worst of all, losing him by letting him finally have his way with her.

There was no fear now, nothing but the hunger, the need of a mature woman. As Alex continued to trail kisses against her throat, her fingers fumbled with the buttons of his shirt. She wanted the feel of that solid, firm chest beneath her fingertips.

As she worked the buttons down his shirt and her fingers moved lower and lower down his chest, he gasped slightly. She finally yanked his shirt from his slacks and unbuttoned the final button. She slid the shirt off his shoulders and ran her hands across his warm flesh.

She wanted to weep because it had been so long since she'd been held, and this moment with this man seemed so right.

Alex gazed at her, his eyes glittering in the moonlight streaming in through the living-room windows. "I keep thinking that your mother will come in, or that you'll tell me to stop."

"My mother is in Florida, and I'm not going to tell you to stop, Alex."

Her words seemed to unleash whatever control

he'd maintained. With a groan he took possession of her lips again and as they shared a deep kiss his hands slid up beneath her T-shirt to cup her breasts.

Even with the barrier of her silk bra between them, she could feel the heat of his hands, and her nipples responded, hardening in anticipation of more.

It was easy to separate the past from the present. Years before, Alex's caresses had been hurried, the frantic fumbling of youth. His caresses and kisses now were confident and masterful, speaking of experience he hadn't had then.

He moved his hands from beneath her T-shirt and instead grabbed the bottom of it and pulled it over her head. As he reached behind her to unfasten her bra, he paused a moment, his gaze once again seeking hers.

"I want you to understand something, Marissa." His voice was thick with controlled emotion. "I wanted you as a boy, and I know that some of that want still lives inside me. But, more than that, I want you as a man. I want you as the woman you've become."

It was exactly the right thing to say, exactly what she'd needed to hear. She leaned forward and pressed her lips against his lower jaw as he unfastened her bra. As the bra fell away, he captured her full breasts in his hands, his thumbs razing across her nipples with exquisite pleasure.

He lowered her to the sofa so she was lying prone, then covered her body with his. He kissed her again, and she lost herself to the sensation of his bare chest against her bare breasts, his hips moving against hers.

Intoxicated. She felt drunk with him, the feel of him, the scent of him, the sound of his labored breathing all combined to steal away conscious thought from her head.

Once again he kissed down the length of her neck, lingering in the hollow of her throat and across her collarbones before moving down to capture one nipple between his lips.

She gasped in complete surrender. His hands moved to her waist in an attempt to pull down her sweats, and in the process they both tumbled from the sofa and to the floor.

For a moment neither of them said anything. Alex was the first to break the stunned silence. A deep burst of laughter exploded from him. Marissa's giggles quickly turned into sidesplitting laughs.

Alex wrapped his arms around her. "I like this better," he murmured against her ear. "I want to have plenty of room when I make love to you."

Any lingering laughter left her as he stood and took off his slacks, which left him clad only in a pair of white briefs. As he slid the briefs off his body, she took off her sweatpants, then her panties.

"You were beautiful as a teenager, but as a

woman you take my breath away." He rejoined her on the floor, and she welcomed his nakedness against hers.

All the hunger he had ever felt for her as a teenager was there, but a new hunger had swept in as he'd spent time with her as an adult.

He loved the woman she'd become, strong and self-sufficient, yet with a soft vulnerability in her eyes that made him want to protect her forever.

The taste of her lips held both the faint memory of familiarity and the exciting newness of discovery. His desire had renewed itself the moment he'd seen her again, and each moment he'd spent with her since then had only stoked the flames of his want higher, hotter.

He felt as if he were not only about to fulfill a young man's fantasy, but also embark on a journey with a woman with whom he just might be able to spend the rest of his life.

He flicked his tongue against the satin smoothness of her skin, reveling in the taste of her and the mewling sounds she made. He explored her body inch by inch, as he'd wanted to do so many years ago, and in turn she boldly explored his, touching him where she'd never dared before, stroking him until he thought he'd lose his mind.

When he could stand it no longer, he moved between her thighs and entered the moist tightness of her. She moaned his name and gripped his back to pull him closer, more deeply into her.

For a moment he held himself rigid, unmoving, afraid that if he did anything it would be over before it began. The feel of her surrounding him, the bewitching scent of her, the sight of her eyes glittering with need, all combined to shove him dangerously close to the edge.

She'd been a part of him for most of his life, and now making love to her felt like a natural culmination of a lifetime of want.

Her fingernails lightly scratched down his back; then she gripped his hips, and with that touch he moved against her, stroking deep and slow.

Her breathing matched his own, ragged and fast. She wasn't a lifeless entity beneath him. She arched her hips to meet his thrusts, then wrapped her legs around his hips and he was lost.

Faster and faster they moved in a frenzied dance. He knew when she reached her climax, saw the widening of her eyes, felt the tension that rippled through her, and that was all it took for him to tumble over the edge. He groaned her name as his release swept over him.

Still joined with her, he leaned his head down and captured her lips in a soft kiss. He'd known the physical desire he'd felt for her, but the depth of his emotional pull toward her surprised him.

"If I would have known what I was missing, I might have been a very bad girl back in high school," she said.

He laughed, rolled onto his side, and propped

himself up on one elbow so he could look at her. "I'm glad you weren't. As much as I loved you then, as much as I wanted you then, it was more than worth waiting for."

His smile faded as he gazed at her. "You know this wasn't enough for me. I don't only want the pleasure of making love to you again and again. I also want all of your laughter; I want all of your frowns. I want all the minutes of each day with you and your children."

She reached up and placed her palm against his cheek, her expression troubled. "This is probably the worst time in my life to bring somebody new into it. With Jennifer's murder and the roses and the phone calls, I feel off center. I know I'm in a vulnerable place right now, and I don't want to let you into my life for all the wrong reasons."

He stroked his thumb down her soft cheek. "I told you before, I'll let you take the lead in this. I'll be as patient as I can, go as slow as what makes you comfortable, just don't ask me to go away."

"I don't want you to go away." She sat up and worried a hand through her tangled hair. "At least not permanently."

He sat up as well, knowing there would be no invitation to spend the night. While he'd love to awaken in the morning with her in his arms, he knew she wasn't ready for that, and he respected her wishes.

She stood and excused herself and disappeared

into her bedroom. When she returned clad in a rose-colored bathrobe, he was dressed and waiting for her.

"I know you need to get to bed," he said as he drew her into his arms once again. She leaned against him, warm and sweetly scented. "Marissa, have the police told you that somehow you might be in danger?"

"Yes and no." She didn't move her face from the front of his shirt, and he tightened his arms around her. "Detective Wilkerson told me that if I'm the Marissa in that note card, then somebody close to me killed Jennifer. I asked her if I was in danger and she couldn't answer."

"You'll call me in the morning after you talk to the phone company?" She nodded. "And you'll call me if for any reason you're scared or need somebody to talk to? Promise me, Marissa."

She lifted her head and smiled up at him. "I promise."

He leaned down, kissed her on the forehead, then reluctantly released her. "I'm not going anywhere this time, Marissa, not unless you tell me to go away."

She shoved him toward the door. "Go away for tonight. I need to get some beauty sleep."

Moments later Alex sat in his car in her driveway and watched as one by one the lights inside her house went off. He imagined her in bed, her fair hair splayed against the pillow, her body warm as slumber overtook her.

Would she dream of him? He hoped so, for he had a feeling his dreams would be full of her.

Chapter 13

"The numbers you gave me come back to pay phones around the city," Detective Wilkerson told Marissa over the phone on Saturday morning. "And there doesn't seem to be any rhyme or reason to which phones are being used. One night it was from the north side of town, the next night the call came from the south side."

"So there's no way to find out who is calling me," Marissa said in dismay.

"That's about the size of it," the woman replied, her tone crisp and cool. "My recommendation at this point would be to go ahead and get a private number. Let us know what the new number is, and that should solve the problem for you."

"Nothing else new on the case?"

Wilkerson didn't have to ask what case she was asking about. "Nothing. We have no trail to follow, no leads to pursue." If the woman's voice had been cool before, it was positively frigid now.

Marissa murmured a good-bye, then hung up, disturbed by the news that there seemed to be no way to identify who was making the strange nightly phone calls to her. It also disturbed her how much Detective Wilkerson seemed to dislike her.

She frowned thoughtfully. No, it wasn't that the woman seemed to dislike her that bothered Marissa; it was the fact that the woman appeared to distrust her that she found bothersome.

Marissa had the feeling the detective didn't think she was being completely honest, was somehow holding something back that might move the investigation forward and crack the case.

If only that were true. If only she did know something that would help. She would beat down the doors of the police station if she had any information that might help them catch a killer.

"Mommy, Justin is making ugly faces at me," Jessica cried from the living room.

"Justin, stop making faces at your sister," Marissa replied.

Both the kids were keyed up, knowing that this evening they were meeting an old friend of their mother's, then going out for pizza.

"I'm not making ugly faces," her son protested. "It's just my normal face. She's just a tattletale and a big baby." Justin's chin rose in stubborn denial.

"Am not!" Jessica replied.

"Are to."

Marissa got up from the kitchen table and went into the living room. "I'll tell you what. You two behave and be nice to each other now while I take care of some business; then we'll go to the park and let you burn off some of your excess energy."

"Okay," Justin agreed, then smiled with sugar sweetness at his sister. "Want to play dinosaurs with me, Jessie?"

"Can I be the big one?"

A mutinous expression crossed Justin's features. He cast a quick glance to his mother, then sighed. "Okay, you can be the tyrannosaurus," he agreed begrudgingly.

Marissa sighed in relief as the two ran down the hallway toward Justin's bedroom. If she were lucky she'd get fifteen or twenty minutes of peace before World War III erupted between the two.

She returned to the table and dialed the number for the phone company. After punching in the appropriate numbers she was put on hold. As she waited, her thoughts turned to Alex, as they had a hundred times since they'd made love.

Making love with him had been everything she'd ever thought it would be. When they were young she'd imagined that he'd be an exciting lover, eager and overwhelming.

In actuality it had been exciting, but it had been so much more than that. Lying in his arms, being possessed by him, had felt like coming home after a long journey in a foreign land.

Certainly she'd never had any complaints about her love life with John, but John was gone, his memory cherished in her heart, but his arms no longer able to hold her, his body no longer able to warm hers.

She hadn't realized how starved she'd been, not just for sex itself, but also for the tactile pleasure of skin against skin. Making love to Alex had awakened her, pulling her from the grips of residual grief and thrusting her into a state of being she'd nearly forgotten existed. She was happy.

Her happiness superceded all other emotions. There had been no more roses delivered, and other than the brief nightly calls there had been no real reason for her to feel threatened.

She'd begun to believe once again that Jennifer Walsh's murder had nothing to do with her, and in any case she was filled with a belief that with Alex in her life everything was fine.

The phone company representative came on the line and she placed the order for a new, private number. There was a satisfying sense of mission accomplished when she hung up, one less unsettling irritation taken care of. While she still didn't know the identity of the caller, at least she hoped now there would be no more calls.

As she got up from the table she gazed at the clock. It was almost one. If she was going to take the kids to the park to play for a while, they needed to get going.

Alex would be arriving around five, and between the park and the arrival of Alex the kids would probably need baths. She hoped an hour or two at the park would wear them out so that by the time Alex arrived they'd be calmer than they'd been since getting up that morning. The best she could hope for was that they wouldn't act like little heathens.

Twenty minutes later she pulled into the parking area of a popular city park. This particular park was a favorite with Jessica and Justin because of the elaborate playground equipment and sandboxes.

As she watched the two kids race ahead of her toward the playground she realized she was nervous about Alex meeting her family. While she thought they were the best kids on the face of the earth, that was in part because they were hers.

It would take a special man to be willing to embrace another man's children. But Marissa was a package deal, and she'd rather be alone than attempt to make a life with a man who didn't love her children.

As the two kids ran toward the sandbox, Marissa took a seat at a nearby picnic bench. The late-May sun was warm on her shoulders, and she decided she was glad Alison had asked her to switch days with her. It had been a long time since she'd spent a Saturday at the park with her two little imps.

They weren't the only people in the park. The warm weekend day had brought out many families for picnics or just to relax. Young women sat in the sun, soaking up the rays, and several men played catch with a frisbee, their boisterous voices riding the warm breeze.

Kids of all ages climbed the slide and swung on the swings, romped in the sandbox and played tag. Jessica and Justin joined the fracas, diving into the sandbox without inhibitions. Definitely baths would be on the agenda when they arrived back home.

Jessica began to build a sand castle with another little girl about her age while Justin remained on the sidelines, eyeing the other kids before joining in. Justin was the cautious one, slow to warm up, but once he made the decision to join in, he would do so without reservation.

She opened the paperback book she'd brought with her and for the next thirty minutes alternated between reading and watching her kids.

Since the night she and Alex had made love they'd talked on the phone every day, sometimes two or three times a day. The conversations had reminded her of the ones they'd shared long ago. Although they had talked about nothing important, each time she heard his voice a giddy excitement filled her and she was amazed that she was lucky enough to feel this way about a man again.

The deep male voice pulled her from her

thoughts. She looked over to the sandbox to see a burly man standing over the kids. He appeared to be yelling at Justin. What the heck?

She slammed her book closed and raced toward the sandbox, the need to protect roaring through her. "What's going on?" she demanded. Justin's eyes were huge, glassy with the hint of frightened tears.

"Is that your boy?" The burly man stabbed a meaty finger in Justin's direction.

"Yes, that's my son. What's wrong?"

"He hit my boy. Paulie, punch him." He prodded the young, frightened-looking boy sitting near Justin. "Dammit, Paulie, I told you to punch him back. Clock him one in the head," he demanded. "You don't take no shit from nobody, you hear me?"

"Are you crazy?" Marissa exclaimed.

"Hell no, I'm not crazy. Paulie, what have I told you about being a wuss?"

"You're a piece of work," she muttered beneath her breath as she motioned Justin to come to her. He scrambled out of the sandbox and to her side, where she placed an arm around his quivering shoulder.

The big man snorted derisively. "That's it, pussy boy. Hide behind your mama."

"Justin, take your sister and go to the car," Marissa instructed. She turned back to the man. "I don't know what your problem is, but how dare you try to instigate a fight between two children, and how dare you use that kind of language in a park!"

"Tight-ass bitch," he said.

"Foul-mouthed bully," she retorted, then turned on her heel and walked toward her car, where Justin and Jessica awaited her.

Her blood thrummed hot when she saw the tears on Justin's cheeks. "Mom, I accidently bumped him with my elbow. I didn't mean to. I didn't do it on purpose."

"I saw him, Mommy. Justin wasn't a bad boy."

"I know that, sweetie. Come on, let's get in the car."

As the two got into the backseat, Marissa stood by the driver's door and watched as the man yanked his son from the sandbox. Poor kid, she thought. He looked as terrified as Justin had.

"Am I in trouble?" Justin asked as she got into the car.

She turned in her seat and looked at her son, his eyes still filled with the gleam of unspilled tears. "No, honey, you aren't in trouble. You said it was an accident."

"It was, and Paulie didn't get mad. I said sorry to him."

"But his daddy was a mean man," Jessica exclaimed.

"He certainly wasn't a nice man," Marissa replied. That poor boy had a long, miserable time ahead of him if that's the way his father behaved on a regular basis.

It didn't seem fair, that John, who had been a good and loving father, had been taken, while men like Paulie's father would probably live to be a hundred.

As they drove home they talked about bullies, and by the time they reached the house once again Justin's tears had disappeared and the incident was behind him.

The next hour sped by as both the kids and Marissa cleaned up for their evening out with Alex. As the time for his arrival grew closer she found herself becoming ridiculously nervous.

It was important to her that he liked her kids and that her children liked him. If that didn't happen, she and Alex were finished and she would feel as if fate had cheated her of happiness once again.

At a quarter of five, Marissa sat the children down on the sofa and gave them a gentle lecture about behaving in public, being polite to Mr. Kincaid, and making her proud.

"Did Mr. Kincaid know Dad?" Justin asked.

"No, honey, he didn't. Mr. Kincaid went to school with me when I was younger and then he moved away to another town."

"Is he a fireman like Daddy?" Jessica asked. With her hair up in pigtails and clad in a pink blouse and matching shorts, she looked as pretty as a picture.

"No, Mr. Kincaid is an architect."

"What's that?" Jessica asked.

"He draws buildings and then people build them," Justin replied before Marissa could answer.

She eyed her son in surprise. "How did you know that?"

He shrugged. "We've been having career days at school, and last week Kim Walker's dad came in to talk to us and he's an architect. Next week Captain Mike is coming to talk to us about being captain of the firemen."

"And the week after that there's no more school for the whole summer," Marissa said.

"And when we go back to school I'll be in the second grade," Justin replied.

"And I'll be in first 'cause my birthday is almost here," Jessica exclaimed.

"Only a week away," Marissa replied, reminding herself she still needed to get party hats and horns and order a cake. They had planned only a small party out at the farm with Jim and Edith. She'd already bought the latest Barbie doll along with enough clothes to make her the best-dressed doll in Cass Creek.

The doorbell rang, and all thoughts of parties and career days flew from her head. Alex had arrived. She opened the door and her heart melted at the sight of him. Dressed in jeans and a short-sleeved dress shirt he looked casual and ready for a chaotic pizza night.

"Hi," she said, grateful that he came empty-handed, that he carried no surprises for children he didn't know, made no attempts to bribe his way into their affections. Children had amazing bullshit meters, and Marissa's children were as intuitive as the best of them.

"Hi," he replied. To her surprise he shifted from foot to foot, looking surprisingly nervous. This only endeared him to her.

"Come on in." She opened the door to allow him inside. As he walked into the living room Jessica eyed him with open, friendly curiosity while Justin's expression was guarded.

"Alex, these are my children, Jessica and Justin, and this is Mr. Kincaid," Marissa said.

"Hi, Jessica and Justin. You can call me Alex."

"Mommy says you're an old friend, but you don't look too old to me, Mr. Alex," Jessica said.

Alex smiled, looking more relaxed than he had moments earlier. "I knew your mommy when she was just about your age, and she wore pigtails just like yours."

Jessica's eyes widened and she clamped a hand over her mouth as if the thought of her mother in pigtails tickled her. The corner of Justin's mouth twitched as he fought off a smile as well.

"Shall we go get some pizza?" Marissa asked.

"Pepperoni pizza. I only like pepperoni pizza, Mr. Alex," Jessica said demurely as she got up from the sofa.

"It just so happens, that's my favorite, too," Alex said.

Within minutes they were in Alex's car, the kids buckled into his backseat and whispering between themselves as she and Alex made small talk.

"Have you ever been to Jazzy's Pizza?" she asked.

"No, can't say I've had the pleasure."

She grinned. "I'm not sure you'll find the experience exactly pleasurable."

"Why not? You said the pizza there was marvelous."

"It is. It has to be to entice parents to enter into the mayhem. The entire interior is filled with video and arcade games and all kinds of things for kids to do. The place is usually noisy, frenetic, and wild."

"If you're trying to scare me, it isn't going to work. I love video and arcade games. I'm a sucker for good pizza, and being in the company of kids always makes me feel young."

He couldn't have said anything that would have made her feel better about the evening. At that moment she felt as if life couldn't get any better.

He had followed her for most of the day. It was rare she wasn't in the store on Saturdays, and since that was one of his days off he'd enjoyed the luxury of feeling as if he'd spent a special day just with her.

When the strange car pulled up in her driveway, a sense of disquiet coursed through him. The man who got out of the car was tall and handsome and walked to the front porch with the confidence of a man sure of his welcome.

Blake wasn't worried. Marissa had several male friends who occasionally came to visit her, most of them old friends of her dead husband's.

He didn't mind her having friends, although she should enjoy them now, for when she became a part of his family she wouldn't be seeing old friends again.

The man was inside only a few minutes before he walked out with Marissa and the kids. They all piled into his car and drove off. Blake followed at a reasonable distance, certain that if Marissa caught a glimpse of his car or of him, she wouldn't recognize either.

He'd bought the car years ago from an auction house and had registered it in the name of an aunt who lived in a nursing home in Kansas City. He kept it garaged in a storage unit several miles from his house.

It was this car that had run down John Jamison in the parking lot of the Food Mart. He hadn't really planned it. He'd been watching Marissa and John for months, his yearning for her growing by the minute, his hatred of John growing as well.

He'd followed John to the Food Mart and had watched as the handsome man went into the store and came out a few minutes later carrying his gallon of milk.

It had been nothing more than an impulse, an impulse impossible to ignore. He'd never forget the burst of euphoria that had shot through him as he tromped on the gas and headed for the solitary figure making his way across the parking lot.

He'd never forget John's eyes in his headlights as the car headed directly for him. First bewildered, then wide with panic, John had dropped the milk and turned to run just before Blake's car had made contact.

He hadn't waited to see the damage, had known by the way the body had flown through the air that John was dead. Instead he had driven directly to the storage unit and parked the car inside.

Over the months he had repaired the damage to the front end, banging out dents, polishing away scratches, and erasing all signs of the incident. Each hair he'd pulled from the fender, every drop of blood he'd scrubbed away, had filled him with a power, with the knowledge that his dreams about Marissa and her children really could come true.

He now followed behind them, his fingers tapping on the steering wheel as he wondered again who the man was and what he was doing with his family.

They pulled into Jazzy's Pizza and Blake drove on by. He parked down the block, then got out of his car and walked back to the busy pizza place.

He didn't worry about Marissa somehow spotting him and recognizing him. The place was packed and he had become a master of disguise. She'd never recognize him with his baseball cap, fake goatee, and dark glasses. As he entered the pizzeria he limped slightly and took a seat at a table on the other side of the restaurant from where they sat.

He ordered a small pepperoni pizza, knowing that was his daughter's favorite, and as he ate he watched them. It didn't take long for anger to stir.

It didn't bother him that the man interacted with the children. He left their table often to play games with the two. The first seed of anger stirred when he saw the way the man looked at Marissa. It wasn't the look of a casual friend.

He also couldn't help but notice that the man touched her often . . . too often. Her hand, her shoulder, her cheek, each touch implied an intimacy that burned hot in Blake's soul.

He would find out the identity of the man and what exactly his relationship was with Blake's family. If he was a problem, he would be dealt with, just as John had been dealt with.

In the meantime, Blake finished his pizza and prepared to leave. He had another chore to take care of before the night was over. There was a filthy-mouthed bully who had signed his own death warrant earlier that afternoon.

Chapter 14

"I don't want to leave," Alex murmured into Marissa's hair as he held her tight against him.

The two of them stood on her front porch. The children had been tucked into bed, exhausted by the evening at Jazzy's Pizza.

Alex and Marissa had shared a pot of coffee and several stolen kisses after the kids had gone to bed, but now it was time to say good night.

"I know. I don't want you to leave, but you have to." She sighed, her face nestled in the warmth of his neck. As his hands moved down her back, evoking a shiver of desire in her, she stepped back, distancing herself from him. "You have to leave, Alex. I have to work in the morning, and besides, it's far too soon for my kids to see you at the breakfast table."

"I know. They're terrific kids. I like them. I had a lot of fun with them tonight."

She smiled, remembering the magic that had seemed to encompass the evening. "They like you, too, and there were several times I thought you were having even more fun than them," she teased.

He grinned sheepishly. "I told you I like arcade games." He reached out and stroked a strand of her hair away from her face, his features radiating a hunger that heated her insides. "You know I want you again."

"I want you, too." The words came from her on a sigh. "But we aren't carefree kids anymore, and I have more to consider than just my own wants and needs."

"I know, and I find that quality admirable if just a bit frustrating." He leaned forward and kissed her on the forehead. "So I'll say good night for now. But I'm hoping we can get some quality time alone soon."

She nodded. "Good night, Alex." She watched him walk to his car, her heart filled as it hadn't been in over a year. When he started his engine, she went inside.

As she readied herself for bed she thought of the evening they had shared. It had been magical. Justin and Jessica, although rambunctious with energy, had behaved well, and it had been obvious that they had taken to Alex without reservation.

She suspected part of the reason was that Alex hadn't tried too hard to ingratiate himself with them. He'd just been himself and allowed things to flow naturally.

Several times during the course of the evening she'd found herself sitting alone at the table, watching as Alex and her kids played one game or another, their hoots and laughter warming her heart. For those few hours she'd felt as if she belonged to something bigger than just herself, she'd felt as if she were once again part of a family.

As she got into bed and pulled the sheet up around her, she reminded herself that while they had interacted like a real whole family tonight that didn't mean things would be peachy from here on out.

Justin and Jessica had accepted Alex as her friend, but there was no way of guessing how they would accept him if he became more, if he eventually became their stepfather.

Despite the fact that she loved having Alex in her life, there was a small part of herself she held back, a piece of her heart she kept hidden and well protected.

Only time would tell where this thing with Alex would lead. But at least for tonight she allowed the sweet magic of the night to embrace her as she fell asleep.

She was getting to him. Luke watched as his partner sipped her beer. She sat on his sofa, looking ill at ease, and he wondered again what had gotten into him when he'd invited her back here for a drink after work.

"You have a nice place," she said, a touch of surprise in her voice.

"What? You expected me to live in a cave?" He eased down on the opposite end of the sofa.

"No, I just didn't expect a cozy house all neat and tidy. I thought maybe you lived in a kind of bachelor apartment. You know, with dirty clothes strewn across the floor and fast-food wrappers littering the floor."

"I bought the house ten years ago. I was thirty-five, had worked all my life, and realized I had nothing to show for it. As far as how clean it is, I have a woman who comes in once a week and picks up my dirty clothes and food wrappers." He took a sip of beer, then continued. "Let me guess. You probably have your spices and your DVDs alphabetized."

"I don't keep spices, since I rarely cook, and no, I don't have my movies alphabetized." She hesitated a beat. "But I do have them arranged by category."

Of course, Luke thought. She was one of the most anal-retentive women he'd ever met. She both irritated and fascinated the hell out of him. And lately, he'd found himself wondering what she'd be like in bed.

Would she hate the mess of love making? Rumpled sheets and wet kisses? She could be such a tight-ass, but there were times when he caught her looking at him and something in her eyes caused every muscle in his body to tense.

She sighed and crossed her long legs. "I'm so glad the Nichols case is closed and the mayor is happy."

They had closed the case two days before, the forensic evidence leading to a business associate and a real estate deal gone bad.

"It's always nice to keep the mayor happy," he agreed. Those long legs of hers taunted him, as did her scent, a vanilla musk that at some point over the last week had worked its way into his very pores.

"I've been thinking about the Walsh case." She set her beer bottle on the coaster on the coffee table and leaned forward, her blouse opened just enough to give him a dizzying view of cleavage.

He fought the impulse to run his cold bottle across his forehead and wondered if the air conditioner was on the fritz, for it felt unusually warm. "What about the Walsh case?" he asked, trying to stay focused on the conversation and not on how badly he wanted to touch her.

She picked up her beer and sat back once again. "I was thinking maybe we should reinterview that cranked-up friend of hers."

"You mean Sam Harmon?"

She nodded, her spiky hair gleaming in the light overhead. He wondered if it was hard with gel or soft to the touch. He wondered if he was losing his mind.

"He was such a slimeball, I can't help wondering if maybe he knew more than what he told me at the funeral that day."

"He was so brain fried, even if he does know something about Jennifer's death he probably doesn't remember he knows," Luke retorted. "Besides, I don't want to talk shop."

"Then what do you want to talk about?"

He wanted to ask her why in the past week she'd been in his thoughts far too often. He wanted to know if she felt the tension that he felt each time she was close to him.

When in the hell had it happened? When had he begun to notice little things about her that made him think of sex? He thought it might have started the first day he'd noticed her perfume.

That's when he started noticing things. Things like the graceful length of her neck and that damnable sway of her hips. Things like the way her tongue licked crumbs off her upper lip when they ate bagels each morning and how she rolled her head on her neck just before leaving work each night.

"Luke?"

He realized he'd been staring at her and that he had no idea if she'd asked him a question or he'd asked her one. For a long moment their gazes remained locked, and in the depths of her dark eyes he saw a flicker of something like smoldering knowledge, like she knew that she was driving him slowly out of his mind and she enjoyed it.

Once again she leaned forward and placed her beer bottle on the coffee table. Then she moved with a sinuous grace closer to him on the sofa that suddenly seemed too small.

"Why did you invite me here, Luke?" Her voice had a slightly husky quality.

He put down his beer and stood, afraid that if he sat next to her another minute he'd make a mistake. Suddenly he was mad. "Lately you're just pissing me off, Wilkerson."

She blinked, obviously surprised by his words. "What exactly am I doing to piss you off?"

He averted his gaze from hers and frowned. "I don't like the way you wipe your mouth after you eat."

"You mean like a normal person? In direct opposition of you mauling your mouth with the back of your hand?"

He ignored her, still refusing to look at her. "And I don't like how you rub your mouth when you're thinking or that red blouse you wear with all those little buttons up the front."

She stood and he finally looked at her once again. "You mean those tiny little buttons that could be ripped right off with a firm yank?" she asked.

Once again the temperature of the room climbed to uncomfortable heights as he thought of those buttons popping off to expose her breasts. She stepped closer to him, close enough that he smelled that damnable perfume, felt the heat from her body.

"Why did you invite me here, Luke?" she asked again.

"I don't believe in partners getting involved."

She nodded. "Neither do I." She leaned toward him, her body making contact with his.

"I told you, I've never been tempted to have any kind of a relationship," he managed to say with his last grasp on sanity.

"I'm not even sure I like you, Luke," she replied. "Now shut up and kiss me."

He did.

He kissed her as he didn't remember ever kissing a woman in his life. She responded, opening her mouth to him. It was as if the kiss unleashed a firestorm of hunger.

They fell back to the sofa, fingers unbuttoning, bodies writhing and mouths possessing. There was nothing gentle, no finesse involved. It was pure lust that drove them.

Within minutes they were both half-naked. He'd known her breasts were small, but he found delight in their minute perfection, in the bold nipples that rose to pebble hardness beneath his hands and mouth.

The spiky dark strands of her hair were soft and smelled like coconuts. The source of the perfume that had tormented him for the last week was the crook of her neck.

The cool competent cop disappeared as she

writhed beneath him, clutching his hair and back in abandon as moans of pleasure escaped her.

Her fingers fumbled at his zipper, her mouth hot and demanding against his. He knew it was going to be fast and furious and that was just fine with him.

She'd just managed to get his pants unzipped when his cell phone rang. She froze. "I won't answer it," he said in desperation.

"You have to. It might be the station." The words came from her all breathy and sexy and filled with regret. The phone rang again. She shoved at his chest. "Luke, answer the phone."

He muttered an expletive, then sat up and grabbed the cell phone from the coffee table. "Hunter," he barked. He listened to the caller, and frustration filled him. He wasn't sure if it was the words he heard that caused the frustration or the fact that Sarah had sat up and was putting on her bra.

"Be there in thirty," he said to the caller, then hung up. What he wanted to do was go back seconds in time and finish what they had begun.

Dammit, why hadn't he put his phone on vibrate, or shut it off altogether?

"What's up?" She pulled on her blouse and began to button it, no hint of the moaning uninhibited woman he'd held in his arms moments before. How quickly she'd transformed from wanton woman back to cool and collected cop.

Reluctantly he stood and zipped up his pants, then reached to the floor for his shirt. "That was Sergeant McCabe. He's on a scene that he thought might interest us. A body has turned up in Oak Ridge Park."

"Why does he think we'd be interested?" She tucked her blouse into her slacks.

"The victim had a big red bow stuck to his forehead."

Chapter 15

It had been a great day at the store. Sundays were funny. They were either good or bad when it came to sales at the shop. There never seemed to be much in between. Today had been one of the good, profitable days, and it had been made better by a phone call from Alex.

She normally didn't work Sundays, but she'd shifted days with Alison this weekend as the older woman had pled a family commitment for today.

A sense of satisfaction carried Marissa from the shop and to her car in the parking lot. On Sundays the shop closed at six, so she'd still have the evening with the kids.

As she drove toward Jim and Edith's house her mind was filled with a million and one things. This was the last week of school for the kids and there would be a flurry of activity involved.

Jessica's birthday was next Sunday, and not only

would they have a celebration with Jim and Edith, but she'd reluctantly agreed to let her daughter have several friends over Saturday evening for a party.

Lists in her head began to form . . . party hats and favors, crepe paper and balloons, she mentally ticked off the items she would need for a successful party.

As always, thoughts of Alex intruded. He scared her more than a little. Not in a physical way, but because she still feared that she'd somehow romanticized their relationship from years ago, that she was still romanticizing him because he'd come along when the first real pangs of loneliness had struck.

What she'd had with John had been good. She didn't want to make the mistake of believing herself in love with the wrong man in an effort to reclaim the happiness of sharing her life.

The problem was Alex didn't feel wrong. He felt wonderfully right and that's what worried her. She smiled and shook her head ruefully, wondering why she was looking for problems.

Maybe, just maybe, fate had decided to be kind to her. Perhaps Alex had been placed in her path to give her that second chance at happiness, to help ease the devastation that John's death had left behind for her and her children.

Maybe she shouldn't look a gift horse in the mouth and should stop worrying so much.

Life was good and there was a sense that things

were only going to get better. She drew a deep breath and embraced that feeling.

By the time she reached Jim and Edith's she felt as if she had the world by the tail. Her business continued to grow; she had the best kids in the world and a man in her life whose eyes radiated both tenderness and passion whenever he looked at her.

She laughed exuberantly as the kids raced out of the house at the sound of her car. She parked and got out as the two ran to give her kisses and tell her that Grandma wanted them to stay for dinner.

"Can we, Mommy? Grandma made fried chicken and mashed 'tators," Jessica exclaimed.

Marissa winked at Jim, who stood nearby. "Well, we can't very well pass up Grandma's fried chicken and mashed potatoes, can we? Go tell Grandma we'll stay."

"Yeah!" The two kids disappeared back into the house.

"Did they give you any trouble today?" she asked Jim.

"Never. Those kids are what make us get out of bed each day." Jim gazed at her with an unusual intensity. "You know we love them."

"Of course I do, and they love you."

He nodded, as if satisfied by her answer.

Strange, she thought as she followed him into the house and into the kitchen, where Edith was putting the food on the table.

"What can I do to help?" Marissa asked.

"Nothing," Edith replied briskly. "Just take a load off and relax."

Marissa did as instructed, sinking into the seat where she always sat when they had dinner there. "Jim, get the kids. It's on the table," Edith yelled into the living room.

Within minutes they were all seated at the table. Marissa wasn't sure when exactly she noticed Edith's unusual quietness or the fact that the older woman wasn't meeting her gaze.

Something was wrong. The kids were just as chatty and happy as could be, but there was a tension in the air Marissa couldn't quite put her finger on.

It wasn't until she and Edith stood side by side at the sink washing dishes that Marissa broached the subject. Edith had a dishwasher but rarely used it. She maintained that washing dishes was a good time for soul-searching, talking to God, and unwinding from the day's events.

It was also during this time that she and Marissa had shared their most intimate conversations. While washing dishes they had talked often about John, laughing and crying together while swishing a sponge and wielding a dish towel.

"Something's wrong," Marissa said after several minutes of uncomfortable silence. "You've been quiet. Are you not feeling well?"

"I'm fit as a fiddle," Edith replied, appearing

completely focused on scouring the pot that had held the mashed potatoes.

"Did the kids misbehave today?"

"Of course not. Those kids are always as good as gold when they're with us." She placed the pot in the drainer and drew a deep sigh. "They told us you have a new friend . . . somebody named Alex?"

So that was what was wrong. Marissa should have said something this morning when she dropped the kids off. She should have known Jessica and Justin would share the fun they'd had with the grandparents who loved them. John's parents.

"Edith, you know how much I loved John," Marissa began. Edith nodded, and to Marissa's surprise, two tears trekked down the older woman's cheeks. "He'll always be in my heart, but Alex has become somebody special to me, too."

Edith bobbed her head up and down as more tears followed the first two. "I didn't expect you to grieve forever for my boy. You're young and pretty, and I knew eventually the men would be after you."

She placed her sponge on the side of the sink and looked at Marissa, the tears flowing as if from a bottomless well. "I'm just so afraid," she whispered.

"Afraid?" Marissa placed her arm around Edith and led her to the table, where they sat down side by side. Marissa took Edith's cold, trembling hands in her own. "Why are you afraid?"

Edith closed her eyes for a long moment, and when she opened them, tears still glittered in their faded blue depths. "I'm afraid that you'll move on with your life and leave me and Jim behind.

"I'm afraid that when you marry again the children will have new grandparents and it will be awkward for you to continue to let me and Jim see them." The words, now that they had started, tumbled from her along with a plethora of fresh tears.

Marissa was stunned by her words. She squeezed Edith's hands, her heart breaking with the other woman's pain. "Edith, that isn't going to happen. I would never allow that to happen," she said fervently. "Why on earth would I deprive the children I love of the best grandparents they could ever have? It doesn't matter what happens in the future, Edith, you and Jim are part of our lives forever. That's a promise from my heart."

Edith drew a tremulous sigh and smiled crookedly. "I suppose you think I'm a foolish old woman."

Marissa leaned forward and wrapped her arms around Edith. "Not at all," she exclaimed. Edith returned the embrace, then she leaned back and said, "So tell me about this Alex."

It was just after eight when they left Jim and Edith's and headed home. Marissa hoped she had put Edith's fears to rest concerning the future relationship between grandparents and grandchildren.

She had meant what she'd told Edith. If and when she married again there were several issues she would not compromise about, and first and foremost was her children's relationship with John's parents.

Second was the fact that she never wanted to live anywhere else other than Cass Creek. Not only was her shop here, but her life was here. The big-city sub-urb with the small-town feel held all her memories.

She'd never had any desire to travel. Even after John's death she'd felt no need to escape the place where they'd met, fallen in love, and married. She loved this place she called home.

As she pulled into her driveway, she glanced at the front porch and breathed in relief as she saw there were no flowers there. The change of her phone number had stopped the calls, and the death of Jennifer Walsh seemed like it had happened a very long time ago.

"Okay, Jessica, bath, and when she's finished, Justin, you go next. By the time you're both finished it will be bedtime."

"When school is over can we stay up later?" Justin asked as they entered the house.

"We'll see." As Jessica headed for the bathroom and Justin to his room, Marissa went into the kitchen to check her phone machine for messages. There were two from Alex. She smiled at the sound of his deep voice and picked up the phone to call him back.

"Next Friday night," he said after they'd said hello.

"What about it?"

"I'd like to invite you to my place for dinner. It can either be a family night or a grown-up kind of night."

Her skin warmed at the thought of being in his arms once again. "I'll get a babysitter," she replied. "Am I cooking or are you?"

"How about if I cook dinner and you bring dessert."

"Sounds perfect."

"Marissa, remember the night we were parked under our tree and I told you I loved you for the very first time?"

Sweet memories cascaded through her. It had been a perfect spring night. A million stars had filled the sky overhead and a cool breeze had drifted through his open window as they had kissed with a longing for more.

"I remember," she replied softly.

"If I was seventeen, I'd tell you that same thing and ask you to wear my class ring."

"But you aren't seventeen anymore," she said.

"I know. Besides, I lost my class ring years ago. I just wanted you to know that whenever we're together that's the way I feel."

"Mommy, I got soap in my eyes." Jessica stood, naked as a jaybird in the hallway, dripping soapsuds and water all over the carpeting.

"Alex, I have to go. I have a soap-in-the-eye emergency."

He laughed. "Go . . . I'll call you tomorrow at the store."

By nine the kids were in bed and Marissa had changed into her nightgown and was at her usual place on the sofa with a book. She hadn't been much of a reader until John's death, when desperate to find something to fill the empty hours between the children's bedtime and her own, she'd picked up a romance novel and had been hooked ever since.

At ten thirty the phone rang. Marissa jumped and stared at the offending instrument in dread. She'd changed her number to a private one. It couldn't be the strange caller. Maybe it was Alex again.

As it rang a second time she forced herself to pick up. "Hello?" she said tentatively. There was a long moment of silence. "Hello?" she repeated.

"You're welcome, my love." The line went dead.

Marissa stared at the receiver in her hand, a cold fist squeezing her heart. The voice had been male, soft, and low. She hadn't recognized it.

What did it mean?

You're welcome. Like he'd done something for her and expected her to be thankful. Was this the same caller who had been making the phone calls to her prior to her changing her number? If so, how had he gotten her new number?

She got up from the sofa and went down the hallway. She stopped at Justin's bedroom doorway and peered in at her sleeping son, then moved to Jessica's doorway.

There had been no forewarning the night that John had left to get a gallon of milk from the store. She'd felt no sense of dread, no impending doom as he'd left the house on his late-night errand.

As she stared at her daughter sleeping peacefully beneath her Barbie sheets, every nerve ending in her body screamed a warning of undefined danger. Dread twisted her stomach into a painful knot.

She often felt this way before one of the severe storms that hit the Midwest. A coppery taste filled her mouth and she realized in nervous tension she'd bitten the inside of her cheek.

Something bad was coming. She felt it as certainly as she felt the bite of her fingernails in the palms of her hands as she clenched them at her sides. Something bad was coming and she was powerless to stop it.

How had he gotten her new number? And more important, what had he done?

Chapter 16

Her phone rang again at eight the next morning. As usual, the morning was frantic as she tried to get the kids ready for school while she got dressed and ready to get to the shop.

She grabbed up the phone in the kitchen while reaching for a soapy sponge to clean up the puddle of pancake syrup Jessica had left in her wake at the table.

"Mrs. Jamison. It's Detective Wilkerson." Marissa's heart dropped at the sound of the woman's voice. "We need to talk to you. Could you come down to the station as soon as possible?"

"Can't you talk to me now? On the phone?" Her heart, which had initially dropped to her feet, now pounded a ferocious beat.

"No. We'll talk when you get here," Wilkerson replied. "How soon can you come?"

"I put the kids on the school bus at eight forty. I

could be there by nine." The words seeped out of her with enormous reluctance. She didn't want to go. She didn't really want to know what had happened, why they wanted to talk to her again.

"We'll be waiting for you." The detective hung up.

The dread that had filled her the night before roared through her now, a hollow wind of fear renewed.

Maybe it was nothing. Maybe they just had some follow-up questions for her. In any case, it would be a good time to tell them about the strange call the night before.

First things first, she told herself. She needed to get somebody else to open the store. She had no idea how long she'd be at the police station.

She called one of her employees, a woman named Kate who had been eager for more hours. "I don't know when I'll be in," she said to Kate when she'd gotten her on the phone. "Alison will come in at noon. You can leave then if I'm not back yet or you can stay until I get in."

"No problem," Kate assured her.

Forty-five minutes later Marissa was headed back to the police station, her heart still pumping an erratic rhythm. She should have eaten one of the pancakes she'd made for the kids. Maybe if she had food in her stomach she wouldn't feel so ill.

She knew she was kidding herself. Whether she'd eaten nothing or half a dozen pancakes, she'd still feel sick by the return trip to the black-and-yellow building.

When she went inside a uniformed officer immediately took her to the same interview room she'd been in before. As she waited for Detectives Wilkerson and Hunter, she wondered how many guilty people had sat in the chair where she sat. And how many innocent people had sat here with their stomachs twisted in knots and their hands sweaty with fear.

She hadn't noticed it before, but now she smelled the room, the scent of stale coffee and perspiration and fear. Her stomach rolled again.

The moment the two detectives walked into the room, she knew that whatever reason she was here, it was bad. Both of them looked rumpled and weary. Detective Hunter held two cups of coffee and he placed one before her.

"I didn't know for sure how you drank it," he said as he took the chair next to her.

"Thank you. Black is fine," she replied.

Detective Wilkerson didn't sit, and Marissa eyed the file folder the female officer held with dread. "Why am I here?" she asked.

"Where were you Saturday night between the hours of eight and midnight?"

Marissa held the woman's gaze. "My kids and I went with a friend to Jazzy's Pizza. We were there from about six until eight thirty or so; then we went

home and my friend left my house around midnight."

"And who is this friend?" Wilkerson asked.

"Alex. Alex Kincaid." She looked from Sarah Wilkerson to Luke Hunter. "Is one of you going to tell
me what's going on?"

Detective Hunter raked a hand through his
blond hair and leaned back in his chair. "We've got
a problem."

"We've got a dead guy named Sonny Farragut.
Do you know him?" Wilkerson's gaze bore into her.

Marissa frowned. "No, I don't know anyone by
that name. Why do you think I'd know him?"

"Our problem is that something about the murder scene ties to the Walsh murder," Hunter said.

"What do you mean?" She looked at him, then at
Wilkerson. "Ties to the Walsh murder how?" Please,
please, don't let this have anything to do with me,
she prayed.

"There's something we didn't tell you about the
Walsh murder." Wilkerson finally sat and slapped
the file folder onto the table. She opened the folder
and withdrew a photo. Marissa steeled herself for
whatever horror she was about to see.

Wilkerson slid the photo in front of her. Even
though Marissa had prepared herself for something
awful, a small gasp escaped her. It was a picture of
Jennifer Walsh, although different from the one
Marissa had been shown on her previous trip to the
station.

"Is that a bow?" The gaping wound across Jennifer Walsh's neck was horrible, but the bright red bow in the center of her forehead seemed even more gruesome. Marissa pushed the photo aside.

"We kept the bow out of the press, but our problem now is that Sonny Farragut had a bow on his forehead, too. We don't know if we have a leak and his death is some sort of copycat killing or if the two vics were killed by the same person," Hunter said.

You're welcome, my love. The caller's words whirled around and around as an awful possibility grew in her head.

"Sonny Farragut, do you have a picture of him?" Her voice was faint to her own ears. She didn't want to see. She didn't want to know, and yet she had to know. She had to face the awful possibility in her head.

Wilkerson pulled a photo from the folder and once again slid it across the table. Don't let it be him, Marissa thought. Please, please, don't let it be the man in the park.

For a moment she squeezed her eyes tightly closed, sending up every prayer she had in her soul. She opened her eyes and looked at the photo.

She jumped out of her chair. The abrupt action sent the chair clattering to the floor behind her.

She stood by the table, senses reeling. It couldn't be. Her mind worked to wrap around it as her heartbeat stalled. The hot sting of tears burned her eyes and the immediate surroundings swam in fog. It couldn't be him, but it was.

"I know him," she whispered. Her heartbeat crashed so loudly in her ears she heard nothing else. She grabbed the edge of the table to keep herself upright as her knees threatened to buckle beneath her.

She was vaguely aware of Detective Hunter standing and uprighting her overturned chair. She felt sick . . . no, worse than sick. Hunter took her by the elbow and guided her to sit once again.

"I know him," she repeated, her mind still working to make sense of the photo she'd just seen. "What's happening? Could somebody please tell me what's going on?" She looked at Hunter pleadingly.

"Marissa, why don't you tell us how you know Sonny Farragut?" Detective Wilkerson's voice was softer, more kind than she'd ever heard it, and Marissa looked at the woman with gratitude. Had she come at her with the usual hard-ass approach, Marissa was certain she would have shattered.

She wrapped her cold, trembling hands around the foam cup of coffee, grateful for any warmth to ward off the icy chill that gripped her. However she didn't take a drink, was afraid that if she did she'd throw up.

"I didn't actually know him. I didn't know his name or anything about him, but I recognize him." Her voice sounded reedy and strained, foreign to her own ears.

"From where?" Wilkerson's voice was still soft, although with an urgent edge.

"Saturday afternoon I took the kids to Oak Ridge Park to play for a little while." She saw the two cops exchange glances with each other. "What?"

"That's where his body was found. In the sandbox at Oak Ridge Park," Detective Hunter explained.

Marissa couldn't stop the moan that left her lips. Of course, in the sandbox where the original altercation had taken place.

"He yelled at my son. Justin was playing in the sandbox with his son and accidentally elbowed the other boy. That man . . . Sonny started yelling at Justin. He was verbally abusive and I intervened and he became verbally abusive to me."

"And then what happened?" Detective Wilkerson stood and began to pace the floor in front of the table, raw energy emanating from her.

"Nothing. I took my kids and we went home." The phone call she'd received the night before now made horrifying sense. "Then last night I got a phone call." Now she was grateful she hadn't eaten any breakfast as she swallowed against a burst of nausea. "At around ten thirty last night my phone rang and when I answered a male voice said, 'You're welcome, my love.' "

"Son of a bitch," Sarah exclaimed and slammed her hand down on the table. "So we now have two murders, both tied to you."

"I swear, I didn't have anything to do with this. I

don't know what's happening. I don't know why it's happening." Tears filled Marissa's eyes. Why was this happening? Who was doing this?

"Don't worry, I believe you." Sarah threw herself into a chair, her gaze holding Marissa's. "But the problem is we have two stiffs with red bows on their forehead and the only connection between the two seems to be you."

"Does the phone company still have a trap on your phone?" Luke asked.

She shook her head. "No, I told them it wasn't necessary when I changed my phone number to an unlisted one."

"The first thing we're going to do is tap your phone lines," Sarah said. She pulled a pad and pen from her blazer pocket and once again sat at the table.

"It appears that somebody is cleaning up the messes in your life," Luke said. "Two people were verbally abusive to you and now those two people are dead. They were even wrapped up with a gift bow to present to you. I'd say you have some sort of a sick champion in your life."

"But that's crazy," she whispered. She felt as if she'd stepped into an alternate universe, where nothing made sense at all.

"Then you give us a scenario that makes better sense," Luke said.

Marissa removed her hands from the coffee cup and instead wrapped her arms around herself and rubbed her upper arms for warmth. "I just can't make sense of any of it. I can't imagine who would do something like this."

"I'll tell you what we need from you. We need a list of everyone in your life. Brothers, uncles, boyfriends, lovers past and present . . . everyone. The mailman, the delivery boy. We need to know every single person you have regular contact with."

Sarah leaned forward. "Do you understand, Marissa? Our killer is somebody around you and we need a list like yesterday. We need to find this nut before somebody else impugns your dignity or calls you a name or in any way offends you and ultimately offends this creep."

Marissa once again grabbed hold of the edge of the table as her head spun dizzily. Somebody in her life. Somebody close to her. It couldn't be possible, it just couldn't. And yet nothing else made any more sense.

She couldn't deny the fact that the two people who were dead had irritated her. Both situations had been ugly, public scenes. "I didn't tell anyone about either of the two incidents," she said.

"Which means somebody was nearby. Somebody was watching."

Sarah's words chilled Marissa once again. Somebody had been watching. That somebody would have had to follow Marissa and her children to the ballpark that night, then again to the park on Saturday. Somebody had been watching her.

"We need that list, Marissa." Luke's eyes radiated weariness. "We need it as soon as possible. And in the meantime we're contacting the FBI to get some kind of a profile on the killer."

"Besides making the list, what should I do?" How did she protect her children from the unknown? How did she protect herself?

"If you don't have a security system at your house, get one. When you leave the house pay special attention to your surroundings. Watch for the same car following you, the same stranger's face popping up again and again, and if you see anything suspicious, call us."

Sarah's advice did little to warm the ice that had taken the place of blood in Marissa's veins. "You think my children and I are in danger?"

Luke shook his head. "At the moment the perpetrator seems focused on protecting you, so my gut feeling is that at the moment you aren't in any real danger. He's killing off people who give you grief. It's the people around you who are in danger."

"So what happens now?"

"You go home, go about your life," Sarah said. "Once we have that list in our hands we do the work and check out everyone on it."

"What about if I don't know the person's name? Like the man who sweeps the mall in front of my shop every day. I see him all the time, but I don't know what his name is," Marissa said.

"In that case you give us as much description as

possible," Luke said. "Same with a car you notice seems to be around too much: Give us a full description and a license plate number if possible."

"I know this is difficult," Sarah said, once again her voice holding more warmth, more compassion, than Marissa had ever heard from the tough cop. "But you seem to be our only link to these murders. Like Luke, I don't believe you're in any danger at this moment. This person seems to be fixated on you in a positive way right now."

"And what happens if that changes? What happens if I'm the one who does something to irritate or aggravate him?" Marissa asked.

Sarah stood once again, her slender body vibrating with tension. "Then we have a whole new ball game and things could get even uglier."

It was nearly noon when Marissa left the police station. She had been afraid after John's death, afraid that she couldn't live without him, fearful that she couldn't raise her children alone, couldn't pay the bills, couldn't provide a good home. The list of fears had gone on and on in the weeks after her husband's death.

But in that fear she knew the answer lay inside her, that it was all up to her to work hard to provide a living, to give her children what they needed, to be both father and mother to Justin and Jessica. Success had chased away those particular fears.

Black and overwhelming, the fear that gripped her now crashed through her on waves of helplessness. *Go home. Go about your life.* Easy for them to say. Neither of them had a psychopath in their lives.

She didn't feel like going back to the shop; nor did she want to go home. She wasn't sure where she wanted to be until she arrived in Alex's driveway.

She sat for a long moment, surprised by the fact that she needed comfort and this is where she had come. Even though Alex had been back in her life only a short period of time, he'd become as important to her now as he had been years before.

As she got out of the car his front door opened. He stood in the doorway, looking both surprised and pleased. "Marissa!"

"I hope you don't mind the impromptu visit," she said as she walked into his foyer.

"Of course I don't mind. I'm delighted."

She turned to face him, and before she knew it she moved into his arms and began to cry. "Hey now," he said softly as he wrapped his arms around her and held her close. "What's wrong with my best girl?"

"Bad morning." She swallowed against the tears, hating herself for crying, hating herself for the weakness that had brought her here to Alex. She stepped back from him and wiped her cheeks. "I'm sorry. I just needed to talk to somebody, I guess."

He took her by the hand and led her into the kitchen, where he pointed her to a stool at the counter. "Coffee, tea, or a good stiff drink?"

"I'm coffeed out, and it's too early for a good stiff drink, but I'd love a cup of hot tea."

She watched as he busied himself preparing the drink. He was dressed in a T-shirt and a pair of cut-off khaki shorts, and there was a solid quality to the breadth of his back, the strength of his long runner's legs. Even though she knew she was being ridiculously feminine, she felt safe here with him.

He set the cup of tea in front of her, then sat on the stool next to her. As she sipped her tea she told him everything that had happened at the police station.

He listened without comment and without interruption. By the time she finished telling him everything she'd also finished drinking her tea.

"The police—you know I'll have to tell them about you," she said.

He nodded. "Of course." His smile was gentle. "Don't look so worried. I have nothing to hide. I'm sorry people have been rude to you, but I didn't kill them."

"I know that. Otherwise I wouldn't be here now."

"I'm glad you came." He took one of her hands in his and for the first time since the police station she felt a welcoming warmth creep into her icy veins.

"Make love to me, Alex. I want you to hold me and make me warm."

"Marissa, I don't want to take advantage of you." His twilight eyes held her gaze, and he reached out and gently stroked a strand of her hair away from her face. "You're afraid and feeling vulnerable."

"Yes, I am," she agreed. "And I want you," she added with a calm certainty.

That's all it took. Without another word he led her into his makeshift office and bedroom in the dining room. As he pulled down the shades, she undressed.

Somewhere in the back of her mind she knew he was probably right, that she was coming to him through vulnerability, with the need to feel as if she wasn't alone in the horror that had taken place.

However, there was another part of her that came to him strong and sure, with a clear and radiant desire. Where before their lovemaking had held the excitement of years of unfulfillment, the passion of new discovery, this time there was a tender quietness, the coming together of two old souls who had found each other amidst the storm of life.

She needed gentle and that's what he gave her, stroking her body with slow, languid caresses. Deep, soulful kisses stirred her just as much as the frantic, hungry kisses that had marked their first physical joining.

She still feared that somehow she was mixing up old emotions with new ones where he was concerned, that somehow the romance of finding an old flame years later colored the reality of her feelings for him.

At least for now that fear seemed inconsequential. He was exactly what she needed now in her life, and for that she was grateful.

Afterward she lay in his arms on the twin bed and waited for her heart to stop racing, her pulse to calm to normal.

"I love you, Marissa. You should know by now that there's nothing I'd like better than to spend my life with you and your children."

She sighed and snuggled closer against him. "It scares me a little bit."

"What does?" He tightened his arms around her.

"How much I care about you, too." She couldn't say the love word, not yet. There was still a part of her that held back, that needed to hold back.

He rose on one elbow and gazed down at her. "Why should that scare you?"

"I don't know, it just does." She closed her eyes and cuddled against him again.

She couldn't tell him that what frightened her at this moment was that somehow, someway, he would gain the attention of the madman who had invaded the spaces of her life.

She couldn't put into words the all-encompassing fear that he would wind up dead with a gaping slash in his throat and a big red bow stuck to the center of his forehead.

Chapter 17

"If there's a fire you're supposed to drop to the floor and crawl to the nearest door," Justin said just before he shoved a bite of fish stick into his mouth. "'Cause the smoke goes up and the fresh air stays down."

"Don't talk with your mouth full," Marissa admonished.

Justin duly swallowed, then continued. "And if you feel a doorknob and it's hot, don't open the door 'cause that means the fire is there."

He'd been sharing firefighting tips since he'd gotten home from school. Captain Michael Morrison had spent the last hour of school talking to the kids about fire safety and concerns.

"I don't want my fish sticks. I want pizza," Jessica whined.

"We're not having pizza tonight, so eat your fish sticks," Marissa replied to the cranky little girl.

"And after Justin's game this evening we need to make a run to the grocery store."

"I don't wanna run to the grocery store," Jessica protested.

Jessica had been a pip since she'd come home from school, and Marissa wondered if maybe she was starting to come down with something. There had been a nasty flu bug going around. Justin almost never got sick, but Jessica was one of those kids who could be in the same state as a virus and catch it.

Marissa sighed. She didn't much want to go to the grocery store either. First thing Tuesday morning she'd had a security system installed at the house and for the past three days her home had been the only place she'd felt safe.

"Baby, we have to go to the grocery store if you want to eat tomorrow," she said to Jessica.

It had been a difficult week, and getting groceries in the house had taken a backseat to other concerns. It had taken her two days to make the list of people the detectives had requested from her. "Besides, Alex is going to meet us at the ballpark."

"He's coming to watch my game?" Justin asked.

Marissa nodded. "He wants to see you play."

"Cool," Justin said.

"Can I sit next to him?" Jessica asked.

Marissa smiled, glad that her kids seemed willing to accept Alex's presence. "I'll tell you what, we'll have him sit in the middle between you and me."

"I'll bet he doesn't like fish sticks," Jessica replied.

Marissa had been pleased when Alex had suggested meeting them at the park, knew that he wanted to be a part of her children's lives.

Tonight they would all be together. Then tomorrow night she was going to his house for dinner and they would get some time alone.

She'd already arranged for the kids to spend the night at Jim and Edith's and suspected she would wake up Saturday morning at Alex's house.

Marissa had nixed the idea of a birthday party with other children for Jessica. With all the uncertainty in her life, she didn't want to put anyone's children at risk. Instead, Alex would go with them Sunday to Jim and Edith's for a birthday party.

The pleasant thought of falling asleep tomorrow night wrapped in Alex's arms carried her through supper and remained with her as they drove to the ball fields.

Jessica remained more than a little cranky, but when they pulled into the parking lot and saw Alex waiting for them, she cheered up.

So did Marissa. It was amazing to her how just the sight of him could put a quiet joy in her heart. It was different from what she'd felt about him when they'd been young. She suspected that what she felt for him now was the adult love of a woman for a man.

They had just gotten settled in their seats on the

bleachers when Marc Carter made his way toward them. His gaze barely flickered to Alex. "Marissa, I was questioned by the cops last week . . . something about an incident in the parking lot here after a game? Some girl got murdered."

He didn't wait for her reply, but continued. "Why did you have to give them my name? What did I ever do to you?"

"I'm sorry, Marc. I had to give the police the names of everyone I knew were here that night," she replied.

"Well, thanks a lot." He shook his head, his eyes glimmering with suppressed anger. "Like I need the police investigating my life. I'm trying to keep my bitch of a ex-wife from getting custody of my son. The last thing I need is this kind of crap."

Before she could say anything more, he turned and stalked away. "I hope the police are looking long and hard at him," Alex murmured.

She looked over to where Marc had sat and caught his angry gaze. Some of the warmth of the evening faded, and she was grateful when Alex covered her hand with his.

Still there was no way Marc Carter could ruin the night for her. It was a gorgeous early-summer evening. A handsome, loving man sat next to her. Jessica behaved like a princess, and for just these few minutes in her life all was well with the world.

Justin's team won, 3–2, and after the game Alex insisted on treating them to ice cream. It was just after seven when they all got settled in a booth at the local Dairy Shack with banana splits in front of them.

As they ate, they talked about the game and school and plans for the summer. Alex kept the attention focused on the kids, and Marissa enjoyed the interaction between them.

"Your mom tells me you like dinosaurs," he said to Justin.

"Yeah. Me and my dad used to study them together," Justin replied, a wistful smile curving his lips. He cast a quick glance at Marissa. "Dad used to say he was like a tyrannosaurus. They're big and strong and he said he had to be a tyrannosaurus to protect his family."

Alex nodded. "Tell me more about the tyrannosaurus. We didn't study dinosaurs much when I was in school."

"Tyrannosaurus rex means lizard king," Justin said, his small, handsome features animated. "They ate meat, not plants, and a man named Henry Fairfield Osborn gave them their name in 1905."

"Wow, you have studied them," Alex said, obviously impressed. A surge of pride welled up in Marissa. Justin was such a bright little boy.

"I like them," he replied. "Tyrannosauruses weren't scared of anything." He lowered his eyes and gazed at his banana split. "Except maybe cars."

Those three words crashed through Marissa. Her heart ached as she realized in her son's dinosaur world, the big meat-eating dinosaurs were frightened of cars.

Before either she or Alex could comment on Justin's words, Jessica chimed in. "I think all the dinosaurs should have been afraid of fish sticks 'cause they're yucky and their mommies made them eat them."

There followed a conversation about most favorite and least favorite foods. By the time they finished the ice cream, Jessica had begun to whine and rub her eyes, a sure indication that it was time to leave.

"As you can tell, my daughter doesn't do tired well," she said as the kids ran ahead of them. "She gets very cranky when she's tired. Woe to the boyfriend who tries to keep her out too late."

Alex laughed. "She's fine. Sometimes I get cranky when I'm tired."

Marissa smiled. "I hope you handle it better than she does."

"I'm sure you'll let me know if I don't. I can't tell you how much I'm looking forward to tomorrow night."

"Me, too. The kids are spending the night with Jim and Edith."

"Does that mean I get to cook breakfast for you Saturday morning?" His gaze warmed her from her head to her toe.

"Absolutely, and no continental-style breakfast

for this girl. I want the full meal deal." They reached her car.

"You got it," he replied. She could tell by the look in his eyes that he wanted to kiss her, but also knew he'd refrain while in front of her kids.

She placed a hand on his arm. "Thanks for the ice cream."

"It was fun." He opened the car door for her and she slid in behind the wheel.

"I'll see you tomorrow night around six," she said, as she started the engine.

"Bye, Justin and Jessica," he said and waved as she pulled out of the parking spot.

"I wanna go home," Jessica said from the back-seat.

"A quick stop at the grocery store, then we'll be home," Marissa replied.

"But I wanna go home now."

"Jessica Marie, no more whining," Marissa said firmly. "I know you're tired, but we're going to the store, and if you continue to whine you'll be in time out until you're old enough to date."

Marissa had never been back to the store down the block where John had been killed in the parking lot. She'd never been able to force herself to return there despite the fact that it was the most convenient place to buy groceries.

Instead she drove an extra fifteen minutes away from the house to go to another grocery store. As she drove she constantly checked her rearview mirror, looking to see if they were being followed.

It was impossible to forget the fact that somebody had been watching her, that somebody knew more about her life than a casual observer would.

She'd spent the past week looking over her shoulder, peeking out windows and into rearview mirrors. Tonight was like all the other nights: She saw nothing suspicious, nobody out of place.

When she pulled into the grocery store parking lot no car followed her in, but each time she went out in public she felt a prickling up her spine, the terrible knowledge that somebody could be near . . . watching her . . . watching her family.

"Stay right next to me, both of you," she instructed as she grabbed a shopping cart and started up the first aisle. There were other shoppers in the store, but nobody who looked suspicious, no reason for her to be nervous. But she was, as she had been every minute of every time she left her house for any reason.

She thought she might hate the person for this as much as anything . . . for the fear that he'd brought into her life, the kind of fear that twisted her gut and weakened her knees and made every moment outside of the security of her home pulse with potential danger.

She filled the basket quickly and tried to ignore Jessica's growing litany of complaints. When they reached the cereal aisle Marissa prepared herself for the usual battle. She was not disappointed.

"I want this," Jessica said and grabbed a box of popular sugar-laden cereal.

"You know the rules," Marissa said and took the box from her daughter. Marissa didn't mind her kids having ice cream after dinner or a piece of cake or cookies, but she drew the line at pouring a bowl of sugar for her children for their first meal of the day.

"You know the choices. They're the same as when we came shopping last week," she said.

Jessica stomped her foot. "I don't like those choices. I want this." Once again she picked up the box of sugar-frosted cereal and threw it into the cart.

Marissa calmly removed the cereal and put it back on the shelf. "If you touch it again, I'll take away your Barbie dolls and you won't be able to play with them for a whole week," she warned.

To her surprise Jessica threw herself to the floor in a complete, abandoned temper tantrum. She wailed and kicked her feet and flailed her arms as Marissa stared at her in surprise. It had been a couple of years since Jessica had thrown such a fit.

"Jessica, get up and stop that right now." Marissa's cheeks burned as an older woman passed them by and shook her head in obvious disapproval.

"Get up right now," Marissa said, as embarrassment battled with anger and the latter won. She grabbed one of Jessica's hands and tried to pull her up off the floor, intent on delivering a crack to her bottom. But Jessica fought her, shrieking as if Marissa was about to physically abuse her.

Marissa was vaguely aware of another shopping cart going by them, pushed by a young man. It was at that moment that terror struck.

Somebody is watching you.

Somebody is watching you, and whoever it is, they are removing people who irritate you from your life. The people around you are in danger. The words whirled around in her head. Her stomach tightened as an invisible fist grabbed her lungs, making it difficult to draw breath.

Was somebody watching right now? Seeing Marisa's irritation? Calculating how best to remove the irritation from her life? Jessica? Her irritation at this moment. Oh God, was somebody watching?

"Jessica, honey. It's okay. Come on, let's go home." Tears of fear blurred Marissa's vision as she crouched down on the floor and reached for her daughter. "Come on, baby. It's okay."

Jessica calmed down, although she continued to cry. She wrapped her arms around Marissa's neck and Marissa stood, bringing Jessica off the floor with her.

"Come on, Justin, let's go."

"But, Mom, what about the groceries?" he asked.

"I'll get them another time."

All Marissa wanted to do was get out of there,

away from anyone watching the family drama, away from any evil that might lurk nearby.

As they headed toward the exit, she found herself murmuring over and over again, "She's a good girl. She's just tired. She's a good girl. She never irritates or upsets me. I love her very much."

Over and over again she said the words loud enough for anyone near her to hear as her heartbeat pounded erratically with the rhythm of fear.

By the time they reached the car, Jessica quietly sobbed with contrition. "I'm sorry, Mommy," she said as Marissa buckled her into the seat. "I didn't mean to be bad."

"It's all right. Let's just go home and get a good night's sleep. Okay?"

The terror that had gripped Marissa remained with her long after they arrived home and she'd put the children to bed. She drifted from window to window in the secured house, looking outside for a nameless, faceless boogeyman.

Had somebody been watching? The thought chilled her as she'd never been chilled in her life.

Blake stood in the middle of the master bedroom and looked around with satisfaction. It was finished. The house was nearly ready for his family. He just had a few last-minute touches and then it would be time to move forward, forward with his destiny.

He was particularly pleased with the master

suite. He'd chosen black and red for the colors of the bedroom he would share with Marissa, black for his masculinity and red for his passion.

He'd added knickknacks and little items to appeal to her femininity. A vase of long-stemmed red silk roses sat on the nightstand next to where she would sleep. Red candles in ornate gold holders lined the top of the dresser, and he could easily imagine making sweet love to his sweet wife in the soft glow of their flames.

Yes, everything was almost ready. He had only a few logistics to take care of and, of course, the fly in his ointment.

A wave of rage swept over him as he thought of the fly. The fly now had a name: Alex Kincaid. Thirty- four years old, a successful architect, and the man attempting to worm his way into Marissa's life.

Blake had known something needed to be done when he'd seen them together at Justin's ball game. He'd seen how Alex looked at her and, even worse, he'd seen how Marissa looked at Alex.

Just like she'd once looked at John: all dewy-eyed and happy. Acid churned in his stomach as he remembered watching John and Marissa together. During that time Blake had known the meaning of coveting. His desire, his very need for Marissa had built moment by moment, day by day, until he knew fate had made an error in giving her to John. She was meant to belong to him.

And now there was another man looking at her

as if he had a right to her, touching her with an intimacy that forced red stars of rage to dance in Blake's head.

He hadn't worked all this time to lose her to another. He hadn't plotted and planned and cleaned up her life to lose it all to a fucking architect pretty boy.

Like an annoying fly, Alex Kincaid needed to be swatted out of existence.

Chapter 18

Alex hit the sidewalk before the sun was up. He loved running at this time of the morning, when the sky was still filled with stars and dawn was just a whisper of promise in the distant east.

He'd awakened before his alarm that morning with the sweet knowledge that tonight he would make love to Marissa and he'd hold her through the night and wake up with her in his arms.

He knew if they continued their relationship and eventually got married, he'd not only become a husband for the first time in his life but a stepfather as well. The thought was both exhilarating and daunting.

He'd never thought much about being a father, probably because there'd never been a woman important enough to him to make that kind of commitment . . . until now.

It didn't matter to him that he wasn't Justin and

Jessica's biological father. What mattered was that they were Marissa's children. He was already half in love with the kids. Jessica, with her love of dance and her sparkling blue eyes was adorable. The more sober Justin, who showed occasional bursts of stubbornness and had initially been aloof, was quickly walking a path straight to Alex's heart.

Slap. Slap. Slap. His shoes hit the sidewalk pavement in reassuring rhythm. The neighborhood houses he passed were mostly dark, although there were lights on in a few, where people apparently worked an early shift.

The air was cool and refreshing. He often came up with his best architectural designs while running. The activity freed the mind and allowed it to wander to wonderful creative places. It was part of what kept him running.

A car passed him on the street, momentarily blinding him by the bright headlights. He didn't break his stride. As the car went by he recognized it as the same car that passed him every morning about this same place.

A dog barked from behind a fence at a nearby house as he pulled in a lungful of the fresh morning air. *Slap. Slap. Slap.* His thoughts returned to Marissa and the night to come.

Steaks for two, baked potatoes with all the trimmings, and a fresh spinach salad. He'd decided not to try anything fancy for dinner, but rather go with easy grill-and-bake items. He didn't want the night to be about dinner; rather, he wanted the night to be about them.

He heard the car before he saw it. The sound came from somewhere behind him, a roar of engine too loud from a car coming too fast down the neighborhood street. But no headlights pierced the darkness.

Odd, he thought. He turned his head to look behind just in time to see the car jump the curb. It roared up the sidewalk directly toward him.

He had no time to think.

He felt the impact, then darkness.

It was just after six when Sarah Wilkerson got the call to meet Luke at the emergency room of Cass Creek Memorial Hospital. He gave her no details, just told her to get there as soon as she could.

Even though it was supposed to be their day off, she'd just stepped out of the shower when she'd gotten the call and she dressed quickly, wondering what was going on. She was accustomed to being called to a morgue or to a crime scene, not an emergency room.

Within minutes she was en route. Was it possible the bow killer had struck again only this time the victim had somehow managed to survive? She was beginning to think that was the only way they were going to catch the son of a bitch.

She and Luke had spent the last week checking out the people on the list that Marissa had provided them. It had been tedious, detailed work, checking alibis and trying to corroborate them, knowing that it was possible their culprit wasn't even on the list.

So far they had managed to clear only a dozen people who had solid alibis for the two nights of the murders. To make matters worse, she'd been dealing with the distraction of remembering Luke Hunter's kisses.

They hadn't spoken of what had almost happened between them in the week since, although she couldn't get it out of her mind. It irritated the hell out of her that he seemed to so easily put it out of his.

She saw him the minute she pulled into the parking lot of the small hospital. Luke leaned against the bumper of his car, sipping from a foam cup with the heavy-lidded gaze of a man not fully awake

"What's going on?" she asked as she approached where he stood.

He grabbed a second foam cup from the top of his car and held it out to her. "An odd coincidence," he replied. "Remember Marissa's first husband was killed in a hit-and-run accident?"

Sarah nodded and took a sip of her coffee, surprised that he'd remembered she liked it lightly sugared and creamed. "So what's the coincidence?"

"This morning Marissa's current boyfriend was out for his daily run and somebody tried to run him down."

"I'm assuming he's alive since we're here. Have you heard what his condition is?"

"All I know is that he's conscious."

"Have you been inside to talk to him yet?"

Luke gave her the half-assed grin that always shot a flutter of warmth through her veins. "Nah, I knew you'd chew my ass from here to tomorrow if I went in to talk to him without you." He raked a hand through his unruly hair. "If I were king of the world, I'd make sure crime didn't happen on my day off and never before nine in the morning."

"Come on, look alive. This might be the break we need to crack this case," she replied with a burst of optimism. "Besides, look . . . it's a beautiful sunrise and you would have missed it if you'd stayed in bed."

They started walking toward the emergency room entrance. "I love this time of morning. Most of the time I take a cup of coffee out on my little patio and watch the sun come up. But sometimes I drink a cup of hot tea. Ginger peach is my favorite. I sit on a wicker chair and breath in the morning air, listen to the birds sing. The world is so peaceful at dawn."

"Wilkerson, anyone ever tell you that you talk too much?"

"Yeah, my ex-husband, but he was an asshole. You think I talk too much?"

"Nah, not me. The last thing I'd want would be to have anything in common with your asshole ex-husband."

She shot him a quick grin as they entered the cool interior of the hospital where a receptionist directed them to room 4 in the ER.

Alex Kincaid sat on the bed in room 4. Obviously not a happy camper, he wore a blue-flowered hospital gown and a deep scowl.

"The doctor is writing up your orders right now, Mr. Kincaid," a young nurse said as the two detectives entered the room. "It should be just a few more minutes." She looked at the two newcomers with relief, then swept past them and out the door.

Sarah instantly recognized him as the man who had been with Marissa when they'd first gone to the mall to talk to her. "Mr. Kincaid, I'm Detective Wilkerson and this is my partner, Detective Hunter."

"I know who you are." He shifted positions, wincing in obvious pain.

"What's the prognosis?" Luke asked.

"Mild concussion, an array of scrapes and bruises, but the doctor has told me I'll live."

"Want to tell us what happened?" Sarah pulled out her notebook and sat in the chair next to the bed.

"I was out for a morning run and a car swiped me."

"Anything unusual about the car?" Luke asked.

"You mean other than the fact that it was driving on the sidewalk?" It was a rhetorical question delivered with a tense, slightly sarcastic tone. He drew a deep breath and released it slowly. "I'm sorry. I'm in a foul mood, and I'm taking it out on you two."

"No problem," Luke said smoothly. "I'd be a little cranky myself if somebody tried to mow me down in a car."

"What can you tell us about the car?" Sarah asked. "Did you get a make, a model? A color?"

Alex's lips compressed together in a grim line as he shook his head. "I got nothing. I heard it coming up behind me and when I turned my head to look, it was right there. I jumped to the side and I guess the fender or the hood caught me on the hip. Flipped me through the air and I hit my head on the edge of the sidewalk as I came back down. I was out. A neighbor found me and brought me here."

"Where did this happen?" Sarah asked.

"About midblock between Cypress Avenue and 81st Street. I made them call for you guys because once I came to and realized what had happened, I remembered how Marissa's husband died."

He shifted positions once again and stared down at the floor for a long moment. "Look," he said, once again meeting first Sarah's gaze, then Luke's. "I don't know if this has anything to do with what's been going on in Marissa's life. I mean, it's possible whoever hit me was coming home after an all-night bender. Left a bar, forgot his headlights, and never saw me on the sidewalk."

"Do you believe that?" Sarah asked.

He released a long, audible sigh. "No. No, I don't.

That car jumped the curb and beelined for me. There was no mistake about it."

"Have you had a recent fight with Marissa? Exchanged angry words with her in public?" Sarah asked.

"Quite the contrary. We're getting along very well. In fact, I'm thinking about asking her to marry me."

"Then you don't fit the pattern," Luke said. "Our other two victims both had negative dealings with Marissa right before they were killed."

Sarah frowned thoughtfully, her mind racing. "He doesn't fit the pattern, but the attack on him makes sense." She tapped her notebook with the end of the pencil, then stood and began to pace in the tiny confines of the room.

"The perp, this Blake, is doing Marissa favors getting rid of the people who are mean to her. He signed his card, Love Blake. I read that as he thinks he's in love with her, and that means you, Mr. Kincaid, are a threat."

At that moment the nurse returned. "You're all set to go, Mr. Kincaid. You just need to sign these papers and follow up with your personal doctor."

Sarah and Luke waited until the nurse had left once again. "You need a ride home?" Luke asked him.

"Yeah, I'd appreciate it." He slid off the gurney and to his feet. "It will just take me a minute to get dressed . . . if you'll excuse me."

"Oh, sure." Together Sarah and Luke stepped out of the room. "Why don't you leave your car here and ride with me to take him home?" Luke asked. "That way we can swing by the place where he got hit and see if we can find anything that might give us a clue to the make and model of the car."

"Okay, as long as you bring me back for my car," she agreed.

"Your assessment of the perp, it makes sense."

Sarah thought she saw a touch of respect in Luke's eyes and a sense of satisfaction filled her. She shrugged. "I think it makes a crazy kind of sense."

"Well, I'd say it's obvious we're dealing with a nutcase." He gave her a lazy grin. "I'd be a little worried if I were you, being tuned into his wavelength."

She slapped his arm, and at that moment Alex eased out of the examining room.

Minutes later the three of them were in Luke's car and headed to Alex's home. Sarah liked sitting in Luke's car, which contained the odor of fast food and his cologne, a scent that had become both familiar and oddly comforting.

Nobody spoke for the duration of the ride. Frustration gnawed at her stomach. If indeed this was the latest work of their Gift Bow Killer, then once again he had managed to strike without leaving any substantial clues behind. They were no closer to finding him now than they had been with the first murder. Hopefully they would find something at the scene of the accident that would give them a clue. Just one damn tiny clue.

Luke pulled into Alex's driveway and cut the engine.

"Thanks for the ride," Alex said, but he didn't move from the backseat. "I'm sorry I couldn't help you with a description of the car. It all happened so damned fast."

"I'd recommend you stay on your toes," Luke said. "If this was our man, then you're in his sights."

"I'm aware of that. What concerns me is Marissa's safety. What happens when this creep decides he doesn't love her anymore and that she pisses him off?"

"We're doing everything we can to catch this guy," Sarah said, aware that her words did nothing to placate his concerns.

"We've told Marissa the importance of being vigilant, of not going out alone, of being aware of the people around her," Luke said. "I'd advise you to do the same."

Alex opened the car door. "You'll let me know if you identify who tried to run me over?"

"Of course," Luke said.

He eased out of the backseat, but stood by Luke's window. "I don't intend to mention this to Marissa. She's frightened enough without knowing about this. I'd appreciate it if neither of you told her, either."

"How are you going to explain to her your physical injuries?" Luke asked.

"I'll tell her I had a close encounter with a car this morning, but I'll make sure she thinks it was just an accident, that I was in the street and the driver didn't see me."

Luke frowned and exchanged a quick glance at Sarah, then turned back to Alex. "I can't promise you we won't tell her. If our investigation requires we speak to her about it, then we will, but at the moment there's no reason why we'd have to mention it to her."

"I appreciate it," he said, then turned to leave.

They waited in the driveway until Alex was safely inside his house, then drove to the area where he had told them the incident had taken place.

For the next forty-five minutes they searched the area, looking for anything that might lead to identifying the make and model of the car.

The grass held not only lingering dampness of morning dew, but also retained the imprint of Alex's body and splotches of his blood. He'd been lucky. Damned lucky, Sarah thought. If he'd zigged instead of zagged, he'd be dead.

"There's nothing here to indicate to me that this was an accident," Luke said as he kicked the grass near the edge of the sidewalk. "No tire skids anywhere. The driver apparently didn't make any evasive moves to try to miss him." Luke frowned thoughtfully. "There's nothing here for us."

Again that gnaw of frustration threatened to chew a hole in Sarah's stomach. "Dammit," she exploded. "This guy is pissing me off. I feel like he's thumbing his nose right in my face. I've never wanted to catch somebody so bad in my life. This is my first big case and I'm blowing it."

She stomped onto the sidewalk, working up a full head of steam. "And I'd love to find the bastard that leaked the information about the bows. That was all we had to separate a real confession from all the wackos who always confess to every crime committed."

For the past three days the newspapers had been filled with the stories of the Gift Bow Killer, the serial killer on the loose in their fair town. "I'd like to find that person and wrap a bow around their neck."

Luke gave her one of his heavy-lidded looks "You through?"

She released a sigh. "For now."

"Good, because I'm starving. Why don't we go to my place and I'll whip us up some of my famous pancakes." There was something in his eyes that let her know if she agreed, she was agreeing to a lot more than just breakfast.

"I'm starving, too," she replied and the look he gave her made her forget all about the Gift Bow Killer and the gnaw in the pit of her stomach.

Chapter 19

"My God, Alex. What happened?" Marissa stared at his thigh, which over the course of the day had turned to an ugly, vivid purple. Scabs had begun to form over the places where the skin had been ripped away.

"It looks much worse than it feels," he assured her as he ushered her through the living room and into the kitchen. He did his best not to limp, although every muscle in his body was sore from his unexpected contact with the ground.

"Sit down and have a glass of wine." He pointed her to the table, then went to the refrigerator to get the wine.

"But what happened?" She sank down on the chair, her forehead wrinkled in obvious concern.

"I was out running this morning when it was still dark. I drifted too far into the street and got clipped by a car. It was my own fault. I didn't have on any reflective clothing so the driver just didn't see me." He smiled as he poured them each a glass of the wine. "Don't look so worried. I'm fine and I've learned my lesson. The next time I jog, I stay on the sidewalk."

He placed a glass of wine before her, then sat at the table. "Now tell me about your day."

Her frown continued to ride her forehead. "It was fine. Where did it happen? Did you go to the hospital? Did the driver stop?"

He'd hoped this wouldn't become a big deal, was afraid of what might happen between them if she thought he was in danger because of her. "Marissa, it was nothing more than an accident, and yes, I went to the hospital to get checked out. I'm bruised and battered but fine."

She took a sip of the wine, her gaze still dark and tinged with suspicion. "I can't help but worry, especially with the way John died."

He reached across the table and grabbed one of her hands. Never had he seen her looking as lovely as she did at the moment. The blue sundress she wore intensified the hue of her eyes and complemented her blond coloring. She'd been wearing something blue the first time he realized his feelings for her were much deeper, much more complicated than friendship. They'd been thirteen at the time.

"Let me tell you something, Marissa. Sixteen years ago I lost you because of powers beyond my control. Now that I've found you again, nothing and nobody is going to keep me away from you. The only way I'm going anywhere is if you ask me to go away."

He released her hand. "And now, why don't you bring your wine outside on the patio where I have a couple of steaks ready for the grill."

Alex was grateful that she didn't bring up the subject again. He didn't want to lie to her, but he also worried that if she knew there had been nothing accidental about the incident then she'd shove him out of her life for his own protection.

Although Alex had a healthy respect for evil, and there was no doubt in his mind that the person committing the heinous crimes was evil, he also didn't intend to run away and hide.

His number one concern was the woman who had swept back into his life, bringing with her the possibility of the happiness and family he'd begun to think he'd never find.

Dinner was a success. The steaks were grilled to perfection, the conversation light and easy but with a simmering anticipation of the pleasure the night ahead held.

After dinner, she insisted he take her into the dining room and show her the plans he had been working on for the community center.

"Why do you have all these topographical maps?" she asked as he booted up his computer.

"The maps show me the pitch and grade of the land around the area," he explained. "I have to take those things into consideration when looking at a particular site."

"I had no idea there was so much involved in your job," she said.

He laughed. "You thought I just drew a little picture and then the construction crew moved in?"

"Something like that." She smiled at him. "But I always knew you were incredibly bright, even when we were little. You always got the highest scores on the math quizzes."

He did what he'd wanted to do from the moment she'd walked through his front door. He wrapped his arms around her and pulled her close against him. "And you always won the spelling bees."

She laughed, but the laughter died as their gazes remained locked and desire flared. Had he ever wanted a woman like he wanted her? Not that he could remember. She'd been in his blood when he was young and she was in his blood now.

He didn't want just her passion. He wanted all of her: her laughter, her dreams, her fears. He wanted her and her children in his life forever.

As he leaned his head down to capture her lips, fear gripped his gut and tightened his chest. He had no idea how to keep her safe. He hated the fact that he felt as impotent now as he had as a teenager when she'd last been taken away from him.

Sarah rolled away from Luke, her body slick with perspiration and her heartbeat still racing with the rhythm of residual passion.

He'd promised her pancakes that morning, but

within minutes of entering his house, they'd tumbled into bed, finishing what they had begun before.

They had come at each other hungry and their joining had been lusty and crazy and more than a little bit wonderful. All that energy he kept pent up during work hours had definitely exploded from him in his love making.

Afterward he had made the pancakes and they'd sat at the table and discussed the case as if nothing had happened between them.

They had decided to get all the files, all the reports and go over each and every one to see what they might have missed. The afternoon had sailed by as they'd argued possibilities, dissected reports, and made phone calls to continue checking alibis.

It was seven o'clock when Luke had leaned back in his chair and gazed at her. "I'm hungry again." She could tell by the look in his eyes he wasn't talking about food.

Three minutes later they were back in bed.

As Sarah's heartbeats slowed, Luke propped himself up on one elbow and gazed down at her. "This doesn't change anything between us," he said, his voice gruff.

"I wouldn't have it any other way."

"I told you before, I've never been tempted to get married again."

"Like I'd want to marry you," she replied dryly. "Luke, I'm a big girl, and this was as much my choice as yours. Don't sweat it, partner. A couple rolls in the hay doesn't suddenly turn me into a clingy, needy kind of female." She popped him on the belly playfully. "And if you aren't going to feed me again, then take me to my car so I can head home."

Half an hour later she parted ways with Luke and got into her own car, which had been left at the hospital early that morning.

As she drove home she tried not to replay those moments in Luke's arms, and tried instead to focus on the case. She didn't want to dwell on the fact that her partner kissed better than any man she'd ever kissed in her life. She didn't want to wallow in thought of how masterful he'd been in bringing her to climax after climax. She needed to think about the case.

The case. The case. It was driving her insane. She wanted this guy so bad she could taste it.

Her mind shot to the taste of Luke's mouth, hot and eager against her own. She often found his laid-back attitude aggravating, and at times his lack of verbosity made her want to pinch his head off, but she could find nothing to complain about when it came to his lovemaking.

He'd managed to curl her toes, not once, not twice, but so many times she'd lost count. She told herself she could deal with this, she could take what he was willing to offer and not hunger for anything more.

She told herself that she could absolutely forget

the fact that somehow, someway, over the last couple of weeks she had fallen head over heels in love with her partner.

What she had to do now was concentrate on not being in love with him, on not wanting anything more from him than his trust and respect as a partner.

She also needed to concentrate on the germ of an idea that was formulating in her head, an idea that might just catch the Gift Bow Killer and earn her the respect not only of Luke, but of the entire department.

Chapter 20

"How come Mr. Alex didn't come with us today?" Jessica asked Marissa as they got settled on the bleachers at the park for Justin's practice.

"Mr. Alex was busy this evening," Marissa said. It was the easiest answer to give a six-year-old. In truth, she hadn't invited Alex to join them.

Spending the night with him, waking up in his arms, had been wonderful, and she knew given different circumstances she would have thrown herself into the relationship body, mind, and soul.

However, the vicious bruising on his thigh and his story of an accident had filled her with horror and disbelief. She didn't believe his story that it had been an accident, and she knew that somehow Alex seeing her, dating her, had put him at risk.

She wasn't willing to lose another man to tragedy. As much as she wanted to be with Alex, she didn't want it to turn out that she'd loved him to death.

At least for the time being, she intended to keep a distance from him. She hadn't told him her decision yet, but she knew it wouldn't be long before he'd demand an explanation for her being too busy to see him.

She shoved thoughts of Alex from her mind and instead focused her attention on her son out on the ball field. As if Justin felt her gaze on him, he looked at her and grinned and waved. Love filled her heart.

With each day that passed Justin looked more and more like his handsome father, and for just a moment she indulged in thoughts of John. Even though she had Alex in her life, there would always be a bit of grief for the man she had expected to share happily ever after with.

She wrapped an arm around Jessica, who cuddled warmly against her side.

"I love you, Mommy," Jessica said.

"And I love you," she replied.

"I had fun at my birthday party."

Marissa smiled. The party at Jim and Edith's on Sunday afternoon had been a rousing success despite the fact that no other children had been invited to attend. They had played games and eaten cake and ice cream and Jessica had been thrilled with all her presents.

The only thing missing had been Alex. Marissa

hadn't invited him after all. She'd feared that any more family time might increase the risk to him.

It had been after the party while the kids carried Jessica's presents to the car that Marissa had told Jim and Edith what had been going on in her life. She hadn't wanted to tell them before, knowing that they would be sick with fear for her and for the children, but she knew they needed to know about the murders, about the dangers.

Again that inexplicable fear welled up inside her. A fear so intense it momentarily stole her breath, iced her blood, and closed her throat.

She looked around, seeking what? Looking for what? She didn't know. Maybe somebody watching her? A reason for the terror that clawed inside her?

People she saw every week . . . parents of children who played ball surrounded her. Familiar faces that on the surface posed no threat. Marc Carter sat nearby, next to a pretty young woman Marissa had never seen before. Maybe he'd finally made a love connection.

In the distance the firefighter ball team was in the outfield, their red-and-white jerseys reassuring to her. As usual, before taking the field the men had sat and watched a few minutes of Justin's game, cheering him on and visiting with Marissa.

Still, there were always strangers at the ballpark. People who had come to watch their friends' sons play, baseball enthusiasts who liked watching for the stars of tomorrow. Was one of those people

Blake? Was he here now, watching her? Watching her children?

She drew a deep breath as some of the terror ebbed away. She was seated in a ballpark with lots of other people. She was safe here. Her children were safe. There was nothing to worry about for the moment. She just needed to calm down and enjoy the practice game taking place on the field.

They were midway through the game when Marissa spied Detective Wilkerson standing next to the bleachers. The spike-haired detective motioned to her, indicating she wanted to talk to her. Marissa's heart jumped in her chest. What now?

"Jessica, you stay right here. Mommy will be right back." Jessica nodded, not looking up from the Barbie Colorforms on her lap.

Marissa made her way to the end of the bleachers and stepped down next to Detective Wilkerson. As usual, the female detective was dressed in crisp dark slacks, a white blouse, and a navy blazer. There was nothing friendly in her gaze as Marissa approached her.

"What's going on? Has something else happened?" she asked.

"The only thing that's happened is that I'm beginning to wonder what you haven't told us." Her eyes were cold, her speech clipped, and Marissa took a step back from her in surprise.

"What are you talking about?" she asked. She

glanced back to check on Jessica, then returned her attention to the detective.

"I'm talking about the fact that I think you know more than you're telling us." Wilkerson stepped closer and jabbed a finger into her chest. "I think maybe you're protecting somebody."

A flush of anger warmed Marissa's cheeks as she swatted away the woman's hand. "Are you crazy? I've told you everything I know. Why on earth would I protect a monster, a murderer?"

"You tell me." Wilkerson practically shouted the words.

Aware that they were drawing attention from onlookers, Marissa took another step back and drew a steadying breath. "Detective Wilkerson, I've told you everything I know. I've written down every name of every person I come in contact with. I don't know what else you want from me."

"I just want you to know that if I find out you've held back from us, then I'll see you in jail for a very long time." With this, Sarah turned on her heel and stalked away.

Marissa turned and hurried back to Jessica's side, her insides churning from the confrontation. What was that about? Why would the woman suddenly think she was holding out on them?

"Mommy, who was that woman?" Jessica asked when she was seated once again.

"Just somebody who wanted to talk to me."

"She looked mad."

"She just needed to talk to me," Marissa replied, still half-angry about the ambush by the detective.

Apparently their investigation was going nowhere and Wilkerson's frustration had needed a scape-goat. Marissa only wished she were keeping some-thing from the authorities. She only wished she knew who was responsible for bringing havoc into her life, for disrupting the happily ever after she might have found with Alex.

They went directly home after the practice game and by eight thirty the kids were in bed and the house was quiet, and in that silence Marissa felt the familiar pangs of loneliness, only this time her lone-liness wasn't so much about John's absence as it was Alex's. And it wasn't so much about making love with him as it was sharing her inner thoughts with him.

She hadn't told anyone else in her life what was going on concerning the murders, hadn't wanted to bring that fear, that horror, to anyone else's life.

The conversation with Detective Wilkerson at the ball field had filled her with a hollow hopelessness. If the detectives were looking at her again, assum-ing she knew something she hadn't told them, then that meant they were not only no closer to solving the crimes, but on the wrong course altogether.

It was almost nine when the doorbell rang. She belted her robe more tightly around her and walked to the door. Peering out the peephole, she saw that it was David.

He was probably here to see why she hadn't shown up at the fire station last Sunday. It had been the first Sunday she'd missed since John's death. For the first time in years she hadn't felt like baking and making the trek to the station.

She started to unlock the front door to let him in, but as her hand reached for the knob a slice of apprehension whispered through her.

David. David had been a friend for many years. He knew everything there was to know about John and Marissa's marriage, their life together. Even now he would know Marissa's schedule.

David, who had declared often that John had been a lucky man. David, who didn't seem to be able to find a woman of his own.

Was it possible David had something to do with the murders? The roses? The phone calls? John was a lucky man. How many times had David said that to her? Why didn't he have a relationship of his own? Was it because he was too busy watching her, obsessing over her, to have a girlfriend of his own?

"Marissa?" he called through the door while at the same time his knuckles rapped lightly on the wood.

Her mouth went painfully dry as she thought of all the conversations she'd had with David, wondered how many times John had shared minute details of their life with his best friend.

"Marissa?" His knock fell louder. She punched

off the alarm and opened the door, but held it firm in her hands, not allowing him inside.

"Hi, David." She was pleased that her voice sounded normal despite the tumultuous emotions that roared inside her. "I'd invite you in, but the kids are already in bed and I'm not feeling well." That was certainly the truth. She felt ill, her guts twisted with her thoughts.

"What's wrong? Is there anything I can do?" Concern deepened his voice. "You didn't seem like yourself at the ball game earlier, so I thought I'd check in with you."

"I've just been fighting off a little flu bug." The little white lie fell easily from her lips. She didn't want him in her house, just wanted him to go away.

"Is that why you didn't make it last Sunday to the station?"

She nodded and gripped the door more tightly. "I've just been feeling a little punky. I thought getting out for the game would help, but it only made it worse. I'm sure I'll be fine, and I appreciate you stopping by." She forced a smile that felt unnatural.

He frowned. "You sure there's nothing I can do? You need medicine? Maybe some chicken soup?"

"No, really. I'll be fine. I just need to crawl in to bed and get a good night's sleep."

"Okay, then tell the kids I said hello and I'll check in with you another time."

She breathed a sigh of relief as he turned to leave. She stood at the door until he got into his car and began to back out of the driveway; then she closed and locked the door and reset the alarm system.

For a long moment she leaned with her forehead against the door, feeling as if something had been stolen from her, something had been ruined.

David had been one of her biggest supports when John was killed. Along with John's parents, he'd helped her pick the casket, arrange for the service. And in the weeks and months after the funeral, he'd been a welcome houseguest, grieving with her when she needed him to and cheering her up when the bottom seemed perilously close.

Now suspicion tainted every moment she'd ever spent with the man who had been John's best friend. Fear darkened every memory.

Tragedy came in many forms. Death, deception, betrayal, and the painful misgivings of distrust. She finally moved from the door and turned out all the lights and got into bed.

It was a very long time before she fell asleep.

It was Thursday night when Alex called, wondering why she had been so scarce the whole week. "I've missed you," he said, his voice a balm smoothed on her soul.

"Things have been busy," she began, then decided to take the bull by the horns. "I didn't buy your story, Alex. There's no way you can make me believe you were jogging in the street and a car didn't see you. First of all, you've been running too long not to know the first rules of safety."

In his ensuing silence she knew she was right and her heart plummeted to her feet. "Alex . . . tell me the truth. What really happened?"

His heavy sigh was audible over the line. "Somebody tried to run me over. It wasn't an accident. It was a deliberate attack."

She sucked in her breath and closed her eyes. "I knew it," she whispered. She opened her eyes and reached for the cup of hot tea she'd prepared before his call. "Did you go to the police?"

"Yeah, I talked to Wilkerson and Hunter."

"I wonder why Detective Wilkerson didn't see fit to tell me? She's been to see me twice in the past two days, once at the ball field on Tuesday night, then again Wednesday at the store."

"Why? Has something new happened?"

"No. Apparently she's just decided to harass me and be hateful. But, Alex, don't change the subject. Somebody tried to run you down."

"Marissa, listen. This changes nothing between us," he said hurriedly. "I'm in this all the way. I know the danger, and some nutcase isn't going to change my course where you're concerned."

She took a sip of her tea, not tasting it but needing the warmth. She set the cup down and slumped against the back of the sofa. As a new horror stabbed her, she shot back up. "Just like John."

Her chest tightened and she began to tremble. It

had crossed her mind before, but now it gripped her in a cold, harsh grasp. "He tried to run you over just like John was run over. That was over a year ago. My God, Alex, how long has this been going on? How long has he been watching me? What does he want from me?" She gasped and swallowed against a rising hysteria.

"Marissa, listen to me. I can't tell you how long this has been going on, but it's coming to an end soon." His voice radiated a calmness that slowly sliced through her frantic thoughts. "The police are after this guy. His presence is known, and it's just a matter of time before Wilkerson and Hunter get a break or this guy tips his hand. We just need to stay strong and not give this creep the power to destroy us."

She drew a deep, steadying breath. She'd needed to hear those words from somebody, anybody, but she had particularly needed to hear them from Alex. Not every man would be willing to risk maintaining an involvement with a woman who was in the sights of a crazed killer.

"You're right," she said. "Of course you're right. But I think it would be smart if we didn't see each other so often for a while."

"Don't do that, Marissa," he said, his deep voice radiating with intensity. "Don't play his game. Don't let him win with his game of terror."

She rubbed her forehead, the whisper of a

headache beginning. "I don't want to play his game, but I'm so afraid. And I'm so tired of being afraid."

"Why don't you and the kids move in here with me until all of this gets resolved?"

The offer surprised her, and there was a part of her that wanted to accept, that wanted the safety of having him by her side, of sleeping in the same bed.

But as inviting as the offer was, she couldn't accept. "I can't do that, Alex. As much as I appreciate the offer, as much as I'd love to just pack up and come over, I can't. I can't just uproot the kids. They aren't emotionally ready for that kind of a move."

"Then let me stay with you for a while," he countered. "I'd feel better if I was there with you and the kids. I could sleep on the sofa. I promise to keep it strictly platonic if that's what you need."

The headache that had whispered moments before now began to shout a little louder, pounding behind her eyes. What to do? What to do? "I don't know. I need to think about it. Can we talk about it tomorrow?"

"You going to be at the store?"

"Yes. I'll be there until nine tomorrow night."

"Why don't I bring you lunch around one? We can talk then."

"That sounds good. And, Alex, thank you for being so understanding."

"Marissa, if you haven't figured it out yet, I'm in love with you. I'll see you tomorrow." Before she could reply, he hung up.

I'm in love with you. His words filled her up and for a moment the headache abated. How had she been so incredibly lucky to be gifted with the love of two wonderful men?

Once again she leaned forward and picked up the cup of hot tea. And how had she been so unlucky to warrant the interest of a person who was obviously deranged?

What had been horrible now appeared even more insidious, much more evil. Somewhere deep in her heart she'd always believed what had happened to John had been a tragic accident. That whoever had killed him had driven off out of fear and shock. She'd never before really considered that it had been a calculated murder.

Was it possible that the same person who had mowed down John in the grocery store parking lot over a year ago had also attempted to kill Alex?

That meant there had been somebody evil in her life for over a year. A killer who knew she liked red roses. A killer who knew what park she liked to take her kids to, that Justin played baseball on Tuesday and Thursday nights. A killer who had already made one attempt on Alex's life.

Why was this happening? What did he want from her? No answer was forthcoming. Only the icy chill of fear replied.

Chapter 21

Sarah bolted upright in bed, heart pounding as the unconsciousness of sleep ebbed away. What? What had happened? What had awakened her?

The telephone next to her bed rang, and she fumbled on the nightstand for the lamp, successfully finding the switch and turning it on. Apparently the ringing phone was what had awakened her in the first place.

A glance at her digital clock told her it was just after midnight. Who in the hell? She grabbed up the phone, knowing whoever it was, they brought bad news. Good news never arrived in the middle of the night. "Wilkerson."

"Detective, this is Captain Michael Morrison with the Cass Creek Fire Department. I spoke to you the other day at the fire station?" His voice was low.

"Yes . . . yes, I remember." She and Luke had spent a day at the station talking to the men, as all of them had been on the list Marissa had turned over to them of people in her life. They had spent several hours interviewing the men and establishing alibis for the nights of the murders. Sarah had interviewed the captain and had found him both concerned and cooperative.

"I'm sorry to bother you so late," he continued.

"That's okay." She reached for the glass of water she kept on the nightstand. "What can I do for you, Captain?" She took a sip of the tepid water, hoping it would drown the last bit of grogginess from her head.

"I've been doing a lot of thinking since last we spoke." His voice was soft and low, as if he didn't want to be overheard. "I need to talk to you, but I can't do it over the phone. It's about one of my men. I think he might be involved."

Adrenaline pumped through her, and she swung her legs out of the covers and over the side of the bed. "Just tell me when and where."

There was a moment of silence. "Fifteen minutes? There's a Taco Bell on Central. I think they're open all night."

"I know it."

"And, Detective Wilkerson? I'd appreciate it if you kept this under your hat. If my suspicions are right, then fine, I don't care who you tell. But if I'm wrong, I could lose the respect and confidence of my men."

"Fifteen minutes, Captain Morrison. See you

there." Raw energy filled her as she quickly dressed, then went into the bathroom to brush her teeth and run a brush through her hair.

This could be it. This could be the break they'd been hoping for. Five minutes later she was in her car and headed for the fast-food restaurant.

She'd been praying for a break, that somebody would come forward with information, that somebody would remember seeing something that would lead them to an arrest and conviction. All they'd needed was one stinking person to come forward. Hopefully that person was Captain Morrison.

She thought about calling Luke, but was reluctant to do so. Her emotions were so topsy-turvy where he was concerned. She'd made the incredible mistake of falling in love with the man. But that wasn't why she didn't want to call him.

For the entire time she'd been with the Cass Creek Police Department, she'd felt as if she were on trial. She'd done nothing to earn the respect of her fellow officers, although she supposed she should be grateful she'd done nothing to earn their disrespect.

She knew that if she were the one who broke this case wide open then she'd truly be welcomed as a member of the force instead of held at arm's length, as she had been. She didn't want to just prove herself to the department. She wanted to prove herself to Luke and to herself.

Besides, it wasn't as if she were racing to meet an

anonymous caller in an abandoned building. Captain Michael Morrison was a respected civil servant, and the Taco Bell where he'd said to meet him wasn't exactly in the middle of nowhere. It was on a major thoroughfare.

She had her gun, her wits, and her cell phone. No whisper of disquiet disturbed her, no sense of impending doom upset her.

She felt only the sweet anticipation of success, the determined resolve to finally get a creep off the streets for good.

As she drove, she tapped her fingers on the steering wheel, eager to get to the meet, get the information from Captain Morrison, and then act on it. Who was it? She mentally ticked off the names of the firefighters who worked out of Station No. 5.

"Make it good, Captain Mike," she said aloud.

When Marissa Jamison had handed in her list of all the people she saw regularly, Sarah had been dismayed to see so many of the city firemen on the list. It was hard to swallow that a person who had committed their life to service could also be a cold-blooded killer.

And yet it made a kind of horrible sense that the killer could be one of the firefighters John Jamison had worked with, had lived with while on duty.

Marissa had mentioned in one of their discussions that she took baked goods to the fire station every week. During those visits she might have garnered the obsession of one of John's coworkers.

Make it good, Captain Morrison, she thought again.

She needed this break to lift her out of the mediocrity of her life.

Central Street in Cass Creek was one of the main arteries of the small city. It ran north and south and bisected the city on the west side.

Businesses lined the street, most of them closed at this time of the night, although several of the fast-food places promised all-night service or late summer hours.

There was little traffic on the street, and she glanced at her wristwatch when she was two blocks from the Taco Bell. It had been fifteen minutes since she'd hung up the phone. Hopefully Morrison would wait for her. Hopefully he wouldn't change his mind about meeting her.

The Taco Bell was only a couple of blocks from the fire station so she assumed Captain Morrison would get there ahead of her.

She could taste an arrest, and the flavor was intoxicating. She needed this. God, how she needed this.

She frowned as the Taco Bell sign came into view. Definitely dark and non-fiesta looking. Apparently summer hours didn't extend beyond midnight south of the border.

Pulling into the parking lot, she immediately spied the car parked near the back of the building. She pulled up in a space nearby and parked, but remained in her seat, unsure if the other car was Captain Morrison's or not.

Her heart banged into her ribs as adrenaline surged inside her. This could be it. This could be the moment that murders were solved, a killer was identified, and Sarah became a hero.

The driver's door of the other car opened, and in the brief flare of illumination from the interior light she saw the tall fire captain climb out of the car. He carried with him a small brown paper bag.

She got out of her car to meet him. The pavement beneath her feet retained the heat of the day and the scent of spoiled vegetables radiated from a nearby Dumpster.

"Captain Morrison," she said in greeting.

"Detective Wilkerson, I'm so sorry about the time. I've been fighting with myself for the past twenty-four hours, trying to decide if what I suspect about one of my men is true. I finally decided I needed to talk to you."

Once again a burst of raw adrenaline flooded through her. "What is it you suspect about who?"

Moore raked a hand through his salt-and-pepper hair and for a moment stared off in the distance with a deep frown. "One of my men told you that he was on duty when he wasn't, and that was on the night of the first murder. He said he was just hanging out at the station on the night of the second murder, also a lie."

His frown deepened and he met Sarah's gaze. His

eyes held the weariness of a man about to give up one of his own. "The lies made me suspicious, but I told myself this was one of my men, certainly not anyone I could ever imagine capable of hurting anyone. Still, I couldn't get those lies out of my head so I checked his locker and found this." He pulled from the bag a large, wicked-looking knife.

"Wow, not exactly a tool for cleaning nails." Dismay filled her as she saw he gripped it without gloves, possibly destroying any prints that had been on it.

"No, it's mostly used to punish the people who give Marissa a hard time."

Without warning he struck. The knife plunged into her gut, deep and hard. For a moment she was so stunned she couldn't make sense of it.

She stared down at the knife protruding from her stomach, and it was only then that she thought to reach for her gun. But before she could put action to thought, her legs buckled beneath her and she fell to her knees on the pavement.

Get your gun! Shoot the bastard! an urgent voice screamed in her head. But the first wave of pain struck her, a pain the likes of which she had never experienced before. She fell from her knees to her side, the pavement gritty and hard against her cheek.

She felt her eyes roll back in her head as she drowned in wave after wave of intense pain. Should have called Luke. Stupid fool.

She wanted to scream as she felt the knife being pulled out. She might have had a chance if he'd left it in, but now she would bleed to death more quickly.

"You were mean to my wife. I just can't allow that." Morrison's voice seemed to come from some distant planet, but she recognized the ring of insanity. "As my wife, Marissa deserves respect. I saw you yelling at her at the ballpark. You shouldn't have done that."

The pain overwhelmed her and she thought she might have lost consciousness for a moment. She came to, but remained perfectly still when she heard footsteps approaching her.

Something touched her forehead. "There," Morrison whispered in obvious satisfaction. "A gift for my bride."

The bow. In horror Sarah knew a bright red bow was now stuck to her forehead. A moment later she heard his car leave the parking lot.

Pain consumed her, along with a cold that seeped through her veins. Dying. She was dying. Who would come to her funeral? Would anyone be there to mourn her? Mama . . . Daddy . . . She wanted to weep as she thought of their tears.

Luke! Her heart cried his name. Luke, I screwed up. I really screwed up. She'd been so stupid, such a hotshot, and now look what she'd done. She'd managed to make herself another victim of the Gift Bow Killer.

Captain Michael Morrison. She never would have guessed. She'd made every rookie error in the book. She'd assumed because Morrison was a respected fire captain, a brother in service, that he wasn't seriously a suspect. Worse than that, she'd left her home in the middle of the night to get a tip on a case without calling her partner for backup.

Darkness closed in and part of her wanted to give in to the darkness that promised no more pain. But there was another part of her that rebelled.

Call Luke. It's not too late. Call him.

Summoning all the strength she could, with one hand she fumbled to find her cell phone, fighting against the unconsciousness that called to her with a siren song.

She flipped the cell phone open, then hit the speed dial for Luke's cell phone number. Answer, Luke. Please answer.

Would he come to her funeral? Would he shed a tear or two?

Crime scene photos of Jennifer and Sonny flashed in her brain. And now there would be a third photo . . . one of her wearing a red bow in death.

"This better be good," Luke barked into his phone. The clock read almost one, and there was nothing he hated more than being pulled from sleep. The caller ID told him the call came from his partner, but all he heard was the sound of heavy, labored breathing.

"Wilkerson, if this is your idea of something sexy, then it sucks," he said. "Wilkerson?"

"Luke . . . help."

Luke shot out of bed. Her voice was almost too faint to hear, but not so faint that he couldn't hear the rattle of death on the line. "Where? Where are you, Wilkerson?" He gripped his phone so tightly he feared it might shatter.

"Taco . . . Central."

"Taco Bell? On Central?" He was already pulling his pants on one-handed. "Can you tell me what happened? Wilkerson, talk to me."

"Fire."

The single word was so faint he thought he must have misunderstood. "Wilkerson, you were in a fire? Hello? Wilkerson, answer me!" he yelled, then waited a long moment. Nothing . . . nothing but the frightening sound of her rattled breathing.

"Dammit!" He grabbed the land phone on his nightstand and hit 911. "This is Detective Luke Hunter. We have an officer down at the Taco Bell on Central. Get backup there and send an ambulance." He didn't wait for a reply, but slammed down the receiver and grabbed a shirt.

He flew out of the house and into his car, the cell phone still pressed against his ear. "Wilkerson, can you hear me? Listen, you hang on. Help is on the way. You hear me, you stubborn broad! You hang in there."

No answer, just the faint sound of her slow, labored breathing.

He drove like a madman, flying through red lights at a speed that was imprudent. His heart crashed against his ribs as panic crawled up in the back of his throat.

What had happened? What in the hell was she doing at a Taco Bell at one o'clock in the morning? Jesus, make her be okay. He didn't want to lose his partner. Hell, he didn't want to lose Sarah.

As he raced to the scene, his head filled with her, the irritating habits that had somehow become oddly endearing and the uninhibited passion he'd never expected. He even liked the fact that she talked too much.

Damn you, Wilkerson. What were you doing out at this time of the night? Fire. That's what she'd said, at least that's what he thought she'd said. Fire. What did it mean? Had there been a fire at the Taco Bell? Why had she been eating fast food at this time of the night? Half the time she bitched at him for eating that junk at normal mealtimes.

He realized he could no longer hear the sounds of her breathing over the cell phone, and he threw the instrument to the floor and accelerated his speed.

As he careened down Central and the fast-food restaurant sign came into view, he saw no flames licking the night sky, no smoke blackening the air.

He got there before any emergency vehicles or other officers. He pulled into the parking lot and stomped on the brakes as his headlights caught her in their glare.

"No." The sight of her prone on the pavement with a familiar red bow shining in the light sucked all strength from his body. "Jesus . . . no!"

He flew from the car, fighting for professional objectivity. At the same time he heard the sirens of help on its way.

Too late? Was he too late? He reached the place where she lay crumpled and his heart seemed to stand still.

Dead.

She looked dead. Her skin was bloodless, pale as a corpse. Emotion flared as he fell to his knees beside her.

It took him only a second to identify that she'd either been shot or stabbed. Blood seeped from the wound in her stomach. Although a terrible grief filled him and he knew it was hopeless, he reached out and tried to find a pulse in the side of her neck.

He jumped as he felt a beat beneath his fingers. Had he really felt a pulse or had he only imagined it? At that moment an ambulance roared into the lot. There! He felt it again.

"Hurry!" he yelled to the paramedics. "She's still alive." He picked up her hand and squeezed it tight. "Wilkerson, if you can hear me, then don't you die. You hear me, dammit? Don't you die!"

He released her hand and stood as the paramedics went to work. Within minutes Sarah was loaded into the back of the ambulance and the vehicle flew from the area, her life in tow.

After they'd gone, Luke raked a hand down his jaw and looked around the dark parking lot. Although he desperately wanted to jump in his car and follow the ambulance to the hospital, he knew there was nothing he could do for Sarah. Doctors now held her life in their hands. What he needed to do was see if he could figure out what had brought her to this place at this time of the night.

Fire. What in the hell had she meant? He had a feeling if he could figure it out, he'd know who had done this to her.

Chapter 22

Marissa heard the reports of the attack on Detective Wilkerson Saturday morning as she sipped her coffee in front of the portable television in the kitchen.

"Gift Bow Killer strikes again. Detective Sarah Wilkerson's body was found early this morning in the parking lot of a local fast-food restaurant. Authorities are not releasing any details of the incident, but sources here at CBNC have learned that a red bow had been placed on the detective's face, making her the third victim of the killer the media has dubbed the Gift Bow Killer." The blond reporter smiled pertly. "And now for today's weather."

"No!" The protest escaped Marissa with a sob as a shock wave shuddered through her. No, please, it couldn't be true. The spike-haired, tough-as-nails female cop was dead? How had it happened?

Tears blurred her vision as she got up and turned

the dial to another news station. Maybe she'd heard it wrong. But she knew she hadn't.

Dead. Detective Sarah Wilkerson had been killed by the person who was watching Marissa, haunting her life. Grief tore her up inside. How many people would die because of this psycho? Because of her?

For a long moment she stood in front of the television, tears washing down her cheeks. A young woman. A father. And now a police detective. Who else would die?

She had to know exactly what had happened. She had to know how an experienced, trained detective could fall victim to a madman. There was only one person she knew to call.

She immediately picked up the phone and dialed the police station. "I need to talk to Detective Hunter."

"Detective Hunter isn't in at the moment," a female voice informed her. "We don't expect him in for the remainder of the day. I can give you his voice mail."

"Yes . . . please." She waited for the click; then Hunter's voice filled the line. "You know what to do," his deep voice indicated, then was followed by a beep.

"Detective Hunter, this is Marissa Jamison. I just heard about Detective Wilkerson. I'm so sorry." Once again tears welled up in her throat, momentarily choking her. "I want . . . I need to know how this happened. Please call me as soon as you get this message. I'll be at home until I hear from you."

She hung up the phone with a trembling hand, grateful that the kids were still asleep, that they weren't awake to see the tears that not only stung her eyes but also coursed down her cheeks.

Sarah Wilkerson. Marissa thought of the last two encounters she'd had with the woman. Sarah had been tough on her, accusing her of holding out, yelling when it hadn't been necessary.

Marissa had thought she was just coming unglued by the pressure to solve the case, using Marissa as a scapegoat for her frustration. Now a new thought blossomed in her head.

Bait. In the last week the detective had chosen public venues to verbally attack her. Had she done so on purpose? To draw the rage of a killer? Oh God. Had Sarah Wilkerson intentionally tried to lure a killer, only to be killed herself?

Once again Marissa picked up the phone and dialed the police station. She asked to be connected to Hunter's voice mail again, then left another message. "Detective Hunter, I just thought you should know that Detective Wilkerson spoke to me several times this past week. In fact, she yelled at me in public places. I just . . . I really need to speak to you." She hung up in frustration.

What did you do? She thought of Sarah again. How could the woman put herself at risk? And when, when would Luke get back to her?

The phone rang and she grabbed it up. "Detective Hunter?" she said.

"It's me, Marissa." Alex's deep voice filled the line. "I guess you've heard."

"Just a few minutes ago. I've left two messages for Detective Hunter. Alex, how could something like this happen? How did this monster manage to kill Sarah?"

"I don't know, honey. I just don't know. Look, you need me to come over? I can be there in fifteen minutes."

"No, no I'm all right. I was supposed to go into the store, but I'm just going to hang out here all day with the kids." She felt the need to hold them close, to circle the wagons against whatever danger might lurk nearby, and to grieve for the woman who had gambled with her life and lost.

"Have you given any more thought to what we discussed last night?"

She rubbed her forehead wearily. "I tossed and turned all night thinking about it. But, Alex, given what I've learned this morning, I can't let you move in here knowing that's just putting a target on your back."

There was a long silence. "How long, Marissa? How long do we put our lives on hold because of a madman? We suspect he's been in your life since before John's murder. As horrible as it is to contemplate, if the cops don't catch this guy, then it's possible he'll be out there for another year and a year after that."

Alex's voice grew stronger with each word he spoke. "How long do we let him and the fear he provokes decide what happens in our lives?"

She heard his sigh of frustration, a frustration she felt mirrored inside her. "I don't know what to do," she finally said.

"Then let me tell you what we do. We go forward together, building a life and being happy. Marissa, what happened this morning to Sarah Wilkerson only makes me more certain that we need to be together. I'll wait forever if you think that's in the best interests of your children, but why on earth should we follow a psychopath's rules?

She closed her eyes and squeezed the phone more tightly against her ear, realizing how much she'd wanted him to talk her into it, to bully away her fears and give her the courage to seek happiness.

"Alex, I want us to be together, and you're right, there's no guarantee the police will be able to find this man. I don't want to put us on hold. I want you here with us." She hoped she never lived to regret her decision.

"Just tell me when." Quiet joy radiated in his voice.

"Is tomorrow too soon? That will give me today to have a talk with the kids and make things all right with them."

"Whatever you think best. I just know I'd feel better if you and the kids weren't in that house alone."

"I'd feel better if you were here, too." Now that the decision was made, the sweet promise of happiness momentarily filled her. She embraced it, knowing it would only last a moment, then be chased away by the reality of a woman's death and the uncertainty of life.

When she'd savored it as long as she could, her mind raced with all the things she'd need to do to prepare for Alex moving in. "I'll take the kids to Jim and Edith's tomorrow. It will be easier to move you in without them underfoot. Then we can all have dinner together here and start this new life."

A new life. Those words resonated inside her when she finally hung up from Alex. At that moment Justin came into the kitchen.

She swallowed the horror the morning had already brought with it and forced herself to smile at her son. "Good morning, champ."

He nodded and slid into his chair at the table. "Aren't we supposed to go to Grandma and Grandpa's today? Don't you have to go to the store?"

"I'm changing the plans and staying with you two today, then tomorrow, if it's all right with Grandma and Grandpa, you'll go out there."

"Can we go to the park?" He got up from his chair and went to the pantry to grab a box of cereal.

"I think we'll just have a quiet day inside today. Maybe I can beat the pants off you and your sister in a game of Crazy Eights."

He grinned and set the cereal box on the table, then went to the fridge for the milk. "You never win at Crazy Eights, Mom."

"Ah, but there's always a first time."

As Justin fixed his cereal, Marissa made a couple of phone calls, covering the two days at the shop, then to Jim and Edith to cancel the day's plans, make arrangements for the next day, and to let them know the latest news about Sarah.

"Do you want us to come in and spend the day with you?" Edith had asked, her voice filled with concern.

"No, I'm fine. I'm going to spend the day with the kids and try to keep things as normal as possible," she'd replied.

But things were anything but normal As Marissa drank her coffee and talked to the kids while they ate their breakfast, her head reeled with all the input that had already taken place.

Sarah Wilkerson was dead. A cunning, vicious killer had managed to take down a cop. Who would be next? Would she get a phone call tonight, a low male voice whispering "You're welcome?"

She watched the phone, willing it to ring, willing Luke Hunter to call her. She mentally tried to decide when would be the best time to broach to the kids the fact that Alex was moving in with them. There was still room in her thoughts, in her heart, for the woman who had lost her life.

She couldn't get it out of her mind, that somehow the tough woman had placed her life on the line for Marissa. It seemed so unfair that she and Alex had decided to move ahead with their lives together in the wake of Sarah's sacrifice.

She'd just sent her kids to their rooms to dress and make beds when the doorbell rang. Looking out the peephole she saw Detective Hunter on her doorstep. She quickly punched off the alarm and opened the door.

It was obvious he'd been up all night. His clothing was rumpled, whiskers darkened his lean jaw, and his eyes held the hollowness of a man on the brink of despair. "I got your messages."

"Detective Hunter, please come in." As she ushered him inside the kids ran from their rooms to see who had arrived. "Justin, Jessica, go and finish cleaning your rooms, then play quietly while I talk to Mr. Hunter." She used Mr. rather than Detective, not wanting to worry the children.

She touched his arm and gestured toward the kitchen as the kids did as requested and disappeared back into their rooms.

Without asking, she poured him a cup of coffee and placed it on the table. He sank down in the chair and wrapped his meaty hands around the mug. "Thanks. Been a long night."

Marissa sat in the chair next to his, tears once again welling up in her eyes. "I just needed to tell you how sorry I am about Detective Wilkerson. I need to understand how this happened." The tears came faster as she realized this was the first time she'd seen the handsome cop without his partner.

He stared at her for a long moment, an assessing gaze that confused her. "If I tell you something, you've got to keep it to yourself. If the media gets ahold of this information it could seriously jeopardize the investigation and I'll come back here and personally arrest you."

She sat back in her chair in surprise. She'd expected his weariness, the grief that darkened his eyes, but she hadn't expected this. "Okay," she said slowly. "I never talk to the press, and I don't intend to start now, so what do you have to tell me?" He had certainly piqued her interest.

He hesitated another moment, then leaned forward. "She's alive."

For a moment his words made no sense. "Who is alive?" she asked in confusion.

"Sarah. Detective Wilkerson."

Marissa gasped softly. "But I heard on the news. They said she was dead."

He nodded. "We planted the story. The truth is she's alive right now, although her condition isn't good. But we knew if our perp thinks she's dead he has a false sense of safety. If he heard she was still alive, he might try to finish the job or go so far underground we wouldn't be able to get him."

"Thank God, thank God she's alive," she said more to herself than to him.

His shoulders slumped as if in weary defeat. "She took a knife to the gut, and they worked all night long to repair the damage. When I found her she'd lost a hell of a lot of blood. I thought she was dead, with that damned bow stuck on her forehead." His eyes were haunted.

Marissa realized at that moment that this wasn't a cop bemoaning the fate of his partner, but rather he was a man mourning for his woman. She reached out and took one of his big hands in hers. "And now? How is she now?"

"She got out of surgery about thirty minutes ago. She's listed as critical, but stable, although unconscious. She was still in recovery when I left the hospital." He released her hand, reared back in his chair, and straightened his shoulders, and before her eyes he transformed from heartsick man to in-control cop.

"You mentioned in your message something about Wilkerson yelling at you this past week. When and where did this take place?" He patted his pocket and again his eyes reflected a hollow darkness. "You got a pen and paper? Wilkerson is the note taker so I never carry anything."

She got up and found a pad and pen in one of the drawers, handed them to him, then returned to her chair. She looked out the window, giving him a moment to regain control.

"Tell me about Wilkerson talking to you. When and where did this happen?"

She looked at him once again and saw the cop instead of the man. His eyes had lost their hollowness and now held single-minded intent.

She explained to him about the visits from Sarah, first at the ball field, then at her shop. "She was loud and hateful," she explained. "She didn't mention any of this to you?"

A muscle ticked in his jaw. "No, she neglected to share this."

"I think maybe she did it on purpose, the yelling at me. I think she set herself up as bait."

He clutched the pen so tightly in his hand his fingers were white. He scribbled a few notes on the pad, then looked at her once again. "And I suppose you didn't notice the same person at the ballpark and hanging around your shop?"

"I'm sorry, I didn't." She'd been so stunned by the attacks from Sarah. She should have recognized what the woman was doing at the time. She should have paid more attention. "What happened, Detective Hunter? I heard the attack on her took place at a fast-food restaurant. Have you been able to find out why she was there? Exactly what happened?"

He set the pen down and drew a hand over his scruffy lower jaw. "We don't know. We've found out that she received a call just after midnight. The call came from a pay phone. Apparently, immediately after the call she went to the Taco Bell. She was attacked there and left for dead. She managed to call me while she was still conscious."

"Did she say who did this to her? Say anything at all that might help find this guy?"

"Fire. She said fire." His frown cut across his wide forehead. "At least that's what I thought she said. By the time I arrived on the scene she was unconscious."

"Fire? What could that mean?" She thought of David Harrold and the unexpected fear she'd felt the last time he'd appeared on her doorstep. "Maybe she was trying to tell you it was a fireman. The list I gave you had all the firemen at the station on it. Have you checked their alibis for the nights of the murders?"

Once again Luke reared back in the chair as a weary sigh escaped him. "We've managed to corroborate several of the alibis, but not all. It's a painstakingly difficult task. People don't always remember where they were on a specific night at a specific time. Several of the men on your list are single, which means their alibis were they were home alone."

"What about David Harrold? Do you remember what his alibis were?"

Luke's gaze filled with interest. "Why? Is there something I need to know about him?"

Forgive me, David, she thought. If he was truly

what he appeared to be, a good and valuable friend, then she hoped he would forgive her for what she was about to say. "David was John's best friend. If anyone knew intimate details about my life it would be David."

She thought of all the times she'd teased him about not having a girlfriend. Was he alone because in his mind he did have a girlfriend . . . her? "He comes here a lot to visit, doesn't date anyone."

Luke stood and ripped off the page of his notes and folded the sheet of paper. "I'll check him out more closely. In the meantime, if you get a call, hear anything that you think might be helpful, call me on my cell phone. I'll be at the hospital if you need me."

She followed him to the front door. "Maybe when Detective Wilkerson regains consciousness she'll be able to say who did this to her."

For the first time since he'd arrived, his eyes held a hard, dangerous glint. "Trust me. I'm counting on it."

Chapter 23

The move began at ten o'clock the next morning beneath a sky laden with thick gray clouds. Alex showed up at Marissa's house with his car filled with clothes and personal items.

Marissa had taken the kids to Jim and Edith's earlier and had explained to her in-law's that Alex was moving in because of the stalker threat. She'd worried about how they would react to her moving in another man, a man she wasn't married to, a man she'd been dating for only a brief time.

"This man, this Alex, he's a good man?" Jim had asked.

"He is," she'd said, then added, "I think he and John would have been friends."

"And you went to high school with him? You knew his parents, where he came from?" Edith asked. "Because you know, this isn't your only choice. You and the kids could move in here."

Marissa had leaned toward the woman and taken her hand. "I know, and I appreciate the offer. But I'm trying to keep things as normal as possible for the kids. I don't want to move them out of the house, but I would feel much better if Alex was there with us."

Edith had squeezed her hand. "Then you know we support whatever decision you make."

Although Marissa would have moved Alex in no matter what, having Jim and Edith behind her made things easier.

She shared this conversation with Alex as she helped him unload his first carful of belongings. She also updated him on what Luke had told her about Sarah.

Alex was astonished to learn that Sarah wasn't dead, and he grabbed Marissa and swung her in his arms as he told her it was just a matter of time now, that once Sarah was able to talk, the murderer would be behind bars.

Despite the gray, oppressive clouds that portended rain, his exuberant optimism set the tone for the day.

"How are the kids with all this?" he asked as he hung his clothes in the half of her closet that she'd cleared for him.

She sat on the edge of her bed. Seeing his clothes joining hers sent a strange combination of happiness and a touch of unease. Were they moving too fast? If she hadn't been feeling an insidious undercurrent of fear, of danger lurking, would she have invited Alex into her home, into her heart so quickly?

"Marissa?" He turned to look at her, and she realized she hadn't answered his question.

"The kids were fine with it. In fact, Justin wanted to know if you'd play catch with him, and Jessica said she hoped you could read because she'd like you to read her a bedtime story sometimes."

"She's in luck. I can read." He flashed her a smile, then turned back toward the closet.

In truth it had surprised her how easily her kids had accepted the notion of Alex moving in with them. They had acted as if it were the most natural thing in the world. In fact, Justin had asked if it meant that Alex was now their stepfather, but she'd explained to him that Alex couldn't fill that role unless they got married.

"That's it for this trip," Alex said, as he turned back to face her. He sat next to her on the edge of the bed, bringing with him that masculine scent that always made her feel like she was wrapped in his arms, the scent that was beginning to smell like home.

He took her hand, entwining fingers with hers. "You know, eventually I'd love for you and the kids to move into my place. I don't want to rush things and I certainly don't want to traumatize the kids, but that house is bigger and holds no memories for you."

Memories. Yes, this house was filled with them, although lately she could go days before one of those sweet memories gave her pause.

"It also has an awesome kitchen," she replied.

He laughed. "Does that mean you'll consider it?"

There was a small part of her that wanted to cling to this house, to the memories, but the more rational part of her knew that letting go was the only way she'd move forward completely. She nodded. "I'll consider it."

"And now you'd better consider this: If we don't get out of this bedroom and off this bed right now, I won't be held responsible for what happens." His eyes held a heat that seemed to unfurl in her stomach.

This man, with his beautiful eyes and wonderful smile, took her breath away. Reluctantly she pulled her hand from his. "Moving? Remember, we're moving you in, and there will be no recreation until the work is done."

"Spoilsport," he teased, then stood and pulled her up with him. "Okay, then let's get the work done so we can have a few minutes of recreation."

She arched an eyebrow. "A few minutes?"

His gaze once again shot heat. "I'll do my best to make it longer, but with you I don't seem to have any control."

Minutes later as they drove to Alex's for more of his items, she wondered if the breathless passion they shared would eventually fade or if it would remain as sharp and exciting as it was at this time between them.

She couldn't remember sharing this kind of passion with John. While she had loved him and loved making love with him, there hadn't been the same intensity that she felt with Alex.

John had been the right man, the right husband for her at that time of her life. Now Alex seemed to be the right man for her at this time in her life, but there was a part of her afraid to celebrate, afraid that the happiness she felt was fleeting.

She worried that their passion, their love, had been built on the past and wouldn't sustain the realities of the present. She wondered if the threat in her life had prompted her to jump at Alex because, despite the years that had passed, he felt safe and familiar. There was still that little piece she kept separate, hidden away to sustain her should things go terribly bad.

"If you don't mind, I'll set up my drafting table in your dining room." He broke into her thoughts.

"That's fine. We never use the dining room anyway. I'll make sure the kids know not to touch any of your things." She leaned her head back against the seat and sighed. "What I'm really hoping is that when we get back to my place there will be a message from Detective Hunter that Sarah has regained consciousness and given them a name and they've arrested the Gift Bow Killer. I was hoping to get a call sometime last night, but I didn't." She was also grateful that she hadn't received any other calls.

"I know. But at least with me in the house I'll feel better about the safety of you and the kids."

"I'm not sure we've ever really been in danger. The danger seems to be for those people around us." A shaft of grief stabbed her as she thought of the innocent people who had already died. "You know most men would run for the hills rather than get mixed up in my life right now."

"Yeah, well, I guess I'm not most men." He pulled into his driveway and killed the engine. He turned to look at her. "I'm also not a fool. Believe me, I know I'm placing myself at risk by being with you, by moving into your home, but it's a risk I'm willing to take. Besides, I do believe it's just a matter of time and this will all be resolved. The killer made a mistake when he thought Detective Wilkerson was dead."

"Thank God he didn't kill her."

"Marissa, the best thing we can do to honor Detective Wilkerson is to go forward and not let this creep dictate our lives."

She sighed. "You're right. Let's get this work done so we can get to the recreation part of the day." She laughed as he jumped out of the car in mock eagerness.

It took nearly two hours to finish loading up Alex's things and get them into place at her house. When they were finished they made love in Marissa's bed-room.

She had somehow feared the ghost of John in this room, but no ghosts whispered to her from the other side, no memories of what had once been intruded in the promise of what might be.

The moment Alex drew her into his arms and pulled her against his naked body, there was only him. His mouth eagerly possessed hers as his hands stroked fire into her veins. He knew precisely where to touch, exactly where to place his lips to steal her breath and weaken her bones. He knew exactly what to whisper in her ear to light a fire that only he could douse.

Afterward they lay side by side, listening to a rumble of thunder in the distance and the wind rustling through the leaves of the trees outside the window as they waited for their heartbeats to slow.

He propped himself up on one elbow and gazed down at her, his eyes so blue and filled with love. "It's going to be all right, you know." His voice held inner conviction. "Justin is going to grow up to be a major-league baseball player. Jessica will be a fa-mous ballerina. And you and I will grow old and gray together, like we planned to so many years ago."

She smiled as he moved a strand of her hair from her cheek. "I'd settle for healthy and happy for the kids and forever blond for me. But I love the part about us growing old together."

"In the third grade, when I first saw you with your crooked pigtails and missing front tooth, I knew that you were going to be somebody special in my life."

"And my first memory of you is that you were an icky boy who pulled my pigtails and followed me around everywhere."

"I was besotted with you at the age of eight."

She laughed. "No, you weren't. You weren't besotted with me until we were fourteen and at Sally Jame's Halloween party."

His dark brows danced up in surprise. "How did you know that?"

Sweet memories flooded through her. "Because that was the night you looked at me for the first time like a boy looks at a girl instead of like a best friend looks at a best friend."

He tightened his arm around her. "You were dancing with Rusty Simpson and it was like I saw you for the very first time. I can see you so clearly in my mind. You were wearing blue jeans and a blue sweater. Your hair was loose around your shoulders, you had on little gold hoop earrings and lipstick . . . pink lipstick."

It awed her, that he remembered such minute details about a night that had happened so many years before. She snuggled closer to him, loving the scent of him, the feel of his arms around her, the sound of his heartbeat next to hers.

They must have fallen asleep. She awoke suddenly, her heart crashing into her ribs as if in the throes of sheer terror. A glance beside her assured her that it must have been a dream that had jerked her awake into panic, for Alex slept peacefully beside her.

She slid from the bed and padded into the adjoining bathroom, where she grabbed her light-weight robe and pulled it around her.

Heart still pounding, she went back into the bed-room and to the bank of windows. The sky looked ominous, with thick black clouds, but no rain fell and she saw no lightning, heard no thunder in the storm.

But the dark sky seemed even more oppressive than it had when she'd fallen asleep. Despite the warmth of the room, she wrapped her arms around her shoulders, wondering what on earth she might have dreamed that had caused her heart to thunder and created the chill that seemed not to walk up her spine but, rather, invade every pore of her body.

She leaned her head against the windowpane, staring out into the woods behind the house. She should be growing accustomed to these spells of in-explicable terror, when her heart pounded unnatu-rally fast and a kind of fight or flight adrenaline raced through her.

She jumped and barely stifled a scream as the phone rang. She hurried to the side of the bed to grab the receiver on the nightstand.

"Hello?" She noticed it was just after three. Apparently they had been asleep for only half an hour.

"Marissa, it's Luke." His voice was a flat imitation of itself. "I just wanted to let you know that Sarah has slipped into a coma. She never regained consciousness after surgery."

He didn't wait for her to reply, but immediately disconnected the call.

Alex sat up as she hung up the receiver. "What? What's happened?"

A wave of hopelessness choked Marissa. "That was Detective Hunter. Detective Wilkerson, she's in a coma. That poor woman." As Alex pulled her into his arms, she buried her head in his warm, bare chest, tears spilling from her as she thought of Sarah.

"What else did he say? Did they get a name from her or anything?"

She shook her head. "She never regained consciousness after the surgery." There would be no arrest. They were no closer to finding the killer, and now Sarah was in a coma.

Michael had watched the day's activities. He'd watched Alex Kincaid drive back and forth from his home to Marissa's, he'd seen him carrying in clothes and other items and the rage that had filled him had been all consuming.

His anger had built throughout the day. As the clouds gathered overhead he'd felt the storm inside him, filling him with a violence he'd never known before.

It had simmered ever since the morning he'd been unsuccessful in removing Alex Kincaid from Marissa's life. He'd known as he'd driven away in that predawn light that the hit he'd made on Kincaid hadn't been a killing blow. But he hadn't been able to take the chance of turning around and seeing the job done right.

He certainly had not spent the last year making things perfect for Marissa so that another man could move in with her. He had not cleaned up her life, made the sacrifices that had needed to be made so that she could belong to another.

This would not be allowed. It was time for him to complete what he had begun, time for him to finally claim forever the family that destiny had chosen as his.

He would begin with the children.

Chapter 24

"I'll be back in twenty minutes. Are you sure you'll be okay?" Alex's concern was evident in his eyes.

"I'm fine. Just go get some sandwiches and hurry back." Marissa had redressed and was curled up on the end of the sofa.

"What time did you tell Edith and Jim you'd get the kids?" he asked as he grabbed his car keys off the coffee table.

"I told them we'd be there around seven. We have plenty of time." It had taken her several minutes to recover from the bad news Luke had delivered. Now all she felt was a weary exhaustion. The day should have been one of celebration, but instead it had taken on a sour note.

Alex leaned down and kissed her on the forehead, his lips warm and gentle against her skin. "Be back soon. I'll turn on the security system as I leave."

She nodded, and a moment later he was gone. She leaned her head back against the sofa cushion and drew a deep breath. Although she wasn't a bit hungry, Alex had insisted that they needed some food. She'd had only coffee for breakfast, but hunger was the last thing on her mind.

Instead her head was filled with thoughts of Sarah Wilkerson. How had a savvy, armed cop been taken down so easily? If the killer could get to Sarah, then nobody was safe.

Once again she found herself drawn to the window as if the charcoal sky somehow drew her, feeding the despair that had begun with Luke's phone call.

She wished it would just go ahead and storm, that rain would fall and thunder would roar. It would be better than this feeling of dreadful anticipation, as if the storm would bring something awful with it.

When would this nightmare end? Would it ever end? The news of Sarah's coma had taken away the last bit of hope she'd been clinging to.

Once again her gaze went to the clouds overhead. The rolling black clouds seemed to reflect the evil she felt surrounded her.

"You're being silly," she said aloud, then turned from the window and padded into the kitchen.

She grabbed a cup from the cabinet, deciding that

a cup of hot tea might hit the spot. The teakettle had just begun to whistle when the phone rang once again.

Moving the kettle off the burner, she reached for the phone with the other hand. "Hello?" she answered.

"Marissa, it's Edith."

She heard the strain in the older woman's voice. "What's wrong?" Once again her heart began to bang the same rhythm it had been beating when she awoke earlier from the brief nap.

"I can't find the children. They were outside playing a little while ago, but when I called them in for their snack they weren't out there." A simmering panic raised Edith's voice half an octave.

"I'll be right there," Marissa said, fighting a flutter of panic of her own. "Edith, you know they've done this before. I'm sure there's nothing to be concerned about." The words were meant to reassure the older woman, but they did nothing to still the screaming fear inside Marissa.

"Jim's outside looking for them now," Edith replied.

"I'll be there in fifteen minutes," Marissa said and hung up the phone. Hands trembling, she quickly scribbled a note for Alex, then grabbed her purse and headed for her car.

For a brief moment she considered waiting for him to return, but was unwilling to waste a moment of time. As she drove toward Edith and Jim's place, she tried to talk herself out of the growing hysteria that threatened to choke her.

This wasn't the first time the kids had wandered off. Last time had been two months ago, when they had chased a rabbit and had gone so far they had been lost in the fields that surrounded the house.

Edith and Jim had called her at the shop, and she'd hurried to their place, only to have the kids turn up thirty minutes later dirty and excited from their bunny chase.

At the time she had given them a stern lecture, warning them that they were never to leave the immediate yard. But, she told herself now, kids were kids and sometimes lectures were forgotten.

If it had been any other time in her life, she wouldn't hear the shrieking fear in the back of her head. If it had been any other time in her life, what she would be feeling now was anger that her children had forgotten her lecture of two months prior.

Probably by the time she got to Edith and Jim's the kids would be sitting in the kitchen, properly contrite for worrying their grandparents and more than a little bit scared about facing their mother's wrath. She wanted to believe this. She needed to believe it.

Fat raindrops splashed on the windshield as she raced down the highway. A roar of thunder followed a flash of lightning as the storm moved closer.

"Please, please, let them be there when I get

there. Please, please." She repeated the words over and over again like a mantra, absolutely refusing to consider any other scenario.

They had just wandered off, like they had done the last time. She was probably panicking for nothing. This time the consequences would be more than a lecture. They'd be grounded for the next ten years.

She was less than a mile from Edith and Jim's when a familiar car approached and flashed its lights at her. It was an official car, white with bright red lettering indicating it belonged to the Cass Creek Fire Department.

She pulled over to the side of the road as she recognized Captain Michael Morrison behind the steering wheel. He turned around and pulled up behind her van. She rolled down her window as he jumped out of his car and approached hers.

"Marissa, I was just about to go looking for you. I've got your kids."

"Thank God." Relief fluttered through her as she turned in her seat to look into his car.

"They aren't there. I took them to my mother's place. Leave your car and get in mine. I'll take you to them, then bring all of you back here."

"I need to tell their grandparents," she replied.

"You can call them from my car." He didn't wait for her reply, but hurried back to his car as the rain began to fall in earnest.

Marissa shut off her engine, got out of the car,

and locked the doors, then hurried to the passenger side of his car.

She got in and looked at him as he pulled away and headed in the direction he had been initially traveling. "Where did you find them? What happened?"

"I was coming back from an appointment and saw them walking along the side of the road." He flashed her a smile. "I couldn't believe it when I saw them. I pulled over and they told me they were lost, that they had been at their grandparents' house and had been playing dinosaurs. I gathered from their story they had somehow wandered off."

"I'm going to spank both of them when I see them," she said with both irritation and relief.

"I never met John's parents and didn't know for sure where they lived, so I figured the easiest thing to do was to take the kids to my mom's home, especially with the storm coming on, and then try to find you."

Marissa leaned back in the seat and closed her eyes for a moment, allowing the fear that had possessed her to seep away. "I didn't realize your mother lived in town," she said, and looked at him once again.

"Not exactly in town, but on the outskirts." He directed his gaze out the window and pressed on the gas pedal to accelerate them to just under the speed limit as rain peppered the windshield.

"When did you find them?" she asked.

A flare of lightning was followed by a deep roar of thunder and in that voice of nature another chill filled her soul. The storm, she thought. She'd never liked storms. Surely it was the storm that made everything a little bit frightening.

"About half an hour ago," he replied. "They were scared, although Justin seemed to be putting up a good front for his little sister. I imagine at this moment they are being stuffed with cookies and milk."

She drew a deep breath, trying to still the fear that still threatened to possess her. What was wrong with her? She now knew her children were safe. There was nothing to worry about, and yet every nerve ending in her body screamed with tension.

She cast a surreptitious glance at Michael. Captain Michael Morrison, or Captain Mike as he was known by the children in the area, had been a huge support after John's death. John had liked and respected the man who had been his boss and mentor, and Michael had helped with the details of John's funeral.

Michael would know many of the intimate details of her life with John. He would have known she liked red roses. He would know her routine.

No, surely her thoughts were leading her down a crazy path. This was the captain of the fire station, a man respected and admired by his coworkers and the people of the community.

Fire. Wasn't that what Luke had said he thought Sarah had uttered before she'd fallen unconscious?

Marissa turned her head to stare out the window, her heart beginning to pound an unsteady rhythm.

Lightning seared a path through the sky, and another boom of thunder resounded. The storm. The storm was making her thoughts crazy. This was Captain Mike, for goodness sake. He wasn't a murderer. He wasn't a psycho. He was a good man, a servant of the people, a man who saved lives.

She fumbled for her purse and withdrew her cell phone, then jumped as he reached out and snatched it from her hands. "You don't want to use that now with all this electricity in the air. Wait, and you can use my mother's phone to contact whoever you need to call."

There was no animus in his voice, no real reason for the scream that suddenly begged to be released. "I'll take my chances with the cell phone." Her voice sounded reedy to her own ears.

He smiled at her and shook his head. "Not with me sitting next to you, you won't." He didn't offer to return the cell phone to her. "I'm a fire captain. Believe me, I know the dangers of lightning. We're only five minutes from the house. I promise you can make your calls the minute we get inside." He made a left turn on a narrow dirt road.

There was absolutely nothing in his voice that should give her pause, but still a rich, thick anxiety filled her. Once again she stared out the window and realized she had no idea where they were.

There were no homes to be seen, no signs of civilization anywhere. The rain came down in earnest now, running in rivulets down the windshield and making visibility more difficult. But even through the rain she could see a huge landmass rising up before them.

Fire. That's what Sarah had said. Had she been trying to say fire captain? Fireman? Had she been trying to tell them that the man they sought was Michael Morrison? But any one of the firemen at John's station would have known personal things about her. Any one of them could be the Gift Bow Killer.

He pulled his car to a halt, and she was shocked to realize there was a house built into the side of the protuberance of land. Pale light shone from the floor-to-ceiling windows on either side of the front door. It was obviously some sort of earth-contact dwelling.

She looked at him in surprise. "This is where your mother lives?"

He unfastened his seat belt and turned to look at her, a smile curving the corners of his mouth. "Well, actually, I told a little white lie. This is where I live. Welcome home, my darling wife."

She stared at him with a growing horror as she recognized for the first time the utter madness that flowed from his gaze.

Her children. Where were her children?

Chapter 25

Alex entered the house and punched in the security code so the alarm wouldn't sound. "Marissa?" He set the bag of fast food on the coffee table in the empty living room. "Marissa?" he called again.

He heard no sounds coming from the kitchen and wondered if perhaps she had gone to lie down. He walked down the hallway, passing first Justin's bedroom, then Jessica's. He went into the master bedroom at the end of the hall, but Marissa wasn't on the bed; nor was she in the adjoining bathroom.

A tiny alarm went off in his head, but he told himself there was nothing to worry about. After all, she'd been in the house with the security system on, and she wouldn't have opened the door to just anyone.

"Marissa, where are you?" he called, as he left the master bedroom and walked through the living room to the kitchen. There he found a note on the table.

Gone to Jim and Edith's. Be back soon.

It was obvious the note had been scribbled quickly, and again the internal alarm rang a little louder. She'd known he was bringing back food for them. Why wouldn't she have waited for him to return before leaving? She'd also told him she didn't plan on picking up the kids until around seven.

He glanced at his watch. It was just a few minutes after four. What had made her change her mind about retrieving the kids?

Although he told himself there was no reason to worry, he pulled his cell phone from his pocket and punched in the number for her cell phone. He waited for the call to connect, but when it did, it went directly to her voice mail. He waited for the beep.

"Marissa, it's me. I just got back to the house and found your note. Is everything all right? Call me." He hung up and fought a growing sense of disquiet.

He went back into the living room and retrieved the bag of hamburgers and fries. He returned to the kitchen and sat at the table, the scent of the food making his stomach growl. There was no sense waiting for her. He wasn't sure exactly where Jim and Edith lived, but he knew it was about a fifteen- or twenty-minute drive.

He pulled his burger and fries from the bag, hoping she'd call within the next few minutes and set his mind at ease. By the time he'd finished eating she still hadn't called, and the sense of disquiet had grown to something bigger, something heavier in his chest.

She should have had time to arrive at Jim and Edith's by now. He wished she'd left him a phone number. He went to the kitchen cabinets and began to check for a phone directory. Surely there couldn't be too many Jim Jamisons in Cass Creek.

The built-in kitchen desk yielded a directory of the area and he thumbed through the pages until he found the J's. Thankfully there was only one Jim Jamison listed. He dialed the number and waited. The call was answered by a woman he assumed to be Edith Jamison.

"Mrs. Jamison, my name is Alex Kincaid," he began.

"Oh, Mr. Kincaid, do you know where Marissa is?"

"She's not there?" Alarm screamed in his head with blaring horns and flashing lights.

"No, she's not. She said she'd be right out when I called and told her I couldn't find the children, but she hasn't shown up yet."

Couldn't find the children? Alex's mind worked to wrap around what was happening. "What do you mean, you couldn't find the kids?"

"They were in the yard playing, and then we didn't see them. They'd wandered off one time before a couple of months ago, but we found them that time. Jim and I both went out and hollered and searched, but we haven't been able to find them this time, and now it's raining and they're gone and where's Marissa?" A hysterical sob choked off whatever else she might say. "She said she'd be right here, but she's not."

"Mrs. Jamison, if you'll give me directions to your place, I'll be there as soon as possible."

Minutes later Alex drove toward the Jamison place, his heart crashing painfully against his ribs. Marissa should have been there; she'd had plenty of time to arrive at the Jamisons'. So why hadn't she?

Maybe the storm had slowed her down. The thought brought little relief. Even if she'd had to slow to a crawl through the rain she should have arrived at the Jamison place by now.

And where were Justin and Jessica?

Damn the rain, which kept him from driving the speed he wanted to drive. But he would be no use to anyone if he sped off the road and crashed his car.

The storm vented its fury, crashing wind through the trees, slicing the black sky with electric streaks and bellowing in a thunderous voice. The wind whipped up the fear inside him, the thunder roared his anxiety and the electricity in the air made all the hairs on his body feel as if they were standing on end.

Something bad had happened. He smelled it in the air, felt it in the deepest, darkest recesses of his heart. Something bad had happened and he'd been unable to prevent it.

Maybe by the time he arrived the kids would be safe and secure inside and Marissa would be scolding them to within an inch of their lives.

He wanted it to be so. He'd never wanted anything so badly in his life. They had to be okay. She had to be okay, for he didn't know if he could handle losing her for a second time in his life.

Finding her again had been a miracle. He'd believed he'd gotten over his love for her when he'd lost her the first time, but in finding her again he'd realized there had been a part of him that had never gotten over her.

He also knew that sexual frustration, and the anticipation of eventually making love to her, had heightened the love he'd felt for her as an adolescent. He'd worried that when they did eventually make love, when that adolescent fantasy had been fulfilled, his love for her wouldn't be as strong, but he'd worried for nothing.

She was in his heart, in his very soul, and the love he felt for her was so much more than that of an adolescent boy for his first girlfriend.

They have to be all right, he thought again as he turned down the road that would take him to the Jamison place. He slowed as he saw a van pulled to the side of the road. His heart beat so fast, so frantically, it felt as if it might burst out of his chest.

It was a familiar van, a dark green Ford. Marissa's

van. He pulled to a stop just behind it, then stepped out into the rain and raced to the driver door.

Locked.

He cupped his hands to peer inside, thankful when he saw no visible signs of a struggle. But why would it be parked here?

He stepped back from the van and looked around in frustration. The road was wooded on both sides and the rain made any real visibility difficult. Had she seen the kids wandering in the woods and gone after them?

"Marissa!" Her name ripped from his throat, a plea for reply.

Nothing.

No answering cry. He looked around again. Why was her car here?

Car trouble. He clung to the idea when it jumped into his head. Maybe engine trouble had forced her to park the van and abandon it. According to Edith's directions the Jamison place was up the road less than a mile. Maybe she'd left the van and had walked the rest of the way.

He hurried back to his vehicle and got in. A tenuous hope accompanied him as he pulled into the Jamison driveway. Please, please, let the kids and Marissa be safe and sound inside.

The hope was dashed as he pulled his car to a halt and the front door flew open. An older man and woman came out of the house, unmindful of the steady rain. As he saw the frantic looks on their faces, he knew, and a swift terror took possession of him.

It took only moments for the three of them to get inside and make terse introductions. As he dried off with a towel Edith had provided, he told them that he'd found Marissa's van parked along the side of the road. When he was finished they told him that it had been over an hour since they'd last seen the children.

"We've looked everywhere," Edith said, tears running down her cheeks. "We've called and searched everywhere. Then we thought maybe the storm had held up Marissa. We were about to call the authorities when you called."

Alex tried Marissa's cell phone twice more, both times getting her voice mail; then he punched in the number for Luke Hunter.

As Jim and Edith held on to each other, their faces radiating the horror Alex felt, he told the detective that Marissa and her two children were missing.

Marissa stared at Michael, recognizing the danger she was in and scared to death for the well-being of her children. Tears welled up inside her as she thought of her babies. "Justin and Jessica," she managed to gasp.

"Are inside waiting for you to join them," he replied. "Don't look so worried, my love. They're fine. I'm sure they're settling into their new home nicely. Now, come, it's time for you to join them."

Her brain worked overtime, processing thoughts in an instant of frantic fear. Should she throw open her car door and run? How far would she have to go to get help?

If he was telling the truth and the children were unharmed, then what might he do to them if she tried to run away?

But what if he'd lied to her about the children? What if they weren't really inside? Or worse, what if they were already . . . her mind couldn't complete the horror of the thought.

The moment she opened the door she knew she'd made her decision. She couldn't run. If Jessica and Justin were inside that house and safe and sound, then she couldn't run and take the chance that she would find help before he could harm them.

Docile, like a lamb being led to slaughter, she got out of the car, and he immediately grabbed her upper arm and guided her toward the door.

She wanted to balk as every instinct of survival kicked in. She needed to do something, but didn't know what to do. Her abject terror made rational thought impossible.

She wanted to kick and scream and do whatever it took not to go through that front door, for she had a horrifying fear that if she entered this house in the earth, nobody would ever see her or her children again.

Chapter 26

Luke was seated next to Sarah's hospital bed when the call came in from Alex Kincaid. He'd met Sarah's parents, who had flown in from Arizona several hours before, and together the three of them had sat by her bed and willed her to come out of her coma.

He would have recognized Sarah's mother anywhere. Tall and slender like her daughter, Virgina Wilkerson had the same take-charge attitude and manic burn in her eyes as her daughter.

Sarah's father, Craig, was a tall, handsome man who seemed content to let his wife chatter and flitter about the room as if by her sheer energy alone she could command her daughter's consciousness.

The entire department was working on Sarah's case, delving through everything they had on the Gift Bow Killer, looking for anything that would

lead them to the creep who had attacked one of
their own.

Luke had spent every moment that he could sitting next to her, but the call from Alex Kincaid gal-
vanized him into action. He made her parents swear
to call him on his cell phone if there was any change
in Sarah's condition; then he left for the Jamison
place.

The storm was passing, and shafts of late-day sunshine pierced through the dissipating clouds as he
sped down the highway. Marissa Jamison had been
at the center of the murders, and the fact that she and
her children had gone missing didn't bode well.

Just as Kincaid had told him on the phone, he
found Marissa's vehicle pulled along the side of the
road. He got out and walked around it, sloughing
through mud and realizing that any evidence of
foul play that might have been on or around the
van had long been washed away by the afternoon's
deluge.

He headed on to the Jamisons', hoping he'd find
all well when he got there. Alex met him at the door,
his eyes haunted and his mouth a grim slash above
the beginning of a five-o'clock shadow.

"They haven't shown up?" Luke asked as the
man ushered him into the house.

Alex shook his head and quickly introduced
Luke to Marissa's former in-laws. Edith Jamison
looked as if she'd been crying for years, and Jim
Jamison looked shocked.

Luke turned back to Alex. "So fill me in," he said.

The four of them sat in the kitchen, and between the three of them Luke got the events of the afternoon from the moment the children had gone outside to play until Luke had arrived at the scene.

"And you've checked the property?" Luke asked.

"As much as we could with the rain, but it's over seven acres, not counting the fields and woods beyond, so we didn't get everywhere," Alex replied.

He leaned across the table, his eyes burning with the intensity of a man on the edge. "We need cops out here, a search party going, and don't talk to me about needing to wait so many hours or the fact that Marissa is an adult and might have taken her kids and gone off on her own."

Luke held up a hand to halt him before he worked himself up into a lather. "Under normal circumstances we'd have to consider the fact that Marissa simply took the kids and went somewhere without her van. But these aren't normal circumstances. It will take me some phone calls to get things arranged."

Luke got up from the table and pulled out his cell phone. Missing kids would get half the county out here, and that's what they needed to search the expanse of land that surrounded the Jamison place.

It took only one call to set things in motion, and after he made the call he moved to the window and stared out into the backyard and beyond. The area beyond the grassy yard was filled with fields and groves of trees with no other houses visible. Lots of hiding places, lots of areas to search.

He was aware of Alex coming to stand beside him at the window. A surreptitious glance showed him a man in despair. Luke empathized. He'd been feeling desperate since he'd found Sarah on the pavement in the Taco Bell parking lot.

"We'll get only a couple of hours or so to search before darkness will make it impossible," he said.

Alex gave him a curt nod. "What if they aren't out there? What if the bastard somehow managed to get ahold of all three of them and took them someplace else?"

Luke frowned and turned his attention back out the window. The rain had worked on the devil's side, washing away any evidence that might exist to help them.

The killer had been fixated on Marissa. What Luke feared was that the madman had seen the children as irritations in her life, nuisances that needed to be removed. He was afraid that they'd find the two children out there in the woods somewhere, dead, with bright red bows on their foreheads. As he looked once again at Alex, he saw the same fear radiating from his eyes.

The house appeared to be a normal earth-contact home from the outside, but inside there was nothing normal about it. Michael guided her through the front door and into an attractive living room complete with sofa and chairs, entertainment unit and coffee tables.

"Where are my children?" she asked, her heart still pounding frantically.

"All in due time," he said smoothly. "First let me show you the kitchen. I think you'll be very happy."

It was when he led her through a doorway into a small kitchen that she realized the house wasn't normal. Each room had a thick steel door that could be closed and locked. The locks were on the outside of the doors, indicating that they weren't for protection from any outside threat, but rather for imprisonment.

"As you can see, I made sure the kitchen has everything you needed to bake. I know John's favorite was always your black forest cake, but I prefer German chocolate," he said.

She stared at him blankly, unable to make sense of anything. He smiled. "I used to listen to John talk about you, about what a wonderful wife you were, what a wonderful mother. The perfect family, that's what John used to say about you and the kids. He'd say he had the perfect family, and I realized it wasn't right, that I deserved the perfect family, not him."

"It was you. You killed him." Tears welled up, not just in her eyes, but in her heart, as she thought of the good man who had been mowed down in the parking lot of a grocery store like a dandelion cut from a lawn. "You killed all those people."

"As you can see, I ordered the best appliances for you in here." He walked over to the oven and opened the door as if he'd heard nothing she had said.

"My children. Where are my children? I want to see them now." If he'd done something to them, if he'd harmed them in any way, she knew she would go mad. She would kill him with her bare hands.

She needed to see her babies now, her arms ached to hold them tight. She needed to know he hadn't lied and they were all right. "Please, let me see my children." Her voice trembled with her need.

"Fine," he said with a touch of irritation. "I'll let you see them for a few moments; then I'll show you the rest of the house."

He led her out of the kitchen and down a short hallway. "I put them both in Justin's room. I thought they could keep each other company until bed time." He withdrew a set of keys from his pocket and unlocked one of the doors.

He shoved open the door and Marissa saw Justin and Jessica seated on a twin bed. Justin's arm was around his little sister, and their eyes were wide with fear. When they saw her they jumped off the bed and ran to her.

She stepped into the room and fell to her knees and hugged them tight, tears of relief coursing down her cheeks. "I'll leave you alone for a few minutes," Michael said, then closed the door. The sound of the lock was audible.

As she held her crying children and tried to soothe their fears, her gaze darted around the room, looking for a means of escape. No windows. Of course, here in the back of the earth-contact home there would be no windows.

The room was painted blue and decorated in typical boy style. A navy spread covered the bed, a small desk sat in one corner and a dresser in the other. Large plastic dinosaurs watched them from the top of the dresser, and the lamp was shaped like a baseball.

Horrified amazement filled her as she realized the extensive planning that had gone into this room, into all of this. He'd built not just a home, but a place specifically designed to keep them as prisoners.

"I want to go home," Jessica cried, her arms wound tight around Marissa's neck.

"I know, sweetie. But we can't right now." She led the children to the bed and sat between the two of them, hugging them close against her sides.

"I'm sorry, Mom. You told us not to get into the car with a stranger, but it wasn't a stranger. It was Captain Mike," Justin said, his little face radiating utter misery. "He told us it was a surprise, that we were going to surprise Grandma and Grandpa and you had told Captain Mike to come get us."

Marissa pulled him more tightly against her side. "It's okay, honey." Of course they hadn't hesitated to get into Morrison's car. She had warned them about strangers, but they had known Captain Mike all their lives. He'd visited their schools and he'd been to their home.

"I need you two to do something for me," she said, unsure how much time Michael would give her with them. "Everything is going to be all right, but for now I need you two to be on your best behavior. You do whatever Captain Mike tells you to, and make sure you don't make him angry. I'm sure everything is going to be just fine, but I need you two to be really, really good." Her voice held a calm assurance that was nothing but a lie, for she'd never felt such despair in her life.

"If we're good, then can we go home?" Jessica asked. "Mommy, I really want to go home."

"I know, I know, and we'll go home as soon as we can, but right now it's just really, really important that you be a good girl."

"We need a tyrannosaurus, don't we, Mom?" Justin said softly.

"We'll be all right," Marissa replied, wishing she could believe her own words.

The three of them tensed as they heard the key in the lock, and the door swung open.

"Marissa, we'll let the children play together for another hour or so; then it will be bedtime. In the meantime we need to get you settled in." He gestured for her to join him at the door.

She didn't want to go. She didn't want to leave her babies, but she knew what Michael Morrison was capable of and also didn't want to incur his wrath. She kissed first Justin, then Jessica on the forehead, then stood. "You heard Captain Mike. Play for a little while, and I'll be back to tuck you in."

She was eternally grateful that when he closed and locked their door once again there were no outcries, no sounds of tears or tantrums. She had a feeling that as long as the two were together, they would find strength in each other.

"I want you to instruct the children that it's disrespectful to call me Captain Mike," he said as he took her by the upper arm. His grip was firm, but not painful. Still, the very touch of his fingers against her skin made her ill.

"Then what are they supposed to call you?"

He smiled. "Daddy, of course."

She wondered how much she could take before she went stark raving mad. There was no way she wanted her beloved children to call this abomination of a man Daddy. And yet she knew their very lives might depend on it.

He opened another door, his features reflecting pride. "This is Jessica's room. I know how much she loves dancing, so I went with the ballerina stuff."

Again a terrible horror swept through her as she gazed into the room. Pink walls, pink bedspread, and pictures of ballerinas on the walls: The room was everything Jessica loved.

How intimately he'd come to know them, their

likes and dislikes, their innermost dreams and thoughts. She felt raped, violated, and dirty.

The next room was a small bath that he indicated the children would share. The final door loomed before them, and a new kind of horror crawled up her throat.

"And this is our room," he said, as he unlocked the door. His words confirmed her darkest fear. He expected them to share a room, share a bed. He swung open the door and gave her a gentle push inside.

"We have a private bath and a walk-in closet. I took the liberty of buying the clothes you and the children would need."

She stared at the king-size bed. She felt like she was going to throw up. The thought of him touching her in any way made her sick. The thought of sharing that bed with him made her want to die. But she couldn't die. She had her children to think about.

"I know this is all a lot to take in," he said from beside her. "And so I've decided I won't share the marriage bed with you tonight. I'll sleep on the sofa and let you get adjusted."

Something snapped inside her, and she turned to face him, her horror, her fear, transforming into an anger she could no longer hold inside.

"You're insane. I'll never sleep with you. You murdered my husband, you bastard."

She never saw his hand move, but she felt it as he

backhanded her with a force that snapped her head back and cut her upper lip. She cried out and stumbled backward, unbidden tears escaping down her cheeks.

"Wives shouldn't be disrespectful to their husbands," he said. "I had thought we could have a nice welcome-home drink, but it's obvious you aren't in the right state of mind." He stepped toward the doorway. "I think you need some time alone to contemplate the right way to treat your husband."

His gaze lost its hard glare, and he smiled once again, and in that smile Marissa once again saw his madness. "You and the kids, you're my family now, Marissa. My own perfect family. And I'll be the perfect father, the perfect husband, as long as you accept that we belong together, the four of us."

Without saying another word he left the room and she heard the lock engaging in place. She touched her lip; her mouth was filled with the coppery taste of blood.

She would have never believed she was capable of taking another's life, but as she found herself in the middle of this nightmare, she recognized that if she got the chance, she could kill Michael Morrison.

With this thought in mind, she began to search the room. She started in the bathroom and again she was stunned by Michael's thoroughness. A bottle of her favorite bubble bath set on the ledge of the deep tub along with an array of candles.

How had he known the brand of bubble bath and the fact that she liked to light candles when she took a bath? She thought of her tub at home, of the window where she had often looked out at the night sky. Had he been there? Hidden in the woods? Watching her? Again a wave of nausea swept over her.

The bathroom yielded nothing that could be used as a weapon. There were no razors, no sharp objects at all, only the bare necessities of a guest bathroom and a drawer full of makeup.

She moved back to the bedroom and began with the dresser drawers. She found sweaters and socks, underwear both for him and those for herself. The nightstand held a lamp too small and too lightweight to be used as a club.

All the drawers to the nightstands were empty except one, which contained a *Glamour* magazine, a box of tissues, and a Milky Way candy bar. My God, the man even knew her secret passion for Milky Ways.

She was no more successful in searching the closet. Clothes hung on plastic hangers and shoes were flats, with no hint of a heel that could be used as a potential deadly weapon.

Sinking to the edge of the bed she fought against a new wave of tears. Trapped. It appeared that he had built the perfect prison for his "family."

Nobody knew where they were. Nobody knew who they were with. She and her children were in a cave with a madman and there appeared to be no way out.

Chapter 27

The search involved dozens of officers and citizens. It was not the best of conditions. The rain had left the area muddy, with standing water in low-lying areas. They worked until darkness forced them to abandon the effort.

When everyone had gone except Luke, Alex stared out the window, aware of the detective moving to stand beside him. "I don't think they're out there," he finally said. He turned to look at Luke. "And if they aren't out there, then where in the hell are they?"

Luke swept a hand through his hair, his features showing the weariness that resonated in Alex's very bones. "I wish I knew. We're doing everything we can."

"But it's not enough," Alex replied flatly.

Luke sighed and returned his gaze to the window. "No, it's not enough," he agreed. He left the window and went into the kitchen.

Edith took his place next to Alex. She worried a dish towel between her fingers. "You want more coffee?" She'd spent the last several hours making pots of coffee and dozens of sandwiches, as if she might be able to find the missing children in the refrigerator or in the coffee tin.

"No, I'm coffeed out." Compassion filled him as he recognized that Edith appeared to have aged ten years in the last couple of hours. "You know, it's not your fault," he said softly.

She shook her head vehemently, tears glistening. "I should have never let them go outside. I should have been with them every minute." She twisted the towel in her hands. "Marissa told me what was going on. I'd been with the kids outside all morning. I'd just gone inside for a few minutes. I should have never left them alone."

Edith used the dish towel to dab at the corners of her eyes.

Alex didn't reply. He knew there was nothing he could say to ease her guilt, her pain. They both turned from the window as the sound of a cell phone ringing filled the air. Alex grabbed for his phone, then realized it must be Luke's ringing.

Marissa, where are you? Once again he stared out at the blackness of the night. They were supposed to have eaten dinner together tonight, the four of them as a family. This was supposed to mark the begin-

ning of something. So why was he so afraid that it
was the end?

Somehow the darkness made their absence only
more frightening, piercing his heart with a pain he'd
never felt before.

He jumped and turned as Luke touched him on
the shoulder.

"That was Sarah's mother. They think Sarah is re-
gaining consciousness. I'm heading to the hospital."

"I'm going with you." For the first time in hours
Alex felt a tiny ray of hope shine through the darkness.

Alex followed Luke to the hospital and prayed
that Sarah would not only regain consciousness but
would be able to speak the name of her attacker.

All his hopes for Marissa and the children now
rested in the hands of a woman who was hopefully
coming out of her coma, a woman who had sus-
tained grievous injuries. Without Sarah Wilkerson,
he now recognized there was no hope.

Despite the fact that the entire Cass Creek Police
Department had been working on the case, they
were no closer to catching the Gift Bow Killer than
they'd been at the time they'd found the first body
with the bow. They had no suspects. Sarah held the
key to saving Marissa and her children.

There was little doubt in Alex's mind that somehow the killer had managed to get hold of both the
kids and Marissa. If he'd killed the kids, the odds
were good the search party would have found their

bodies someplace near the house. If he'd killed Marissa, surely they would have found her body in the vicinity of where her van had been left.

He could have taken them far from here and killed them, a little voice taunted. Their bodies could right now be rotting in a shallow grave or in the middle of one of the parks the city boasted.

Gripping the steering wheel more tightly, he shook his head to dislodge the voice of doom. They weren't dead. He absolutely refused to entertain any doubt about that fact, for if he did, he feared his despair would consume him and he would never crawl out of the black hole of grief.

"Sarah, open your eyes. It's time to wake up."

The voice came from very far away, seeping through the layers of sleep that embraced her with loving, gentle arms. Sarah recognized the voice. It belonged to her mother.

Fifteen more minutes, she wanted to say. Just let me sleep for another fifteen minutes; then I'll get up and get ready for school.

A sliver of anxiety tore a layer of sleep away. Did she have a math exam this morning? She couldn't remember. She hadn't studied for it. She hated being unprepared for a test.

"Sarah Louise, I'm not going to tell you again. It's time to wake up." Her mother sounded angry with her.

"Princess, you really need to open your eyes and

wake up now." The deep voice flowed through her. Daddy! How odd. He was always at work already when she woke up for school. Why was he home this morning?

More voices added to her confusion. What did they want from her? Why was everyone yelling at her? She clung to the darkness, to the sweet oblivion of sleep, and knew no more.

There was no passage of time in her darkness, so she had no idea how long it was before she heard the voices again.

"Sarah Louise, can you hear me?" Again it was her mother calling through the murkiness. "We want you to wake up now."

Consciousness came on a sharp stab of pain in her gut and she opened her eyes and blinked, momentarily blinded by the light in the room.

"Sarah?" A hand took hers, familiar in its strength. Her mother's face appeared in front of her, and Sarah was stunned to see tears on her cheeks. Her mother was the strongest woman Sarah had ever known. She never cried.

Her father took the place of her mother and once again confusion spun Sarah's head. "Sarah, honey. You're going to be fine. You're going to be just fine."

It was all too confusing and she wanted to sink back into the darkness, away from the pain and bewilderment. She closed her eyes.

"Sarah."

Luke. His voice called to her through the dark,

summoning her upward through the layers of noth-ingness that had been her home.

And in Luke's sweetly familiar voice, the confu-sion fell away and clarity rang in her mind.

The parking lot. The knife. Oh God, the knife. The pain, that jagged thrust of steel to flesh. She'd thought she died in that parking lot. But she was alive! Obviously in a hospital, but wonderfully alive.

She opened her eyes once again, and this time she saw Luke's face. How odd, his eyes were filled with tears, and he looked like hell. There was nothing laid-back in the way he stared at her, in the way his hand clutched hers.

"Sarah," he said. "Can you hear me?"

She recognized somewhere in the back of her mind that it was the first time he'd called her by her given name. Sarah. She'd never loved her name as much as when it fell from his lips.

Luke. Her lips worked to form the word, but her mouth was too dry. She raised a hand and pointed to the water pitcher on the stand next to her.

He jumped up from the bedside, poured a glass of water, stuck a straw into it, then returned and held it to her lips. She took only a little, discovered that swallowing was difficult. She took another small sip; then he set the glass back on the stand and faced her once again.

"Sarah, honey. Talk to me. Tell me you're okay."

"I hope there hasn't been any brain damage," her mother whispered.

"You look like hell, Hunter." The words fell from her lips on a faint sigh.

Luke grabbed her hand once again, joy leaping into his eyes. "She's fine." A short bark of laughter left him. "Jesus, Sarah, you gave us all quite a scare."

"Sorry." She touched her stomach, where most of her pain radiated. "Am I . . . am I okay?"

"You're going to be fine, just fine." He squeezed her hand. "Sarah, listen, honey, Marissa Jamison and her two children are missing. We think whoever attacked you has them. Do you remember what happened in the parking lot? Can you tell me who did this to you?"

Fire. Her brain screamed the single word, and for a moment it made no sense. A blaze of fire didn't stab her in the belly. A lick of flame hadn't tried to eviscerate her.

Fire.

Fireman.

Fire captain.

Images exploded in her brain and she gasped and held tight to Luke's hand as memory returned with a jolt. The knife plunging into her, the blood, the taste of the grit of the pavement.

"Morr . . ." her voice cracked.

Luke frowned and gestured toward the water pitcher. "More water?"

She shook her head. "Morrison. Michael. Fire."

"Captain Morrison?" A new voice made itself heard. She turned her head a bit to see Alex Kincaid standing just inside the room.

"Yes. Captain Morrison," she confirmed.

Luke squeezed her hand tightly, his gaze holding hers for a long heart-stopping moment. "Sarah, remember when I said I'd never been tempted?" His gaze bored into hers with meaningful intent. "Remember?" She nodded. He released her hand and brushed her cheek with the back of his hand. "I just want you to know that I'm tempted. Okay? I'm really, really tempted."

The words were as sweet as any "I love you" she would ever hear. She reached up and touched his cheek in return. "Go. Go find Marissa. Get that bastard." The words took the last of her strength, and she watched as Luke and Alex flew from the room and prayed they'd find Marissa and her children in time.

They had a name, and within minutes they had an address and the information that today had been one of Captain Morrison's days off. Luke arranged with a fellow officer to obtain a warrant and get it to the scene as soon as possible.

Although Luke attempted to try to talk him out of tagging along, there was no way Alex intended to sit idly by while the people he loved were in danger. He climbed into Luke's car despite Luke's protests. "If Marissa were your woman would you be able to just go home and sit patiently?"

"No," Luke admitted.

"Then just drive, and let's get Marissa and her kids home safe with me."

They didn't speak another word until they reached Michael Morrison's apartment complex. The complex was quiet, most of the apartment windows dark, as occupants had already gone to bed for the night.

"I've got to wait for the warrant," Luke said as he parked the car.

Alex was already out the passenger door. "Well, I don't. I'm not bound by the same rules you are. I'll go through the door if it's locked, and you can charge me with trespassing after this creep is in custody."

"Kincaid, wait."

Alex heard Luke curse, then was aware of him following, but Alex didn't slow down. If Marissa and the kids were in that apartment, then Alex was determined to get them out. He didn't give a damn about legalities.

Michael Morrison's apartment complex was a community of two-story brick buildings, four apartments to a building. Morrison's apartment was on the bottom level and a light burned in one of the rooms in the front. Alex was about to hit the door when Luke grabbed him from behind.

"Slow down, cowboy," Luke breathed softly in his ear. "Marissa and her children aren't just visiting in there; they're hostages being held by a nut, and we don't know if Morrison is armed or not."

Some of the manic energy seeped out of Alex as he recognized the wisdom of Luke's words. He nodded and Luke released him. "So what now?"

"I want to try to get a look in the windows, see if we can locate Marissa and the kids inside a particular room," Luke said.

"I'll go this way." Alex pointed to the north side of the building.

Luke nodded, his eyes gleaming in the pale illumination of a nearby porch light. "And I'll go the other way."

The two men parted. Alex moved slowly, knowing that if Michael were to catch sight of him or Luke, then all bets were off as to the safety of Marissa, Justin, and Jessica.

A side window to the living room was the first Alex approached. Cautiously, holding his very breath, he peered into the window.

A lamp burned on an end table next to the sofa, but nobody sat there. There was no sign of anyone in the room. The next window was dark, making it impossible to see what was inside, but he sensed no movement, no indication of human presence.

The other windows on that side of the building belonged to the apartment behind Morrison's. He met Luke at the back of the building. "I don't think anyone is in there."

"I placed a call and found out Morrison drives a

fire department sedan. It wasn't in the parking lot," Luke said. "My warrant should be here anytime."

"I'm not waiting," Alex said. "They aren't in there, but the information we need to find them might be."

Luke didn't stop him as he turned on his heel and walked around the building to the front door. Alex had a feeling Luke wanted him to break down the door and get in sooner rather than later.

When they reached the door Alex tried the door-knob. He expected the door to be locked, and it was. He lowered his shoulder and rammed into the door, bouncing backward as pain shot up his arm. "Dammit!"

"Together," Luke said. "On the count of three." When he said three the two men hit the door with the power of enraged bulls. The lock disengaged as the doorjamb splintered. If there had been any question about somebody being in the apartment, it was answered when nobody came running to see what was going on.

Luke stepped in first, gun drawn. "Wait here," he said to Alex, then he proceeded through the apartment, clearing it one room at a time.

"We're alone," he said as he returned to the living room. "No apparent sign that either the kids or Marissa were here."

"There's got to be something," Alex said. "I intend to tear this place apart. Somewhere there's got to be a clue as to where Morrison is now, and wherever he is, that's where Marissa and the kids will be."

The first thing he noticed were the Spartan living conditions. The sofa was a simple beige, the end tables polished and without a single adornment. An entertainment system held a small television and a radio, but no CDs or DVDs lined the empty shelves.

The whole place felt as impersonal as a motel room, but according to what Luke had learned, Captain Michael Morrison had lived here for years.

The kitchen was no more telling about the occupant. The refrigerator held the usual staples, as did the cabinets; nothing out of the ordinary and nothing that yielded any real information about Morrison the man.

"I'll check out the master bedroom," Luke said and pointed across the hallway. "You can check the spare room."

Alex's frustration grew by the second. It wasn't normal for a man to live in the same apartment for years and not have left a mark of himself. The spare room held a treadmill and a desk.

He sank down in the desk chair. Surely the desk would yield something. He opened first one drawer, then another, finding citizen citations and awards, a group photo of the captain and his men, and a handful of paid bills for rent and utilities on the apartment.

"Anything?" Luke appeared in the doorway.

Alex leaned back in the chair. "Nothing. It's like a

ghost lives here." He tossed the handful of bills he'd found onto the top of the desk. "This place doesn't feel real. It feels like a facade, a front. He's got to have someplace else, someplace big enough to hold a woman and two children."

Neither of them voiced the fact that it was possible he'd taken them and killed them and didn't need a place to keep them at all.

Alex got up from the desk, and as he did, his gaze fell on a cardboard tube in the corner. He leaned over and grabbed it.

"What's that?" Luke asked.

"I don't know." Alex pulled the end off the tube and reached to get the papers rolled up inside. "House plans," he said as he unrolled the large sheet of paper. Adrenaline kicked in as he eyed the drawings.

Luke looked over Alex's shoulder. "Looks like gobbledygook to me."

"That's because you aren't an architect."

Why would Michael Morrison have house plans unless he was building or had built a house? "It's not a traditional kind of house," Alex said, more to himself than to Luke. "It's an earth-contact." He frowned as he studied the dimensions. He looked at the second sheet of paper, which was a topographical map of the building site.

"I think I can find this," he said, urgency ringing through him. "You need to get me to Marissa's so I can look at my maps of the area. If I can match up the surface areas, then we'll know where this place is located."

"In the meantime, I'll have somebody check to see if Morrison owns any property and we'll set up a wiretap on Marissa's phone. Maybe we'll get a call and this guy will want money."

"A kidnapping for ransom?" Alex eyed Luke grimly. "Is that what you really think this might be about?"

"No, I think it's about a man who wanted Marissa no matter what the cost."

"Yeah, well, he's got competition," Alex replied as he headed for the car.

Michael awoke to a keening cry. He shifted positions on the sofa and tried to go back to sleep, but the irritating wail continued. It sounded like his memories of his mother railing against her misery, screaming at him as if he were personally responsible for all the injustices of her life.

Stop. He needed it to stop. He sat up, vaguely surprised that the noise sent a trembling through him, as if he were still a powerless child. STOP!

He got up from the sofa, grabbed the ring of keys from the coffee table, and with the aid of the moonlight drifting in the bank of windows made his way through the doorway and down the hall.

The sound came from Jessica's room. He stood outside her door and placed his hands over his ears. This wasn't the way daughters were supposed to act. They weren't supposed to wake up in the middle of the night and scream and cry.

He paced in front of the door. "Stop," he said softly.

Why can't you be like Blake? Why can't you be a perfect son to me like he is to his mother? I should have had an abortion when I got pregnant with you.

His mother's voice mingled with the wails until Michael thought he'd lose his mind. "Make it stop," he said as the anger inside him built. He slammed a fist into the wall. He had to make it stop!

Marissa sat up, appalled that she had fallen asleep. Instantly she became aware of the sound of Jessica's cries. They were the hysterical cries of terror, and they ripped through Marissa like a knife in her heart.

She jumped off the bed and raced to the locked bedroom door. She'd just reached the door when she heard a loud boom, like fists banging on a door.

"Stop it!" Michael's rage-filled voice etched terror in her soul. "Stop it now," he screamed. "I can't take it."

"Michael!" Marissa screamed and used her fists to bang on the bedroom door. "Michael, please. Open the door. Let me go to her. I can make her stop. Michael, can you hear me? Let me handle it."

She nearly sobbed as she heard the rattle of keys in the lock of her bedroom door. Jessica's wails still filled the air.

"Make her stop," he said without preamble, as he opened the bedroom door. "Make her stop or I'll make her stop."

She nodded and flew past his to Jessica's door. He unlocked the little girl's door and Marissa went immediately to the bed, where Jessica sat crying.

"Shhh," Marissa gathered her daughter in her arms. "It's all right," she said, her heart still thundering with fear.

"I had a bad dream, Mommy," she cried.

Marissa glanced up to see Michael standing in the doorway, his face a twisted mask of rage. Quickly, she placed a hand over Jessica's mouth, muffling the cries. "It's okay, baby. I'm here now. It was just a dream, just a bad dream."

Jessica pulled her hand off her mouth. "I want bunny ballerina. I want to go home."

Michael took a step into the room, and Marissa once again clamped her hand over her daughter's mouth.

"I know. I know, but for now you need to go back to sleep." Marissa rocked her little girl and smoothed her hair away from her forehead. Please go back to sleep, she mentally begged, aware of Michael standing too close, looking too stressed.

"Shhh." Marissa rocked faster and Jessica's cries faded to faint whimpers. She was vaguely aware of Michael taking a step backward.

Jessica's whimpers stopped, and still Marissa clung to her, refusing to meet Michael's gaze. She didn't want to leave Jessica. Her heart still pounded unsteadily.

When she'd heard Jessica crying she'd been afraid, so terribly afraid that Michael would hurt her. She certainly knew what he was capable of and had feared the consequences if Michael hadn't let her come to her daughter.

"Marissa, come. She's asleep now." The tension that had been evident on his features before was now gone.

With reluctance Marissa released her hold on Jessica and gently lay her back on the pillow, hoping, praying she didn't wake up again until morning. She didn't want to think about what might happen the next time. She couldn't allow herself to think what might have happened if Michael hadn't let her go to her daughter.

"You didn't change into your nightclothes," Michael said as he relocked Jessica's door.

"I guess I fell asleep before I could change," she lied. She wasn't about to put on one of the slinky nightgowns she'd found in the room.

"Jessica was a bad girl tonight. I won't tolerate such behavior in the future."

"You have to understand, she's in a strange place, in a strange room. It may take her some time to adjust. She sometimes has nightmares." I'm trying to reason with a madman, she thought.

His features still held a trace of irritation. "John never mentioned anything about nightmares."

"She didn't have them before John's death." Marissa tried to keep the bitterness from her voice.

"I will not tolerate that kind of caterwauling. I had enough of that from my mother when I was growing up."

He led her back down the hall to her room. "We'll all have breakfast together in the kitchen in the morning before I leave for work," he said. "We'll eat at seven. I'll wake you at six so you can shower and prepare for the day. Sleep well for the remainder of the night."

Once again she found herself locked into the room. She returned to the bed and sat on the edge. She realized she couldn't wait for help to come. Nobody knew where they were. Nobody knew who held them. She was on her own to save her children.

Breakfast in the kitchen. That was fine with her. Surely in the kitchen there would be knives. If she could just get her hands on one sharp knife, she'd make sure that no red bow ever adorned the foreheads of her children.

Chapter 28

Alex jerked up, appalled to realize he had drifted off. The house was silent except for Luke's faint snoring. The detective had fallen asleep in one of the dining room chairs while Alex had been poring over his maps.

Checking his wristwatch, Alex saw that it was nearly four a.m. He got up from his chair at the dining room table and padded into the kitchen, where two more cops sat at the table drinking coffee and talking in low voices about the Kansas City Royals baseball team.

They had a dozen cops on standby, just waiting for Alex to give them some direction, to find the place where Michael Morrison might have built a house of secrets.

Tax records had yielded nothing in his name, and their only hope was that Alex would be able to identify the area where the house might have been built by the surface characteristics of the land on the plans.

"Anything?" One of the two at the table looked at him as he moved across the kitchen to the coffee-maker.

"Not yet." He poured himself a cup of coffee and for a moment leaned tiredly against the kitchen counter.

The map work was beyond tedious, and he knew the importance of getting it right, of being certain. The last thing he wanted to do was send a force of officers on a wild-goose chase.

He took a sip of the black coffee and tried to shrug off the weariness that threatened to claim him. "You guys doing okay in here? Help yourself to whatever you can find in the refrigerator if you get hungry."

"We're fine," one of them assured him.

Alex carried his coffee cup back into the dining room and set it next to the maps he'd been studying for most of the night. Instead of sitting down and resuming his work, he walked back out of the room, needing a stretch to ward off exhaustion.

He walked down the hallway, stopping first at Justin's room, then at Jessica's. Jessica's room was tidy, her bunny ballerina in the center of her bed.

If there was anything that would have convinced him that Marissa had absolutely, positively not somehow taken the kids and run away, it was the presence of bunny ballerina. Marissa had told him how much Jessica loved the stuffed animal, which had been given to her on her third birthday by her father. There was no way bunny ballerina would have been left behind.

He walked into the master bedroom and thick emotion filled his chest. The bed was still unmade from their earlier lovemaking. He sat on her side of the bed and grabbed her pillow. Raising it to his nose, he breathed deeply, taking in Marissa's scent.

The emotion he'd kept tightly in check since first speaking to Edith on the phone surged up inside him. A sob choked in his throat as tears welled up in his eyes.

He'd begun to think that a family wasn't in his cards, that he'd never find a woman with whom he wanted to spend the rest of his life.

At thirty-three years old he'd resigned himself to a life alone, to drinking milk straight from the carton because nobody cared, to leaving his dirty socks on the floor because nobody saw them but him. He'd believed his life would be filled with occasional meaningless sex, TV dinners on a tray, and a king-size bed that was always cold on the other side.

It wasn't until the moment he reconnected with Marissa and discovered she was a widow that he realized fate had known what it was doing in keeping him single. He felt as if he'd been waiting for her all his life.

Now, with happiness but a breath away, she was

gone. Her children were gone. Another sob escaped him as he buried his head in her pillow.

He should have never left her to get those damn sandwiches. He should have insisted she go with him or not gone at all. He should have never left her alone in this house.

It was a killing guilt, eating him from the inside out. The guilt that he'd screwed up and now she was gone. The knowledge that if his actions had been different, she would be with him now.

Suck it up, he told himself. He lifted his head and tossed the pillow aside. He had no time to wallow in his grief.

Swallowing his emotions, fighting his tears, he stood and left the bedroom. He needed to get back to work. He was the only one who could help them, and he couldn't afford to waste time indulging in emotion.

In the back of his brain was a taunting voice telling him it could be too late for Marissa and the children, but he refused to entertain that voice.

He rubbed his eyes tiredly and took a sip of the coffee. Then he set his cup down by the maps and began to search again, comparing his maps to the ones he had found in Morrison's home.

In the hours that had passed, they had discovered very little about Michael Morrison's personal life. On the surface he was a dedicated civil servant, with folders filled with awards and citations.

He was respected by the men who worked with

him, praised by his landlord as being a clean, quiet tenant. But nobody seemed to have any real sense of the man beneath the facade. Nobody seemed to know anything about his life away from the fire station. His personal life remained a mystery, and they hadn't been able to figure out why the notes he'd left with Jennifer Walsh's body had been signed as Blake.

An optimist, laid-back and slow to anger, Alex had always considered himself a reasonable, rational man. In the last several hours a rage had been born inside him, a rage the likes of which he'd never felt before.

It was a rage against a world where a fellow human being could callously take the lives of others, where a man could steal that which didn't rightfully belong to him.

Alex had known despair when he'd buried his father, but that grief had been tempered by the knowledge that it was the natural order of things that children buried their parents. The idea of having to bury Marissa or either of her children was an outrage that knew no boundaries.

He focused his attention again on the maps, knowing that at the moment he seemed to be the only hope, and praying that when he finally discovered a location it wouldn't be too late for the three people he had come to love with all his heart.

It was five thirty when he found it, an area of land south of town that appeared to be a match for the land on the drawings he'd found in Morrison's apartment.

"Luke." He touched the man's knee. Luke came awake in the blink of an eye, looking surprisingly alert for a man who had been snoring for the last hour and a half. "I think I found them."

Luke came out of his chair with his cell phone in hand. "Where?"

Alex showed him on the map. "All the land characteristics match those on the house plans. If Michael Morrison built this house, then this is where it's located."

"Let's go find out."

Marissa was already awake when Michael knocked on her door. She'd been awake most of the night, dozing off only in the wee hours of the morning and awakened by nightmares.

The night had seemed endless, and with every hour that ticked by on the bedside alarm clock, a piece of hope faded away.

Nobody knew where they were. There would be no rescue. It frightened her that she was losing hope, for without it she would have to face the hollowness of utter despair.

She'd watched the clock on the nightstand, the digital minutes changing as if in slow motion. She'd wondered what Alex was doing. He must be frantic. And Jim and Edith, they must be beside themselves with worry, with guilt.

Were the police out searching for them? By now they would have found her van parked on the side of the road, but there would be no clues inside or out, no leads for them to follow to her.

She heard the lock to the door disengage and tensed. Michael opened the door and smiled at her. "Good morning. The coffee's ready in the kitchen. I thought it would be nice if you and I shared some time together before we got the kids up for breakfast."

The crazys have taken over the world, she thought as she followed him out of the bedroom and into the kitchen. This time she eyed her surroundings more thoroughly than she had the night before.

Weapons. She needed to find weapons. She couldn't wait for rescue; she had to somehow figure out how to save herself and her children.

Her heart sank as she sat at the table and noticed that several of the drawers had padlocks on them. He'd thought of everything, and desperation grew by leaps and bounds. She swallowed against it, knowing that if she gave into despair they would have no chance at all.

If he left her in the kitchen alone for long enough, she'd find some way to break open those locks, rip open those drawers, and get a weapon of some kind.

He poured her a cup of coffee and set it before her. For just a brief moment she considered what would happen if she tossed it into his face. She stifled the impulse, afraid that it would only serve to incapacitate him for a moment and would stir his wrath. If she were in this all by herself she might have taken the chance, but she couldn't risk it with her children here to bear the brunt of his rage.

She couldn't forget the rage that had twisted his features when Jessica had been crying the night before. The emotion she'd seen emanating from his eyes and distorting his features had been the blackest, rawest anger she'd ever seen.

She couldn't forget the unexpected sharp crack of his hand across her mouth. Her upper lip was still slightly swollen and sore.

He sat across from her at the table, a cup of coffee in front of him as well. He was clad in his fire captain uniform. He wore a crisp white shirt complete with emblems of the department on the sleeves. His navy slacks were neatly creased, and he looked like the respectable fire captain that everyone knew and admired.

"I've dreamed of this moment for so long," he said. "When I was a boy my mother used to tell me that I'd never amount to anything; she used to beat me for not being as wonderful, as perfect as Blake, one of the characters on her favorite soap opera. But I have become Blake, with the perfect job, the perfect life, and the perfect family."

"But it's not perfect." She couldn't help herself.

She couldn't sit here and play a role in his fantasy. "You've built this all on the murders of others."

He waved his hand as if to dismiss the dead. "That girl who cursed at you in the ballpark, she was nothing but a drug addict. She would have never been useful to society. And that man was a bully. His son would thank me if he got the opportunity. As far as Detective Wilkerson is concerned, I saw the way she yelled at you. She was a vile woman."

"It doesn't matter. What you did was wrong."

He nodded as if conceding the point. "I'm not crazy, Marissa. I know I broke the law. That's why I was so careful when killing those people. Police and fire officials, it's amazing how people trust them."

He leaned back in the chair, looking inordinately pleased with himself. "The girl was easy. She'd talked to me several times at the ball field. All I had to do was tell her I had some drugs that we'd seized from a fire scene, and she went willingly with me to Penguin Park to partake. Farragut was a bit more of a problem. I had to go to his house and tell him I needed to discuss some fire code violations with him. He stepped outside to talk to me and I took him down there. Then I had to transport the body back to the park, back to where his crime against you and Justin had occurred."

"And Sarah? Detective Wilkerson?" She wanted to keep him talking; as long as he was talking he wasn't hurting anyone.

"She was the easiest." He paused to take a sip of

his coffee, then continued. "So eager to solve the crimes, she would have met me anywhere when I offered her a tip. She was an aggressive bitch, no big loss to the world."

"And John. What about John? He wasn't a drug addict or a bully." Emotion rose up inside her. "He was a good man."

"John was unfortunate," he agreed. "He was a good man, a good firefighter, but he was in the way." He paused to take another sip of his coffee, his expression no more troubled than if he were talking about the weather.

"I listened for years as John talked about you and the kids. I feel like I was there when Justin spoke his first word, when Jessica took her very first step. John shared with me each and every milestone. Then he'd talk about you and his face would take on a light and his voice held a lilt."

Each word was like a piercing arrow in her heart.

"He'd tell me about the little thoughtful things you'd do for him, about the laughter you two shared. He was so happy, and as I listened to him I realized fate had made an error. You and the kids were supposed to be mine, not his."

Her heart felt as if it bled. It had been John's love and pride in her and the children that had placed him in the center of a killer's sight.

And in the memory of John's sweet, shining love, she found her full and complete love for Alex. Until this very moment in time she'd been afraid to accept what she'd felt in her heart for him. That little piece that she'd held back now opened and embraced Alex and the love he offered her.

With his love flowing over her, she knew if she managed to get herself and her children out of this alive, she'd willingly tie her life with his. No more doubts. No more fears. Life was too short, and if John's death had taught her anything, it was to embrace life and love.

"Anyway," Michael continued, "I know this is all still new to you, and it will take some time for you to completely adjust to your new life. But I'll be a good husband, Marissa. And you and I and the children will eventually become the perfect family."

"Never." She wasn't even aware that she'd spoken the word aloud until he grabbed her chin and squeezed so tightly tears sprang to her eyes.

"Don't make me angry, Marissa." A knife appeared in his hand, and the tip pressed into her throat, pricking sharp enough that she felt a thin trickle of blood.

"You aren't acting like the perfect wife, Marissa, and that makes me angry, real angry. I hate to think about me being a single parent to our children, but if I have to, I will."

They parked nearly a mile away from the location where Alex suspected Michael Morrison held Marissa and her children. They met half a dozen other cops there along with members of the SWAT team.

The morning sun was just etching the sky with slivers of pinks and oranges, but the beautiful promise of a new day did nothing to staunch the agonizing fear that consumed Alex.

The police intended to approach the house as if it was a hostage situation, but Alex knew conventional measures wouldn't work. There were no windows for a sniper to get a shot, no way for a SWAT team to approach other than a frontal attack.

Michael Morrison had built the perfect fortress. Alex just prayed it wouldn't become the perfect tomb.

They had learned that the property was owned by Rhonda Hicks, an aunt of Michael's who suffered from Alzheimers and was currently in a nursing home. Rhonda also had a vehicle tagged and licensed in her name and a storage unit. Officers were checking the storage unit at that very moment.

When Luke and Alex had left Morrison's apartment, other officers had moved in for a more thorough search. Hidden behind a heater vent, they had found an elaborate kit for applying false facial hair, a blond male wig, and a red one.

The disguises indicated how Morrison had managed to spy on Marissa without her recognizing him.

Alex listened as the officers discussed the best way to handle the current situation. Luke had tried to get him to stay behind, but Alex had told the detective that the only way to stop him from being there was to arrest him.

He now stood in front of Luke's car, the map spread out on the hood, looking for any weakness in the structure that could be exploited.

"There's a couple of vents somewhere in the hill," he said to Luke, who stood next to him. "But, unfortunately, they'll be too small for anyone to get inside."

"What about using them for dropping in smoke bombs?"

Alex turned to him and frowned. "Are you crazy? With two little kids inside? Surely that's not a viable option."

Luke raked a hand through his hair in obvious frustration. "We don't even know if the kids are in there. He could have already . . . they might already be . . ."

"No." Alex shook his head vehemently. "No. If he killed them, we'd already have found them."

"I think you're right," Luke agreed. "Morrison is proud of his work. He has left his victims in public places where they would be found quickly. If Jessica and Justin were dead we'd know it."

"I just can't help but believe I'd know it," Alex said hoarsely and touched his heart.

Luke touched his arm, as if to steady him, and Alex drew a deep breath to control himself. He couldn't lose it now. He couldn't give in to the emotions that choked his throat, twisted his gut, and ripped at his heart.

They were so close now. Hopefully within hours Marissa and the children would be back with him, back where they belonged.

"It looks like the only choice we have is to make phone contact with Morrison and see if we can get him to release Marissa and the kids."

Alex looked at him in disbelief. "You really think he's just going to give them up and turn himself in peacefully? He's killed at least three people that we know about. He even attacked a police officer. He's gone to great lengths to get Marissa and have a place to keep her. He wants Marissa, and I wouldn't put it past him to kill her, then kill himself in some sort of crazy suicide deal. Surprise is the best weapon we have, and the best way to go in is through the front windows."

He paused, drawing a deep breath after the lengthy diatribe.

A new sense of urgency filled him as Luke walked away to speak to the other officers. The cops were going to screw this up. They were going to try to play by the rules. Alex knew there were no rules with Michael Morrison.

He didn't intend to wait for the cops to decide what they were going to do. He could hear Marissa's and her children's cries in his head and knew he couldn't wait another minute, another second.

He took off across the wooded area toward the steep rise in the earth that was the back of the earth-contact home. He walked quickly, half-expecting Luke or one of the other cops to yell "Halt" or take him down and handcuff him.

Loose cannon, that's what they'd think he was, and in a sense, he was. He was a loose cannon fueled by fear, driven by desperation, and he couldn't wait around for the cops to make a final decision on what to do.

From his vantage point nobody would know that the steep mound of earth contained a house inside its depths. The sheer face on the other side would display the windows that would let somebody know the rise was more than just an unusually steep hill.

The dawn brought with it the sounds of nature awakening as Alex hurried to make his way around the incline of the mound. Birds sang in nearby trees, bees buzzed around newly bloomed wildflowers.

A beautiful, normal morning except that the woman he loved and her children were being held by a killer and he was acting like the Lone Ranger riding to the rescue.

As he hiked closer to the front of the structure he spied a large chunk of concrete and picked it up. Behind him he heard the faint sound of footsteps against grass and knew the cops were making their way toward the place as well.

He had no idea what plan they'd settled on, but

knew that if they called Morrison, if they told him they were out there, then the results could be deadly.

He came around the side of the hill and saw the windows of the living room gleaming with the morning light. Knowing he was taking a chance, but also unwilling to leave things to the authorities, he crept closer to the bank of windows.

Tempered glass. The huge windows were tempered glass, and that was a good thing. One solid hit and they would crackle and crumble like glass dust. He also noted that no interior light seemed to be on inside.

Holding his breath, he crept closer and peered inside, at the same time envisioning the house plans in his head. The front living room was devoid of human presence, but down the hallway he could see a light shining from a room on the left. The kitchen.

Surprise was the only way, he thought. If Morrison got wind of the fact that he was being surrounded, Alex feared what he might do.

Despite the fact that he might be facing the potential charge of interfering with an investigation, or trespassing, or myriad other crimes, he knew he had no choice. He needed to get inside now.

If he was wrong, and Michael Morrison wasn't inside this place, then he would deal with the consequences later, but he couldn't wait for the police, couldn't wait for the mistakes he feared they would make.

He backed away from the windows and hefted the chunk of concrete in his hands. There was only one way into the house, and that was the way he was going in. He was armed with only one real weapon . . . surprise.

He ran toward the window, the concrete held out in front of him. When he was a foot away, he threw the chunk with all his might. The glass crackled, but before it could splinter to the ground he raised his arm to shield his face and burst through.

He didn't stop. Driven by adrenaline and rage, he flew down the hall and into the room he knew to be the kitchen. They were all there.

Marissa and the children were at the table, and Morrison stood just inside the door, a knife in his hand. Alex had no time to celebrate the fact that they were alive. In one quick glance he saw Marissa's reddened upper lip and a trickle of dried blood on her throat.

A roar filled the air, and Alex realized it came from him as he rushed toward Morrison. Morrison jabbed with the knife, managing to connect with Alex's forearm, but Alex felt nothing, nothing but his own rage.

He grabbed Morrison's hand that held the knife and the two men crashed to the floor, each fighting for control of the weapon.

"You can't have them," Morrison cried. "You can't have them. They're mine. They're my family."

The words further enraged Alex. He managed to

punch the knife from Morrison's hand and grab it as several police officers swept into the kitchen.

He held the knife at Morrison's neck, his hand trembling with the need to end the life of the man who had caused pain not just for him, but who had also caused Marissa and her babies fear and anguish.

"We've got him, Alex." Luke's voice seemed to come from very far away. Morrison lay perfectly still beneath him, and still Alex didn't get up, didn't pull away the knife from his throat.

"Alex, don't." Luke's firm voice barely penetrated Alex's brain.

All his darkest fears, all his impotent rage, seemed to crystallize to form tears that half blinded him. He became aware of several things. The children were crying, and Marissa softly called his name over and over again.

A large droplet of blood fell from him and plopped on the center of Morrison's forehead, a scarlet blossom like the red gift bows Morrison had placed on his victims.

The sight of that blood drop broke the killing spell that had momentarily gripped him. With a strangled cry he stood, and two cops immediately moved in to secure Morrison.

It was Justin who reached him first. The little boy threw himself at Alex and hugged him around the waist. Justin looked up at him, his bright eyes shining with hero worship. "You were just like a tyrannosaurus," he said. "You saved us."

Then Marissa was in his arms, wiping his face with a cloth and weeping. "You're hurt," she said. "Your face is all cut up."

He held her close. "I don't feel a thing except relief. I thought I'd lost you again."

"Never," she replied. "You'll never lose me again."

Luke approached the four of them as other officers secured the scene and led Michael Morrison away in handcuffs.

"You okay?" he asked Marissa.

"We are now," she replied and touched the top of Justin and Jessica's heads, as if to assure herself that they really were okay.

"We'll need you and the kids to come down to the station for statements," Luke said.

Alex tightened his arm around her, wishing he could shield her, protect her from having to relive the past eighteen hours. But she nodded at Luke, her gaze strong and steady.

"I'll do whatever it takes to make sure Captain Morrison spends the rest of his life in prison," she said.

Hours later Marissa, Alex, Justin, and Jessica left the police station. Marissa had answered all the questions, explaining how Morrison had gotten her into his car and how he'd managed to lure the children away from their grandparents' home.

She was thrilled to learn that Sarah had come out of her coma and had given them Morrison's name. Although Sarah had a long recovery ahead of her, Luke assured Marissa that Sarah would be fine.

Luke also told her how Alex had found the house using his skills as an architect. An EMT had cleaned up Alex, who'd been covered with slivers of glass and had dozens of cuts on his face, arms, and shoulder.

She'd listened as Luke Hunter admonished Alex for acting like a kamikaze, throwing himself through a window and into a situation that could have ended very differently. "You were lucky," Luke had said. "Damn lucky that Morrison didn't kill you."

Alex had accepted his lecture good-naturedly, nodding his head in agreement with everything Luke had said.

"I want to go home. Can we just go home now?" Jessica whined as they walked out of the police station and into the early-afternoon sunshine. That familiar whine was music to Marissa's ears. She'd been afraid, so afraid that all their voices would be silenced once and for all.

"Yes, we're going home," Alex replied and picked up the little girl and swung her around so she rode on him piggyback. She giggled and wrapped her arms around his neck.

As Justin grabbed one of Alex's hands, Marissa took the other and her heart swelled with happiness. This was her family, complete with a whiny daughter, a stubborn son, and a man who looked as if he'd used his head to grate glass.

Yes, this was her family, and as they walked toward her car, which had been brought to the station at some point that morning, she felt the sudden presence of John nearby.

It was a benevolent feeling, as if he were smiling at her, as if he were telling her to reach out and embrace her new man, her new happiness, and the very imperfect family that was just perfect for her.

Epilogue

Eight months later

The wedding was beautiful, a small intimate affair in the backyard of the Victorian house that would now be home. Jessica had served as flower girl and Justin as best man, both taking their responsibilities very seriously.

Jim had walked Marissa down the aisle and into Alex's awaiting arms. The minister had been wonderfully brief, and the reception afterward filled with the warm wishes and love of their closest friends.

Now Marissa and Alex stood side by side on the porch and waved at the last departing guests. Jim and Edith had left a few minutes earlier, taking the kids with them to their house for the night.

When the last car had pulled out of sight, Alex turned and smiled at Marissa. "Alone at last," he said, then scooped her up in his arms for the traditional walk across the threshold.

When they were inside the house he placed her feet back on the floor. His eyes glowed as his mouth sought hers in a kiss that spoke of their future together.

The last eight months had been busy ones. Not only had they finished refurbishing Alex's home, but she'd sold her house as well. She'd also stopped making deliveries to the fire station. It wasn't because she couldn't face the place where Captain Michael Morrison had worked and presented himself as a normal human being. Rather, it was because it was time to say good-bye to the past.

There was only one more difficult task ahead of her, and that was in facing the trauma of Michael Morrison at his trial, which was scheduled to begin in a month. But she knew with Alex at her side they could get through any difficult times that might lie ahead.

"Hi, Mrs. Kincaid," he said as he broke their kiss.

She smiled. "Hi, Mr. Kincaid."

"Shall we adjourn to the master suite where I have a bottle of champagne on ice?"

"Ah, Mr. Kincaid, I can tell by the light in your eyes that champagne isn't all you have on your mind." She took his hand and together they went up the stairs.

They first walked past Jessica's bedroom, a

charming room done in bright yellows and greens. Justin's room was down the hall, sporting the red and gold of the Kansas City Chiefs football team.

In that single night in Michael Morrison's madhouse, her babies had outgrown the traditional colors of their sexes and had wanted nothing to do with pink and blue rooms. They had each chosen the colors for the rooms in their new home.

"Guess what I heard today," Alex said as he drew her into the master suite, a lovely room decorated in rich burgundy and deep greens. He moved to the dresser, where an ice bucket held a bottle of chilled champagne.

"What?" Marissa sat on the foot of the chaise that had come from her shop.

"I heard that Luke Hunter and Sarah Wilkerson are no longer going to be partners." He popped the cork on the bottle, then hurriedly filled the two fluted glasses that awaited.

"Really? I thought they worked so well as partners." She accepted the glass he handed her.

"Apparently the department has some sort of a rule that husbands and wives can't be partners." He joined her on the chaise.

"They're getting married?" Marissa hadn't thought it possible that she could feel any more happiness, but this news brought a new wave sweeping through her.

"That's what Luke told me." He held up his glass toward hers.

"That's wonderful. I can't believe Sarah hasn't mentioned a word to me." During the last several months Sarah and Marissa had become close friends.

"Enough about them, now let's talk about the really important things."

"Like what?" she asked, half-breathless by the look in his eyes.

"Like how long I'm going to have to make nice and sip this champagne before I get lucky."

She touched her glass to his. "To getting lucky," she said, then downed the drink in three fast swallows.

He laughed and emptied his glass. "To being lucky," he replied, and as he gathered her into his arms she felt like the luckiest woman in the world.

Michael Morrison lay on the bottom bunk in his jail cell and stared up at the bunk above him, where his bunkmate was reading his latest letter from his wife.

The man, Simon Burrell, was awaiting trial for armed robbery. During the past three months that the two men had been sharing a cell, Michael had grown to like Simon. The man gave him his space and didn't seem inclined to play pissing male posturing games.

"Daisy lights a candle for me every night," Simon's voice drifted down from the top bunk. "Isn't that sweet?"

"Yeah, sweet," Michael agreed. Week after week he'd listened as Simon spoke of his young bride, about how she liked to cook and keep a clean home, how she was a pretty brunette with a killer smile.

Michael closed his eyes and thought about his future. He was optimistic about his trial. He had a top defense lawyer and even though it had been Sarah Wilkerson's survival that had spelled his doom, he was now grateful she hadn't died. They'd never be able to prove he killed John, so he was facing only two murder charges.

He knew he'd do hard time, but he'd be a model prisoner and eventually memories would fade. He'd find God—parole boards seemed to like that. Yes, he'd do some time, but eventually he'd be out again.

"She says she's going to bring me some magazines when she comes to visit on Saturday," Simon said, interrupting Michael's thoughts. "You like to read?"

"Sure."

"Then whatever Daisy brings we can share."

Yes, Simon was a nice guy. Too bad he'd never make it out of jail alive.

Although Michael hadn't figured out how yet, Simon was going to have an accident and wind up as a jailhouse tragedy. Then, when Michael eventually got out, he intended to look up Daisy Burrell, who sounded like such a fine, upstanding woman. Michael was already half in love with her.

He had the feeling she'd make the perfect wife for him.

PROMISE HIM ANYTHING

by award-winning author
CARLA CASSIDY

She promised not to leave him.

But some promises are made to be broken.

For a year, Juliette Monroe and her son have
been on the run from her abusive
ex-husband. But when he finally tracks them
down, he must confront local cop Nick
Corelli. When sparks fly between Juliette and
Nick, they know they must face the
madman threatening their lives—and
their blossoming love.

0-451-41143-9

O284

All your favorite romance writers are
coming together.

SIGNET ECLIPSE